# The Spell of Summer
## (Once Times Thrice)

DIANNA HARDY

The Spell of Summer
(Once Times Thrice)

Published by Satin Smoke Press, June, 2014
First Edition
ISBN 978-0957540422

This print updated August, 2023

This book is set in 11.5 pt Cormorant Garamond Medium by the Cormorant
Project Authors, licensed under the SIL Open Font License, Version 1.1

Written in British English.

Satin Smoke Press
*(an imprint of Bitten Fruit Books)*
Hampshire, UK

www.satinsmoke.com

# Acknowledgements

Where do I start? I am blessed with so many good people in my life that make writing and publishing easier than it would otherwise be.

Ninfa Hayes and Elizabeth Morgan – fab authors, writing advisers, my Beta readers (*my preeeecccioussss*) – I would go insane without you there!

I am endlessly grateful to Jeris Quinn (and also Panu, Javolenus and unreal_dm) for allowing me use of his magnificent song, *The Living Game*. Hearing that song was like falling in love for me and I could listen to it forever.

A huge shout-out needs to go to my small and cosy Street Team who share my promo and spread the word about my books with untiring enthusiasm. I am so, so grateful: Becky Johnson, Lynn Worton, Samantha McGrath, Maggie Gill Frank, Rhonda McGuire, Jennifer Moorman, Tracey Constant, Nikki McCarver, Claire Taylor, Tiffany Webb ... I'm talkin' about you! I should also mention Carly Chambers and Laurie Garrison for always making time for me and my books.

To editor, Mandy Pederick, aka The Picky Bitch: thank you for being so damn picky, and for proofreading this little experiment of mine.

Thank you to anyone and everyone who leaves a review of my book – you might have no idea just how priceless that is. It is gold. It is one of the most valuable ways of spreading the word and I cherish hearing your thoughts.

Thanks to those of you who always comment, or *always* click Like on my statuses – I love you!

I want to acknowledge my readers and fans, both new and old. Thank you for letting me write; for sticking it out with me. Every book is a journey in its own right, from start to end, and this one ... this one has certainly been like no other for me. I started writing this book at the beginning of January, this year. Those of you who have been with me since then ... know.

I hope you all enjoyed it.

Dianna Hardy
*May, 2014*

To those who have reached the summit:
don't ever forget the view.

To those still trying:
it's worth everything it takes to get there.

~\*~

# The Spell of Summer

# Prologue

She knew it was coming. Could feel it in the air, like when she watched something on TV and knew a scary bit was about to happen, and she'd get all tense inside while she waited for it.

The sound of something smashing downstairs made her jump; her daddy's voice, shouting, on the tail of it, forcing anxiety to the top of her throat. "For fuck's sake, Penny!"

She wished she was older than five. Everything was so much bigger than her.

Looking towards the window, through where the curtains didn't quite meet, she could see the night only just giving way to dawn; the darkness turning grey. The dreamcatcher hanging from the window railing cast a very faint shadow on the far wall of her bedroom, and the amethyst on her windowsill glimmered just a fraction in the low light.

She reached out behind her and found the textured threads of Blue's hair.

Clutching her beloved rag doll to her, she crawled out of bed, her toes finding the carpet before the rest of her feet, and she stayed on her toes, maybe to ensure no one would hear her; maybe to ensure she was that little bit taller.

"Don't you dare do this again! Not again!"

Mummy was using that voice she used when she was trying to be angry instead of crying.

"Penny..."

Daddy sounded sorry. He was sorry quite a lot.

"If you go, you stay gone."

That anxiety in her throat suddenly tightened into a hard ball that lodged a scream of panic. *He's leaving again.*

"Penny—"

"I mean it! I'm not your god-damn yoyo! I don't care what you feel inside. I don't care what your *instincts* are telling you ... you have responsibilities. *Here.* I need you here and so does Meredith. Be a fucking father."

Meredith snuggled Blue tighter into her chest as she peeked out her bedroom door. The stairs were tall and steep and she couldn't make out her mum or dad at the bottom, but her mind played out the picture her eyes couldn't see, their hurled words as bright as any colour.

*Words can hurt,* Mummy had once told her when a girl had said something bad to her at school and she had said bad things back, *and words can also heal. We must be careful with our words – we're like superheroes and words are like our super powers. Super powers should always be used to help others.*

There were a lot of words she didn't understand though. Like reponsa ... responsa ... 'responsibilities'.

She rubbed Blue against the beat of her heart to ease the slight ache there. She thought she *might* know what the word meant, but she wasn't sure. Mummy and Daddy used it a lot when they were talking about her when they thought she wasn't listening, so she was pretty sure it was something to do with her, and her daddy didn't like reponsa ... that word ... so it must be because of her that he kept leaving.

"I can't ignore my work. It's my *work* – my *life* work."

A plate came flying towards the stairs and smashed into the middle step, Meredith just catching sight of the top of it as it broke into pieces. She jumped as the smash sent vibrations through her little body from under her feet, and then retreated into the shadow on the landing at the far end of the bannister, her breath frozen in her throat as she sat.

She hugged Blue and curled her knees up against her chin.

Her parents' heads bobbed in and out of view as they shouted and paced.

"*This* is your life."

"You knew who I was before we married."

"Don't you throw that in my face! You think *I'm* the same person I was then? Things change, life changes, *children* change things and we all need to make sacrifices."

She tugged on Blue's dress nervously, that not-nice feeling pressing on her heart again. She didn't know how she changed things – she tried hard not to change things because that was another word that they said a lot when they argued. They didn't like when things changed, so she always tried extra hard to make sure everything was the same every time: she *always* washed her hands and brushed her teeth the same way, she *always* put her clothes on in the same order, she *always* made sure her toys went back to the same place she'd gotten them from. And she didn't know what that other word meant – 'sacrifice' – but it sounded a bit like fire and a bit like ice.

"I can't give up my life's work, Penny."

"Chasing ghosts?" said her mummy, her voice sounding hard and coupled with a laugh that sounded not like laughing at all.

Daddy was a ghost hunter. When he talked about

ghosts, his eyes lit up and he was happy. He said that he helped them when they became trapped in this world. She didn't completely understand everything he said, but she always nodded and smiled with him when he talked about it because she loved seeing him so happy.

A strange silence filled the hallway downstairs, and Meredith braved shuffling a few inches forward on her bum.

"Penny..." whispered her dad, and he sounded really sad.

Her mum wiped her face and crossed her arms. "I mean it, Mitchell. I get that you love what you do – of course I get it. But I need you here with the *living*. This time, if you go, you stay gone."

The big clock on the mantelpiece – the one that had mermaids carved either side of it – ticked loudly in the quiet of the breaking dawn.

Meredith heard a shuffle, and then a rustle, and then she saw the back of her dad's head as he opened the front door.

"Mitch..."

He was wearing her favourite coat – the one that felt like a big, fluffy jumper. She loved to snuggle with him when he wore that.

"*Mitchell...*"

The door closed behind him, and the thing pressing on her heart was really hurting now.

She gripped a wooden bannister railing with one hand, and made sure Blue's eyes were shielded from everything that was happening. She didn't want Blue upset.

A wail left her mother, and she bent forward, clutching her tummy and started sobbing.

Meredith felt torn.

She wanted to go downstairs and hug her. She wanted to run outside and stop Daddy from leaving. She wanted to crawl back into bed and under the covers, because that's one of the places she felt safe.

Instead, she stayed where she was and watched her mummy open the big chest that she called her 'magic box'. She thought it was a bit like a pirate's chest, but where pirates kept gold, her mum kept candles and crystals and oils and incense and other things that she didn't know the names of. The wooden chest smelled lovely, but it also scared her a little because Mummy never talked to her about anything inside it – not like her daddy talked to her about ghosts.

Still crying, she pulled out a funny-looking feather that was also a pen, and some red ink, and then began writing words on a yellow piece of paper, whispering them through her tears as she wrote them... *"Once times thrice, I bind thine heart to mine, to hold, to never part. Once times thrice, I bind thine heart to mine, to hold, to never part. Once times thrice, I bind thine heart to mine, to hold, to never part."* And she repeated it, and repeated it, and repeated it, until she was clutching the piece of paper to her chest the same way Meredith clutched Blue to hers.

Finally, she howled out a last, angry-sounding sob, screwed up the paper and threw it in the box. Her shoulders slumped in defeat, and Meredith couldn't stay where she was any longer. Still on tiptoes, she made her way down the stairs until she was next to her mother, and placed a hand on her shoulder.

Startled, her mummy looked up. Her face smoothed out, but her eyes filled with tears again. "Merri..." She held her arms open for her.

Meredith climbed into them, holding Blue.

Her mum rocked her in her arms and kissed the top of her head. "I'm so sorry, baby."

"It's okay, Mummy. It's okay."

It *was* okay, because Daddy had left before and he had come back. Daddy always came back.

The days turned to weeks, until summer became autumn, and then winter. Christmas came and went, and then, somehow, the daffodils emerged, the songbirds sang their yearly tune, and it was summer once more.

Daddy never came back.

Dear Diary,

Okay, I admit it. I've never found these entries useful. My therapist said I should write it all down – just a small paragraph – of stuff that happens, at least once a week if I can't manage it every day. Apparently, it'll help to balance things out in my mind and reduce the mountains to molehills again: reduce the anxiety ... but I've always been dubious. My mind's pretty stubborn, after all.

Today, however, is different. Today, I realised that I've been doing it all wrong for years. I've been writing about the ordinary things, when I'm not ordinary. None of us are ordinary – we just settle into ordinary lives. We have the hopes and dreams of childhood knocked out of us; we have our personalities moulded and polished without our realisation, so we can fit into 'ordinary'. And because ordinary ends up being easier, we stay there, some of us never reaching all those heights we promised ourselves we would.

So, today, I'm writing about the extraordinary; those 'moments' in life that reach us, and change us. Those moments take place all the time, really – it's just that we're taught not to notice. We're taught that whims are for the foolish; that instinct and passion are more akin to fairy tales than reality; that they won't get us very far, and everyone would laugh at us if they knew what we really held close to our hearts.

It's a lie we allow ourselves, and it's understandable.

But it's simply not true.

Do I dare say that my mother was right? Magic does exist. But it's not in the ether, and it's not some intangible thing we can't see or sense. It's the extraordinary hidden in the ordinary, playing out before us often, but only in small amounts, so that we're tricked into missing it when it happens.

But sometimes, if we're lucky — or perhaps luck doesn't have much to do with it — it grabs us and shakes us so we can't miss it, even if we want to.

Then, things get hard, because once you know magic exists, you have to decide whether to be the bystander, or the magician … and we were all born to be magicians.

# I
# *Last Night of Freedom*

## ~ PRESENT DAY ~

The shrill sound of the doorbell made her jump, just as she leaned into the mirror, wide-eyed and holding her breath so she wouldn't get it wrong.

The black mascara missed her lashes and landed on her eyelid.

Meredith groaned.

*Crap.*

She was uneven now – she hated being uneven.

Diving into the bag of cotton wool, she fished one out, knocked the hot tap on with the side of her hand, held the cotton ball in the stream for a couple of seconds, then squeezed and attempted to get rid of the error, ignoring the way her chest tightened over it.

*Breathe ... it's not permanent. Nothing's permanent.*

The doorbell rang again.

"Fuck."

No. She had to deal with this first.

With the black gloop gone, she reapplied the shimmering brown eyeshadow – one sweep over that small, ruined part of the eyelid – *no, not ruined ... different; just different* – then blended it in with the blending brush.

Her breathing had become laboured. She could feel the heat build under her armpits and across her chest.

*It's easy to fix ... it's not permanent...*

The mascara went on once more, her panic at getting it wrong again forcing her hand steady. It helped that this time, she was anticipating the doorbell.

It rang a second after she'd finished, the bell depressed for a good ten seconds.

Candace was early, and she'd obviously been let into the lobby downstairs or she'd be buzzing her intercom.

"I'm coming!" she yelled as loudly as she could.

There. Done. No longer different, but the same.

The prickling heat across her chest dissipated and she sighed in relief before turning and making her way down the stairs to greet the friend she hadn't seen for ten years.

She still didn't quite know why she'd invited her to the hen-do having not seen her for so long, but they *had* been the very best of friends once. She suspected it was part of her last goodbye to her old life, and out of all the friends from her past she could have invited, it would only have been Candace – Candace had always been sensible, providing solid ground for her to land on throughout her reckless teen years.

She shook away the brief anxiety that the memory of her childhood self brought up. Yes, that's why she'd invited Candace – it was time to say goodbye; lay it all to rest.

She hurried down the stairs and across the large hall, the clicks of her heels echoing across the expanse of the room, then she unlocked the top latch, followed by the bottom one, and swung her front door open.

An insanely wide smile showing off pearly white teeth greeted her. They nestled in a face that had always been round and jovial, easy to redden and ... *oh my god* ... she'd only gone and gotten her dark brown hair dyed blue and cut short. The choppiness of it suited her, but Candace's hair used to be so long that Meredith couldn't help but blink at the new style.

"Merri!!!" Candace bulldozed right into her despite the bottle of champagne in one hand and the huge, paper shopping bag in the other, and squeezed her in a bear hug. "I hope you don't mind – someone let me into the lobby downstairs and I just couldn't wait to see you so I raced up here."

An unexpected laugh ripped out of Meredith as everything that made up her best friend took her back to the good old days – the days that really *had* been good. Tears rushed to her eyes, and when Candace finally let her breathe, she could see the same mistiness in her friend's. "Wow, Candy! Look at you!"

"Look at me? Hell, girl, look at *you*. Talk about glam."

"Oh, I was going for classical and smart."

"Well, yes, I meant 'classical glam', and totally smart, but also sexy as always, and definitely far from slutty." She pulled a face, but it was in good spirit. "You know what I'm trying to say – you look *gorgeous*."

"Thanks," smiled Meredith, as she reached for the bag and champagne. "Can I unload you?"

"All for you," said Candace, handing them over. "Congratulations, honey. I'll haul my own rucksack to my room as soon you show me where to ... Jesus Christ..." Her eyes widened as she took in the light, beech wood floor, decorated with two lines of spotlights running along the edge of opposite walls. She moved to stare at the matching spotlights on the ceiling before taking in the apartment as a whole. "Jesus *Christ*!"

"Oh, wait, Candy – would you mind taking your shoes

off?" she asked as she closed and locked both latches on the door, bottom one first and then the top.

"Oh, yeah, sure." She absent-mindedly kicked them off, her gaze now on the 1930s-styled French doors that led out onto the fifth floor balcony overlooking the Docklands. "Bloody hell, Merri, you said you were an accountant? Are you the accountant for the Queen of England?"

She laughed. "I work for the *Bank* of England, not the Queen of England. And, actually, I'm moving into independent financial advising next month and will be starting with a new firm – one of the top wealth management firms in the country. Michael and I talked about it. He only has partial ties to the bank nowadays as he spends a lot of time working with his parents in the family business. This opportunity came up for me and we agreed that having our work places completely separate from each other's once we're married and living together would probably be a good idea; help to maintain a healthy relationship."

Candy's eyebrows shot up. "You don't live together yet?"

"Well, we may as well have. I mean, we've been in and out of each other's apartments for weeks at a time over the last two years. The next step is to buy a place together."

"The next step?"

She straightened Candace's shoes and placed them onto the shoe rack. "After marriage."

Her former best friend looked at her quizzically for the briefest of seconds and then threw her another huge smile. "Well, you look awesome. Clearly, this upmarket London lifestyle is working for you. I can't wait to meet Michael."

Something inside her squirmed as she imagined exactly what Michael would have to say about Candace's blue, cropped hair. *Michael Fortune of Fortune Airs, meet Candace North of ... er ... Cornwall.*

"How's your mum?"

The squirmy feeling got bigger. Michael and her mother got on politely, and for her sake alone. "She's good."

"Not blown up the Houses of Parliament yet, then?" grinned Candy. "Your mum's a hoot!"

*Yeah ... my self-confessed, anti-capitalist, 'white witch' mother and my London banker fiancé – heir to his family's multi-million pound global enterprise – really don't mix.* "She's got a permanent weekly slot as the Clairvoyant for a large and well-known New Age shop near Covent Garden, and she finally set up her own online business selling her potions and what-not when I finally convinced her the internet wouldn't bite. And it's doing well – she's developed a small name for herself."

Candace's tone grew a touch more gentle. "How's her health?"

"Good," she repeated. "She's been in remission for almost ten years now."

"That's great! I wasn't sure. After that last time I saw you, I went backpacking on my Year Out before uni, and we lost touch and—"

"I'm so sorry," they both said in unison and some of the slight awkwardness disappeared from the room.

Meredith shrugged, tilting her head in apology. "I should have made more effort to keep in touch – I really, really missed you. It's just ... with my mum the way she was back then and all the shit I got myself into..." She inwardly cringed, battled a swell of guilt, and then straightened her shoulders, with effort, to stave off the familiar tightening heat that liked to take her prisoner. "I needed to put all my focus into turning my life around, you know?"

Candace approached her and slipped both her hands into hers. "And it's paid off, right? I mean, look at you, here, in this place..." Oddly, a small frown creased the centre of her eyebrows.

Merri wanted to erase it. "Yes. Everything's perfect now."

"Excellent." The crease disappeared, and so did the anxiety that formed a vice around Meredith's ribcage – squeezing... "So ... hen-do! Where are we going? What's the plan?"

~*~

~ THIRTEEN SUMMERS AGO ~

"Merri! Merri! Merri!" came the chant from below her, cushioned by drunken cheers and stoned clapping.

A wisp of her pink-tipped blonde hair smacked lightly into her face with the wind, as she risked a look down at her audience.

"*Meredith*," hissed Candace, her hand on her hip as her eyes, barely visible from this height and angle, stared daggers at her. "This is the most idiotic plan ever! Get the fuck back down!"

*No way.*

"You're stoned and drunk, you stupid bint!"

"I'm not drunk!" she called back down, singing the declaration to the crowd twenty feet below – friends she might never see again.

"Even a little drunk is too drunk to go climbing cliffs!"

"It's not a cliff. I'm already half way to the top."

"You'll break a limb if you fall – or *die* – that makes it a fucking cliff."

Meredith rolled her eyes and then gripped the ragged granite a little tighter when a wave of dizziness washed over her.

*Whoa.*

Maybe she was a *little* drunk. But this was her last night of freedom; the final curtain before the scenery, along with her life, changed forever, and the hard rock suited everything that awaited her: London was cold. Busy and bustling and full of life and wonder ... but hard and cold. Like granite. Except the granite that protected the Cornish coast encased a land that was expansive and ... the only word she could think for it was *free.* How could it not be? The sea was right there, waves crashing into rock, then rolling out into the ocean; a furious, raging dance of foam and water that met the horizon. The ocean was free and she wondered how long it would be before she saw it again.

She closed her hand around the next jutting piece of wall and hauled herself up another foot.

She heard Candace mutter a curse into the wind, but then Candace was always worried about something. If it wasn't the additives in food, it was pollution in the air. God forbid *she* ever live in London; she'd have a friggin' nervous breakdown.

*And you're gonna be just fine, right?*

The next gust of wind stung her eyes, and tears rose to the surface.

*Right.*

Because she wouldn't let the stoniness of the capital keep her trapped there. Not for anything. She belonged here where the winters stoked your fire and the summers ignited your passion, where the cliffs and the sea reminded you of the greatness of life; the swelling hills and fields that the earth could breathe.

*And what if Dad comes back and I'm not here?*

She quenched that thought as quickly as it had sprung up, frowning at its mere existence, knowing it was nothing but a futile illusion – the last hope of a five-year-old. By all accounts, that hope should have died a long time ago, but when she looked out towards the skyline, she still felt it: a small flame, burning, that the persistent wind could not extinguish. *He's out there somewhere. Why has he never kept in touch? Maybe I'll go look for him as soon as I've finished my studies.*

More thoughts that needed to be quenched before they brought a whole load of hurt with them.

She was old enough to know it was only ever going to be a matter of time before her mum found another man – not just a boyfriend, but one for whom she was prepared to make changes. She had met Rick two years ago. He lived and worked in London – as a nutritionist and Yoga instructor in Harley Street – coming down to Cornwall for the big eco and alternative festivals, two or three times a year. Meredith had seen their spark, had been happy for her mother – of course she had. But the move to London was breaking her heart. Why couldn't they wait three more years? She had turned sixteen yesterday. In three years, all her schooling and exams would be behind her and she'd be able to choose where she lived.

But asking her mum to wait three years felt selfish – she'd already waited ten; done everything in her power to make Meredith feel safe and happy.

So, the protest lodged at the base of her throat, frothing like the foam did when the ocean slammed into rock, and growing bigger by the second. Dope alleviated it.

So did doing crazy things.

She brushed away the guilt that enveloped her. Yeah, her mum would have a heart attack if she knew she was climbing forty feet of vertical rock with no protection, but she just ... *had* to. Had to let it out. This was her protest; this was her expression and *this* she had control of.

The next ten feet were a doddle.

She grinned, looking up. Ten more to the top.

If she could conquer this, she could...

"Shit," she mumbled as the first drop of rain hit her right cheek. This was going to make things slippery, and she couldn't exactly go backwards.

*Just get to the top.*

"Merri!"

*Give it a rest, Candy.* "I'm fine!" she hollered over her shoulder, unable to tell if she could be heard.

Shaking her head to bring some focus to her mind, she took in a deep breath and continued hauling herself up. She'd only had a couple of drags on the joint – her head was fine; the night was young and the sun hadn't even set yet.

Her fingers were getting cold, the summer rain bringing a chill to the wind that hadn't been there before.

*Five more feet to go. This is nothing. This is easy.*

Her left plimsoll-clad foot slipped.

Her heart skipped a beat, but both her hands had good hold on the granite and her foot found its place again with ease. Still ... it took a good few seconds for her heart rate to slow down again. It wouldn't slow that much – she was only twenty-odd inches from the top now, and this was *exhilarating*.

She'd known the granite was stable. Shame she'd never stopped to think about the very top of the cliff – no longer granite, but dirt and grass.

She clamped her fingers around the grass, wedged her feet into the side of the cliff as well as she could on the next foothold, and heaved herself up with as much force as she could manage, preparing to land on the grass with her upper body.

The earth under her hands gave way.

A scream ripped from her before her brain fully registered the predicament, because instinctively, she knew she was fucked. She was in the wrong position for her feet to save her and she was already teetering backwards.

More screams echoed below her.

She tried to push her weight forwards with the force of her body alone, and reached for the top of the cliff once more.

Her middle finger brushed soil, but it was just out of reach, and her throat was still working out the scream when a hand clamped around her wrist.

Before she could think about what was happening, she was hoisted upwards. The ground winded her when she landed hard on her stomach and chest, and then she was dragged along the beautiful, safe dirt some more until the edge of the cliff was a good few feet away.

Her rescuer grunted and fell to his knees in front of her, panting for breath.

She looked up and met a mass of dark brown hair, most of it in a ponytail, and some of it whipping across amused, liquid brown eyes. Her breath caught in her throat ... or maybe she was still winded.

Perhaps the world had slipped away after all.

The stranger – a boy, verging on man, about sixteen or seventeen at a guess – threw her a cheeky grin, and then reached into his coat pocket and pulled out a smoke and a lighter.

He drew from the roll-up as he lit it, then handed it to her.

Tentatively, she brought herself up to her knees, facing him, having no idea what to say.

*Say thank you, you bimbo.*

Right.

Except no words came out.

But then, he hadn't spoken either. He just stared at her with eyes that seemed to read her like a book.

She reached forward and took the rolly he offered, and so began the last twelve hours before her life, as she knew it, ended.

# II

## Out of the Blue

### ~ PRESENT DAY ~

"Your life as you know it is about to end," pressed Candace, the wrong side of tipsy.

Meredith cocked an eyebrow. "I don't feel that way about it. Nothing's going to change that much – it's just a ceremony ... some words."

Candy stared at her with that quizzical look again – the one that had made an appearance a few times that night – and pushed her glass of Sambuca towards Meredith. "Drink," she ordered.

"What? Why?"

"This is your hen night and you're being boring."

"It's a chance to catch up with friends before coupling off. I can hardly do that efficiently whilst drunk."

"And," Candy looked around her from where they sat at the cocktail bar that had been hired out for the do, "these are your friends."

Merri tampered down a slither of annoyance.

"Which is cool," she continued, "they're very nice. But I haven't heard anyone here say more than a few words to you since we got here."

"We work together," she replied defensively. "We saw

each other this morning – there's only so much you can say in one day that hasn't already been covered."

"Are all your friends people you and your fiancé work with? Are they all his friends too? Have they at least hired a stripper for you?"

"Candy!" she exclaimed, aghast.

"There was a time when *you'd* have been the one stripping."

Her mouth dropped open. "I have *never* stripped!"

"Maybe not, but you'd have been the first to try it if someone had dared you." Her blue eyes took on a mischievous haze. "Want me to dare you?"

"Don't you dare!" she snapped, the crippling sense of panic already rising, but right there with it, was also a rise to the unspoken challenge and it was even more unsettling – she thought she'd curbed that side of her. "I invited you here because you were always the sensible one."

"Still am," she grinned, "although you may just be stealing the title from me. Look, I *am* the sensible one, and I hereby solemnly vow that I will make sure you get into no trouble tonight, so just let your hair down a little, okay? Speaking of which, since when did you start to straighten it?"

She glanced down at her ash-blonde strands. Naturally wavy with a tendency to curl when damp, it had always been a pain to get the knots out, especially living by the sea, so she had never bothered too much, instead letting it grow long and unruly, and then chopping most of it off once a year. Starting her job at the bank though, she'd had to look neat, and her hair was anything but, so she'd taken straighteners to it and had kept it straight since. "It's more acceptable this way."

Candace frowned. The Sambuca was pushed another

inch towards her. "Drink."

"Candy," she warned. "Listen, I didn't want to mention this tonight, but I've been getting counselling for ... it's sort of like an anxiety dis..." her voice trailed off as wolf whistles and clapping erupted from the far side of the room near the entrance.

A tall man walked in, a bag slung lazily over his shoulder; his white shirt unbuttoned down to the middle of his well-defined chest. He wore his dark hair back in a short ponytail, and for a second the air sort of wavered in front of her. The smell of salt, sand and sea, combined with cool summer wind, hit her sharply – one of those anomalies of how the brain worked, where it could conjure up a smell from memory so readily.

*It's him.*

When his eyes finally landed on her, they were a start-ling blue and not the liquid brown that she hadn't thought about for over ten years. *So why think about him now?*

Her breath whooshed out of her in relief, even as a baffling disappointment made itself known in the centre of her chest. "It's not him," she whispered.

Her sense of relief was short-lived.

The man zeroed in on her, taking in the sash she'd been forcefully encouraged to wear, with Bride-To-Be stamped all over it, and threw her a devilish grin. Chanting filled the room ... "Strip, strip, strip, strip..."

Candace squealed in delight. "Oh, you *do* have nice friends!"

"They promised they wouldn't do this." Damn. She should have told them; should have told someone about her problem with ... surprises. She didn't think they'd do this – not here of all places – in this swish, sophisticated venue. She hadn't wanted a hen-do. Simply imagining all the things that could go wrong was enough to start her off, but all her bridesmaids had insisted; Michael and her mother had both encouraged it, and when she'd finally decided to invite sensible Candy, she had conceded.

"Go on, get up! It's you he's here for... Merri?"

She turned to find Candace staring at her with concern.

"Honey? You okay?"

Her breaths were shooting out in short, shallow bursts. She must be pale – she felt pale ... and faint.

With a little whimper, she gripped the side of the bar and tried to stand; tried not to double over at the stinging restriction across her chest. She needed to get to...

*Under the covers, where everything's safe.*

"The bathroom," she croaked out.

She lost her footing on the rung around the base of the bar stool as she rose. Stumbling two steps forward, she was already seeing multi-coloured sparks, which were fast fading to blackness, before she hit the ground.

~*~

~ THIRTEEN SUMMERS AGO ~

The rolly was a nice one – it was welcome; grounding. "What are you doing all the way up here?"

His eyebrows went up a fraction. "Watching a crazy girl climb a small cliff with no ropes." He plucked the smoke back from her hand and took a drag as he leant to the left and stared behind her at the drop. On his exhalation, his lips curled up in a wry smile. "You're fucking insane."

That smile looked like a secret – like he knew something she didn't – and it caused an unexpected flutter low in Merri's abdomen, which in turn pissed her off, although she couldn't quite fathom why. "I needed to know if I could do it."

"Did you?"

"What?"

"Do it?"

She frowned. "Well, yeah. You saw me climb up – here I am."

"That doesn't mean you accomplished whatever it was you set out to accomplish."

*What the fuck...? Who is this guy?* "I did," she snapped, then strode past him, looking for the path down from the cliff.

"Was my saving your life part of your accomplishment?"

*Smart arse.*

"You're welcome, by the way."

Irritation rose fast. "You didn't—" she began, but had to cut herself short and bite her tongue. He *had* potentially saved her life, but *only* potentially – it was more likely she'd have survived and had to deal with broken bones. Still... She involuntarily shuddered as she pictured her mother's devastation at hearing the news of her (potential) death. Fuck. "Thanks."

He grinned, and those little flutterings conspired with each other, merged together, and turned into a somersault. "No problem. It's over here, by the way."

"The path down? Hang on..." She ran back to the edge of the cliff, careful to avoid the bits of earth that had fallen away. Peering over the edge, she whistled down to Candace and the others.

"You're a cow, Merri – a stupid cow! I fucking hate you! Are you okay?"

"I'm great! Listen, I'll catch up with you all further down the beach a bit later, okay?"

"What are you doing up there?"

"Saying goodbye to home," she yelled back, not really understanding why she didn't want to mention her rescuer. He was just suddenly there – poof, like magic. If she gave him away, he might poof into nothingness. The idea of him suddenly disappearing on her didn't sit well with her at all. "See you in a bit, okay?" She turned as she retreated, refusing to look the boy in the face. Instead, she strode past him, towards the path. "Where is it?"

"Pardon?"

"You said the path was here."

"No, I didn't."

She crossed her arms. "Yes you did."

He took in her defensive stance, bemused, and threw the butt of his expired roll-up under his heel. "No, I didn't. My *ride* is here ... and yours."

He led her further down the slope and a Piaggio scooter that looked like it had seen better days came into view on the right. Meredith laughed. "No way. You rode all the way up here on *that.*"

"Treat an engine right and she'll treat you right."

"Bet you say that to all the girls."

He bellowed out a laugh and it was her turn to grin. She kept it plastered on her face as he, once more, got all deep with his stare.

*Nope – not affected.*

As if he'd heard her silent statement, and received it as a challenge, his mouth moved up again in that secretive smile – *oh, to hell with that smile* – and he motioned to the scooter with his head. "Hop on."

"And what makes you think I'm going anywhere with you?"

His annoying smile widened. "Because I've only got one

helmet and you're insane."

Oooo ... he was good.

She cleared her throat. "Where would we go?"

All the sudden, he seemed to turn serious, his voice coming out low as those brown eyes – an old soul's eyes, she realised – shone with things she might never know about him. That thought punched a hole through her – she wanted to know everything about him. Which was stupid because she'd met him little over five minutes ago. She looked away from him and his haunting gaze as he spoke. "You have great things you need to achieve. How would you feel if you never did?"

She kicked dirt with her feet and kept her eyes glued to the ground. How weird that her heart ached – just a little, but the ache was there. She hated it when her heart ached. It reminded her of when her dad had left.

"I just wanted to climb that wall, that's all."

"Why?"

She sighed. Fine. "Because we're leaving to go live in London tomorrow – my mum and me. Nine in the morning and," she looked out across the summer sky, only just starting to grow dusky as the sun lay to rest, "all this is gone, replaced by ... hell, I don't know what. But the sky's gotta be harder to see with all those tall buildings surrounding me, right? I wanted to leave a part of me here; maybe take a part of here away with me ... I don't know exactly."

Ten seconds of silence was too long.

She gave in and looked at him. Yep, there he was, still staring at her.

"See anything you like?" she snapped.

He smirked. "I'll let you know. Hop on then," he added, quietly.

She cocked her head at him in question.

"The night's still young, and the world is ours. We have twelve hours for you to make your mark in it."

*Ours?* A thrill ran through her. "Ours?"

He shrugged. "I find myself intrigued by your desire to fall off cliffs – I can't look away. It's sort of like trying to look away from a bad accident. I want to know how you got this way and what happens next." He held out his helmet to her. "Come on, I dare you."

The thrill got bigger. Damn it, he knew – somehow, he *knew* those were the magic words.

She snatched the helmet off him. "You're comparing me to an accident? I knew what I was doing. I've climbed indoor walls fifteen metres high – that cliff was no higher. It's barely a cliff."

"They let you climb indoor walls without ropes?"

*Smart arse. Again.* "I get the helmet? I thought you said—"

"I said you were insane." He took the helmet from her hands, pushed it down over her head, and then adjusted the straps. "I, however, am not insane. All passengers wear helmets."

"Smart arse," she said, aloud this time, behind the visor.

If he heard her, he didn't react.

"How does you *not* wearing a helmet make you sane?" she shouted through the head gear, wishing breathing was a bit easier trapped in this thing.

"Because I'll drive all the more carefully without one. You, on the other hand..."

She flipped him her finger and he laughed. "You getting on then, or what?"

Yeah, he was right – she was insane. For all she knew, he was some kind of psycho – Ted Bundy's grandson. She waited for her sensible half to turn around and walk away, but her sensible half hadn't really been around much the past few months. Instead, she got on the small two-seater and found herself snuggled into him, closer than she'd expected.

Boys were the last thing she should be thinking about with her leaving tomorrow – she'd deliberately ignored Jason, her major crush since middle school, since finding out she'd be leaving her home behind – but *this* guy had just appeared out of nowhere and blind-sided her a little. He was totally different to the boys she knew and her curiosity was getting the better of her. That, and her need to fulfil every last second she had in this beautiful part of the country with everything she could.

*And so you should. What's the big deal, Merri? He's not Jason. He's totally new and just for now. He's the last you'll have of this place, and maybe that's good – better than spending it with friends and going through all those cruddy feelings at leaving them behind. You won't have to deal with so much this way. You won't have to say heavy good-byes and make 'see you soon' promises. Nothing's permanent. For the next twelve hours, you just get to be free.*

"Ready?"

She curled her fingers around the rear hand rail and shook away the urge to wrap her arms around his waist. "Yeah – ready."

~*~

### ~ PRESENT DAY ~

"Merri…"

A small crowd had gathered around her. That was the first thing she knew as the neon sparks in front of her eyes faded. Had she passed out? No – almost.

The world had gone black, but, somehow, her body had been able to utilise the oxygen it needed, and the black had only been passing – a two-second spell.

"Already feeling the effects of the cocktails, or the effects of the hot stripper guy?" grinned Laura, a friend from work she'd only known about three months, but she was nice enough and they got on well.

"Er..." She looked up, embarrassed. The stripper was there among the crowd, looking as if this kind of thing happened to him often. Heat flamed her cheeks ... and he now looked *nothing* like who she'd thought on first seeing him. Her brain was clearly having an off-day. Maybe it was easier to play drunk. "Both? Whoops," she laughed, shakily.

"Come on," said Candace, placing an arm under hers. "Let's get you up."

She smiled a thanks at her long-time best friend. She could see she wasn't fooled – concern shone through her eyes.

"So," Candy said to the huddle, "who's gonna show our handsome entertainer where to set up?"

"Ooo!" Laura practically leaped up. "That'll be me!" She wandered towards him – sprinted was more like it – and the crowd dissipated, drunken giggles rippling throughout the room.

"It'll all be forgotten in half an hour, as soon as the clothes start coming off," winked Candy.

"Thanks."

She hauled her up and the two of them made their way to the washroom.

"What was that about, Merri?"

Meredith sighed. She hated explaining, which is why she never did. Her mum and Michael were the only two people who knew – she had never wanted anyone on tenterhooks around her if the slightest thing went wrong. "It's not as bad as it sounds, okay?"

Candy rose her eyebrows, waiting.

"I get panic attacks, that's all."

"Since when?"

"Since I found my mum that time when you last came down."

"You've had panic attacks for ten years? Ten *years*?"

"They come and go," she added quickly. "It only happens when things get unpredictable. With the wedding and everything, it's all been a bit ... you know." She turned the cold tap on and ran both her hands under the water, the coolness of it calming her down. "I'm not usually this bad. Can you get me a paper towel?"

"Sure ... so, the attacks only come on when things happen that are out of the blue?"

She nodded and took the towel that Candy held out to her. Folding it in four, she soaked it under the water, then squeezed it dry and placed it on her forehead with another sigh – this one of relief.

"Ever since you found your mum passed out?" Her question was whispered sympathetically.

Meredith had slowly lost it over the first three years after moving to London. Her need for controlling uncontrollable things had seen her in precarious situations she had put herself in over and over again, with the help of some very unsavoury peers. Cannabis had led to the occasional line of coke and Ecstasy tablet. It was E she had been high on when she'd stumbled home one night, earlier than planned because her 'friends' had left her high and dry, and found her mother collapsed on the kitchen floor.

She'd been complaining of dizziness, nausea, shortness

of breath... Merri hadn't listened. She hadn't really been there most of the time – her head was always somewhere else. Meredith had shrugged at her complaints, and her mother had kept mentioning that she should maybe see a doctor, but she'd never gotten around to it, and Merri was in no place to care – she couldn't *give* care; she couldn't even care for herself and lord knows, she certainly didn't care for her new London life. Not after what she'd learnt the morning they'd left Cornwall, and not after ... no, she couldn't think about that.

She couldn't remember much of what happened after she'd found her mum passed out – she couldn't even remember how she'd gotten home that night. She remembered laughing at the sight of her on the floor, 'cause drugs fucked you up like that. She remembered nudging her mum with her foot to get up ... or maybe the nudges had been kicks, 'cause later, the doctors had found bruises on her stomach. The guilt still ate her up over that. She didn't remember calling 999, but she must have done. She didn't remember riding to the hospital in the ambulance, but she had woken up the next morning in a hospital bed with a hydration drip in her arm, trying to thread together pieces of a broken night.

Primary glioblastoma multiforme – a brain tumour. That's what her mum had had.

It had been in an accessible location, isolated, and the spreading wasn't as bad as they had feared – surgery had been possible and successful. Candace had been there throughout the surgery, because she was the first person Merri had phoned as soon as she had been of sound mind.

"You're lucky we got to your mum when we did," one of the doctors had said to Merri, much later, with reprimanding eyes, the message, clear and written between the lines of her medical notes for all eternity: *you fucked up – we could have gotten there sooner if you hadn't been high. She might have died.*

It had been one scare too many.

That was the last time Meredith ever took drugs.

She had started seeing a counsellor after that and gotten her life back on track. The panic attacks had started two months later.

"Ten years, Merri?"

"They're a small sacrifice. I'll take them over what could have happened any day of the week."

Candace came up behind her and rested her chin on her shoulder as they stared at each other in the bathroom mirror. "Why the hell didn't you tell me? I'd have talked you into a quiet night watching old movies," she smiled, "like we used to do while we ransacked your mum's magic box in secret and went through all the spells."

Merri laughed. "Don't you think we're a bit old for that?"

"No way! You're never too old for magic."

"Anyway, I felt dumb not having a hen night – everyone here wants to celebrate and—"

"Come on," said Candy, suddenly, tugging at her sleeve. "Let's get out of here."

"But—"

"Can you hear that?"

She strained her ears. "Music?"

"Not just any music – dance music. The stripping has begun, my darling, and I *promise* you that all eyes will be on him when we walk out the bathroom. Sneaking out will not be a problem."

Oh, leaving here would be *heaven*. "They'll all hate me for leaving them."

"I recall that never used to be a problem." A hint of resentment lay in that statement, and Merri knew why. Candace was referring to her never having made it back to the beach that last night she'd spent in Cornwall. She'd been so fucking selfish. "Oh, Candy..." she started, apologetically, but her friend just leaned forward and took her into an embrace. Too much had happened the past decade to let teenage selfishness stand in the way of friendship.

She squeezed her back, tears skimming her eyes. "I'm glad you're here."

"Me too."

"Okay," Merri released her, "let's go. I have popcorn and Baileys at home."

"An excellent combination! And spells?"

She snorted. "That's my mum's area of expertise, not mine."

# III

## Sea Whisperer

The runway to Heathrow airport came into view as he stared out of the aeroplane window.

He'd never been a natural flyer, preferring the depths of the ocean to the expanse of the sky.

"Are you a nervous flyer?" came the voice to his right. The woman – older, maybe about sixty – had been a meek passenger, only now making conversation when they were about to land, but that was the way with people, wasn't it? You only really got to know them when it was too late.

"Not nervous, just ... let's just say it's not my forte."

"I know what you mean. My husband loves flying; me, not so much. He's meeting me at the airport. We've been apart for the first time in twenty years," she smiled, knowingly, as if he was supposed to know whatever it was that she knew.

He returned her smile politely and looked away, back out the window, at the country he'd left a decade ago to go study abroad. He'd ended up living abroad.

Home is where your heart is, that's what they said. As far as he was concerned, it was never a good idea to connect the two, for if you lost your heart, you lost your home too.

"Are you visiting family?"

He supposed conversation was impossible to avoid in

such close quarters. "No, I ... I just split up with my girl-friend of ten years, actually."

Fuck. That hurt. Saying it out loud.

"I'm sorry."

He shrugged. "They say these things happen for a reason."

"Oh, they do happen for a reason," she nodded.

"The reason is called, Pierre."

"Oh."

"Sort of rhymes: Pierre and Claire."

She clamped her lips shut and looked down at her fingers on her lap.

He'd always rather enjoyed making people feel a tad uncomfortable – it tickled his funny bone – so he carried on. "We met when we were both very young – nineteen. We were on the same university course, studying Oceanography. I guess I should have taken the hint: ten years together and she never wanted to marry; didn't want to have kids. We had both always put our work first, determined that our relationship wouldn't get in the way of our studies; I thought she just didn't want to settle down yet. More fool me.

"So, this is my coming home in a way. I'm from Cornwall; a little village near the coast. I'm heading back to see my parents ... to regroup. Figure out where to go from here."

"Good idea."

"Yeah."

"Was she – I mean, your girlfriend of ten years – was she your first?"

He stared at her, intrigued at her question. Maybe she wasn't so uncomfortable with the conversation after all.

"Sorry. It's a personal question isn't it? You said you were nineteen when you met, and I was just curious."

He shrugged. He'd been the one to make it personal by mentioning Claire – her question was valid.

The image of green eyes, a stubborn chin and pink-tipped hair blowing on a cliff top on a windy summer's evening, filled his mind and brought the first genuine smile to his lips for weeks. He hadn't thought about *her* in years.

He pushed the image away, coming back to the present as the plane's wheels came out for landing. "No. She wasn't my first."

~*~

Candace squealed with laughter and Merri tried not to tip over the glass of Baileys as she lay, shaking in fits of giggles, on the sofa.

The television was on, but muted, and old photograph albums were scattered, open, on the floor. The photograph at the receiving end of the snorts of laughter was one of Meredith and Jason. Her and Jason had been on and off as an official couple for a year – mostly on because of her and off because of him.

"Jason was *so* clueless, Merri, I don't know what you ever saw in him."

"He wasn't clueless! He just got so focused on one thing that he'd forget everything else."

"He forgot *you* repeatedly – he forgot your sixteenth birthday, for Christ's sake."

"Because he had a game with the lads – football was important to him."

"More important than you." She reached forward for the bottle of Baileys.

"Yeah, well, he was sixteen. Didn't he get a football scholarship or something? Into one of those clubs?"

"Mmm-hmm," nodded Candy. "Up in Cheshire."

"Well, there you go – he kept his focus and achieved his goal – didn't let some blonde bimbo get in the way of his career."

"What a charmer."

Merri laughed, and then sighed. "Honestly, Candy, it never bothered me as much as people thought. In the end, it was easier that he was focused elsewhere. I was always off doing my own thing anyway, and it would have been harder to deal with leaving if he'd been all attentive and solid boyfriend material."

"Yeah, but no one wants to know they gave their V-card to someone who never appreciated it."

"What? Candy! Jason wasn't the one to get that!"

Candy's eyes widened as she gulped down her double-shot of Baileys. "No waaaay ... Merri, after you left he went and told everyone that you and he had ... you know."

And now Meredith's mouth fell open. "Jerk!"

"Hello? That's what I've been saying for the past half hour."

"Did everyone believe him?"

"Well, yeah. You and he were a couple – mostly – and why would they not?"

"Give me that." Merri snatched the bottle from Candy and topped up her glass.

"So if *he* didn't get it, then who did? You never mentioned any boyfriend to me after you moved to London."

*"This is one of those bad ideas," he protested, "like climbing cliffs with no ropes."*

*"Look how that turned out." She pressed her lips against the side of his neck, delighting in his appreciative sigh, barely able to keep from shivering with anticipation. The*

*last five hours had been the most perfect five hours of her entire life. Everything about this boy swallowed her up – his scent, his wit, his humour, the way he looked at her... Her stomach was doing somersaults all over the place now, and for a second, she hesitated, even though she'd been the one to initiate this. On a deep level, this felt meant to be – she wanted this with a ferocity that was almost scary – but in the cold light of day, she was a sixteen-year-old about to have a one-night stand. This wasn't how a girl was supposed to lose her virginity.*

*She took a step back and looked up at him. "Is this wrong?"*

*Warm brown eyes she'd never forget in a million years speared her own. They should be spearing her heart too, because she'd never see them again; yet, somehow, they made everything better. She'd wanted to leave something of herself behind; take something with her ... granted, this wasn't what she'd had in mind, but from falcon-watching, to stargazing, to skimming rocks across the sea, this is where tonight had led and...*

*One hand came up to tenderly grasp the back of her neck. His thumb stroked her cheek. "The thing is, Merri, with you ... everything that's supposed to be wrong, is right."*

A cushion hit her square in the forehead. "Hey! I almost spilled my drink!"

"You are sitting there, zoned-out, with a huge, Cheshire cat grin on your face, saying nothing – spill!"

"There's nothing to really tell."

Candy grabbed another cushion and Merri screeched in protest as it came down over her defending forearm. "Don't you tell me it's nothing when you have *that* look on your face."

Merri's hoots of amusement turned silent as she grabbed the stitch developing on her right hand side.

A third cushion took aim.

"Okay! Okay ... it was that night. My last night when I disappeared on you all."

"With who? Craig? Oooo ... Simon?"

"Nuh-uh," she shook her head, the wonderful pain in her side not letting up. When was the last time she'd had a stitch from laughing? God, it seemed too long ago to count. "You don't know him – I met him that night."

Candace gasped. "You slut!"

"Oh, no, no, no," Merri put down her glass and rolled onto her stomach, "don't you do that."

"Do what?"

"Cheapen the best night of my life with your judgyness."

Another gasp, this one quieter. Candace shuffled towards her across the floor on her bum, intrigue colouring her alcohol-reddened face. "Seriously? The best night?"

Their eyes met and Merri nodded, her laughter fading into a contended smile. "His name was Jamie. I hadn't thought about him in years until that stripper walked in – he looked a bit like him."

"Oh, my god, he looked like the stripper?"

"Well, a seventeen-year-old version of ... his eyes were a different colour. He was at the top of the cliff. When the earth gave way and I was falling backwards, he grabbed me and pulled me up."

An odd silence filled the room.

"I swear, Candy, he was just ... *there* ... I'd never seen him before. He took me to see the Peregrine Falcons feeding their young – he knew where they all nested, then we skimmed rocks for a while, collected cuttlefish bones and shells... It was a clear night and we lay for over an hour naming constellations and giving the ones we didn't know stupid names—"

"Are you kidding me?" interrupted Candace. "You said he was seventeen, not seventy."

Meredith giggled. "That's exactly what I said to him. And he told me off for being all prejudiced despite my pink hair and black nail varnish."

*"You think the only boys in existence are the ones who like football, farting and telling bad jokes? Some of us are word-smiths, or musicians; we have dreamers' souls – we just know how to hide it 'cause we don't want the shit kicked out of us when we could be spending our time more wisely."*

*She turned her attention from the sky and onto him, leaning on her right elbow so she could see his face. "Are you a musician?"*

*"Nah," he smiled, "I'm a sea whisperer."*

*A laugh burst from her. "A what?"*

*"The sea talks to me – tells me things."*

*"You just made that up!"*

*"Sort of, but not really. That's what I want to do: re-search the ocean."*

*"Like, a marine scientist or something?"*

*"Yeah – I'm hoping to get a scholarship to go study in Australia. I love the sea. It's full of secrets just waiting to be discovered," his gaze met hers, "kinda like you."*

*And suddenly she forgot how to breathe – it was the best kind of oxygen starvation.*

"Holy hell, Merri," sighed Candace. Her head landed on the arm of the sofa, her blue eyes, dreamy. But Candy had always been a hopeless romantic. "Why did such a cynical, reckless bitch like you end up with the sweet guy?"

"Nice!"

"I'm kidding! Sort of."

And now Candy took a cushion to the head.

"I didn't 'end up' with him, I had to leave the next day and I never saw him again."

"Was it good?" Candy yawned, which had Merri following suit.

"Was what good?"

"Duh ... the sex."

*The full weight of his body was followed only by the full weight of his groan against her ear.*

*Tears pricked her eyes as she clutched him to her, not because of that sharp sting between her legs that was fast giving way to ... something else ... but because she never wanted to let him go; never wanted herself empty of him now that she'd known him.*

*She whimpered as he moved, the feel of it all so unfamiliar, still a little painful, and yet, so singularly amazing that nothing else could ever compare.*

*He stilled inside her and dropped a kiss on her lips, uncertainty shining through the need in his eyes. "Are you all right? Am I doing this right?"*

*She moved beneath him in encouragement; stroked his hair, now loose from its tie ... "It's perfect."*

"It was perfect."

"For real?"

She looked down at her friend. Her eyes were closed as she leant on the sofa's arm.

"You know how it's never supposed to be good the first time? Well, everything that was supposed to be wrong about that night, was right. It was perfect."

"Bitch."

Merri smiled at her slurred insult.

"Did you use protection?"

She rolled her eyes. Forever Miss Sensible. Trust her to bring that up now when it had happened thirteen years ago. "Yes, Candy, we did." She pushed away that *other* memory she could do without having. Luckily, the Baileys was hitting the spot nicely. Another yawn slipped out of her, her own eyes closing. "Of course we did."

*Only just, though,* she thought, wryly, as she pictured that one, almost out-of-date condom she'd kept in her wallet for months in case her and Jason had ever gotten that far. Through her dozy haze, she smiled as she remembered Jamie's face when she'd produced the slightly tattered foil packet. *"Er ... and that's how old?"*

*"It's use-by is tomorrow – see? Meant to be."*

She chuckled, half-asleep.

Candy made some sort of protesting noise at the sound.

The light of the silent television glared through her shut eyelids, but all she saw at this moment were constellations and brown irises staring down at her.

*Why am I thinking about him now, after all these years?*

*'Cause you're getting married tomorrow,* came the faraway reply.

A faint sense of panic seized her, but it was as far away as the voice in her head, and fast taking its place was the dim roar of an engine – a 50cc engine. A rust-bucket of a thing that had defied all odds motoring up and down the steepest of terrain...

*They pulled up one street down from hers, the grey of dawn getting lighter faster than she'd like. Her heart was a* strange combination of free and aching when he switched the engine off. The subsequent silence was deafening.

"Well..." they both started in unison, and then laughed.

"Ladies first?" quipped Jamie.

She pursed her lips. "So not a lady."

"You were last night." He took her left hand in his right – just the tips of her fingers folded under his.

A furious blush exploded in her cheeks.

"Thanks for the best night of my life," he said.

She thought he must be joking, but when she looked up, he was all solemn and serious, his eyes seeking hers out in question.

On impulse and almost as if led, she took a step forward and planted a kiss on his lips, pouring everything she couldn't say into it. And she really could say nothing ... there were no words for something that meant everything, yet couldn't mean anything.

'Yes there are,' betrayed her mind.

His hand snaked around her waist and he pulled her into him as he returned her kiss for like, both of them leaning against the invincible Piaggio scooter, now covered in sand and dust.

Pulling away was a small kind of torture.

He still searched her out with his stare. "What are you thinking?"

Her face grew hotter, if that were even possible, but he stilled the shake of her head with his hand cupping the side of her jaw. "Tell me. You're never gonna to see me again, so spit it out."

Fuck, she'd already told him everything anyway – stuff about herself she'd never even told Candace, because she was never going to see him again. "Remember I told you about how my dad left?"

He nodded.

"And remember I said about my mum saying those words?"

Another nod.

She risked a glance up to see if he was listening. Hell, he wasn't just listening; he was drinking in everything she said as if the syllables were spun out of gold.

Her reservations left her. "I was thinking about the words."

Understanding lit his eyes from brown to what almost looked like bronze ... or maybe that was the light of the sun coming up. "You wanna say them?"

Her mouth went dry and she barked out a cynical laugh. "It's so stupid."

"No it's not. They mean something to you. And last night meant something. Feelings aren't stupid."

Seriously, dude, where the almighty fuck did you come from? You're like my dream guy, and I didn't even know I had a dream guy.

"Say them."

"Whoa ... no. Na-uh. It doesn't work anyway – I mean, the magic. If my mum really does magic like people think she does, then ... well, Dad never came back."

"Then it doesn't matter if you say them, does it?"

"You want me to say them? Even though it's a ridiculous thing to do?"

He gave her that cheeky grin of his, complete with dimple, his eyes twinkling. "I want you to have no regrets for the rest of your life, starting from now; starting with me. So, if regret is something you're gonna feel if you walk away without saying them, then say them."

She stood there against him, like a statue, for what felt like an age.

He laced his fingers through hers, then whispered, "No regrets, Merri."

She swallowed the lump in her throat right along with her sense of foolishness at her childhood hopes and fears. "No regrets."

He tightened his fingers around hers and she took in a breath, recalling the words forever scarred into her memory bank.

The birds seemed to cease their dawn chorus...

"Once times thrice, I bind thine heart to mine, to hold, to never part."

No sound existed except for their breathing.

Strangely, a weight lifted off her heart, and then a huge gust of wind came in from the right and batted the side of her head with grit.

She squealed, and Jamie laughed and held a side of his jacket up against it, shielding them both. "See?" he said. "Easy."

She grinned against his final kiss, and then he sat astride his ride and put his helmet on.

She didn't want to get all teary, but her eyes were misting up anyway. Sod that. She blinked the tears away and smiled instead.

He took hold of her chin between his thumb and forefinger. "Love that stubborn smile." And then he winked at her through his open visor. "Have a good life, Merri."

"You too."

The roar of the small engine filled the street once more, he kicked the stand up and a few seconds later, he was gone.

Wow.

Merri turned and strode purposefully home.

Wow.

Some part of her felt like she should be bawling her eyes out, yet she found herself grinning like a maniac, a bounce in her step.

Just ... Wow.

Next door's ginger cat stared at her haughtily as she made her way up her drive, and then she froze.

An unfamiliar car was parked at the top of the driveway and the lights were on in the living room. Who the hell was here at this time of the morning? Or had they arrived last night after she'd left?

Crap.

She was hoping to not have to explain to her mum why she was coming home at—she looked down at her watch—5:27 a.m.

However, that wasn't the sense of trepidation that grew as she opened her front door – it was ... some other dark thing. She couldn't name it, but it filled the air.

"Merri?" Her mum's weak-sounding voice travelled across the hall from the living room at the sound of her closing the front door.

Her heart, which had felt so free just seconds ago, now sunk into her chest like a leaden weight. "Yeah, it's me." She walked into the living room.

Her mum looked ashen, and was leaning against the sideboard with her arms wrapped around herself. Two men she didn't know were seated on the sofa, both of them gloomy-looking and dressed in black. For one ridiculous moment, she wondered if they'd been invaded by aliens.

"Merri." Her mum left her position and walked up to her, stopping short of touching her, seeming unsure of what to do. It looked like she'd been crying.

"Mum?"

"We're going to leave for London a couple of hours later than planned."

"What's going on?"

She sighed, or maybe it was more of a stifled crying, and brought one trembling hand up to her shoulder.

Merri flinched at her touch even though she didn't mean to.

"Last night ... um... Oh, god. Honey, I'm so sorry – it's your father. He suffered from a heart attack last night. He was on his own so..."

"No..."

Her mum's eyes filled with tears before putting out that last flame of hope and confirming what the child in her had feared for ten years.

Magic. Didn't. Exist.

"He's gone, baby. I'm sorry. He's gone."

# IV
## Like the Wind

"You're baaaaaaaack!"

"Uncle Jamiiiiiiie!"

Well, it was fucking hard to be morose with three bouncing, half-sized Homo sapiens tackling you at the arrival gate.

"Good god! *What* are you three doing out of bed?" he gasped in mock shock. "It's nearly midnight – you'll all turn into pumpkins!"

Liam looked skywards in exasperation. Ten was *far* too old for that. Nevertheless, his grin remained on his face.

Samuel, at seven, started rolling around on the floor, making spooky Halloween noises and announcing to anyone who would listen that he was a pumpkin, and little Rebecca, at four years old, stared at Jamie with wide-eyed fright and a thumb in her mouth because the last time he'd been back home she hadn't even been born.

"Jamie..."

"Hey, Pippa." He brought his sister in for a tight hug, tearing up unexpectedly as he also took in his mum and dad just behind her.

"Son," nodded his father, holding his name up on a card: James Corbin.

Jamie arched an eyebrow. "You have a sign for me?

Afraid I wouldn't recognise you?"

"Well it's been five bloody years," was the grumbled reply, said partly in jest, as dry as it was.

His mum was already in bits, blubbering.

He sighed into Pip's hair, the first glimmer of hope finally shining through his emotional armour. For the first time in weeks, he felt like he'd made the right choice coming back home. He'd wondered endlessly if he should have stayed and fought for Claire; somehow, some way ... ten years was a lot to give up. He'd even tried those first two weeks and his efforts had been met with nothing but her cold shoulder and the occasional sympathetic glance. It was hard admitting he was the idiot whose girlfriend had been screwing around behind his back for three years.

Three. Fucking. Years.

Other people had known, so maybe the fault had been with him – maybe he had been blind. He had finally swallowed his pride – what was left of it, which wasn't much – and accepted that he couldn't fight for someone who didn't want to be won.

"How's sis?"

Pippa pulled back, months of exhaustion in her eyes. "I'm good. It's hard, but I'm good. David's with the best doctors possible – he's in the best place."

Jamie nodded as he pulled his mum in for the next hug.

His dad carted his bags onto the trolley.

"I can't believe you all came. And *you* three..." Jamie half-lunged at the talking pumpkin, but he rolled away.

"Liam and Samuel *so* wanted to see you. There was no way I could get them to sleep, so we all came out. *Sammy*," scolded Pip. "For goodness sake, get up! People will fall over you."

Rebecca darted behind her mother's legs and stayed

there.

"You don't need to be scared of Uncle Jamie, sweetie."

"She does," piped up Liam. "You said his girlfriend's a monster."

Ah.

Nice.

Pip sucked in a breath and gave her oldest the death stare before turning to Jamie, panicked. "I didn't mean *monster*. I just meant—"

"Evil!" squealed Sammy, finally up off the floor. He made two horns on his head with his fingers and growled at Rebecca. "Evil Monster Claire – she chews on hearts and spits them out!"

Pippa made her 'oh, shit' face. "Er..."

"It's all right, Pip," smirked Jamie. "I've already told Claire not to come anywhere near you for the rest of her life."

"Well, good! Cheating trollop!"

"Oh, do speak louder – there are some people at arrival gate 42 who didn't quite catch that."

"Sorry," she whispered.

"Okay," boomed Dad, "we're in a hotel ten minutes away, and then we drive home tomorrow."

"I made sure you got a nice room, Jamie," cut in his mum.

He squeezed her to him harder.

"Now, to the people-carrier before I get a ticket!"

"You drove The Beast? She's still running?" The Beast was an eight-seater Hyundai i800. His dad had won it in a draw, much to his mother's amusement since he was always entering contests for god-knows-what and had never won a dime until that car.

"Six years and counting!"

Sammy bulldozed ahead of them and cleared a path through the people with a roaring chant of "Evil Monster Claire", and the seven of them bumbled towards the exit ignoring a number of heads being shaken at them for the racket.

Jamie found himself chuckling.

Pippa snorted into his right arm as she threw him a knowing look, and he still had his mother on his left – the quiet lifeline to his broken heart without having to say a single word. 'Cause mums were awesome like that.

"Welcome home," grinned Pip. "Did you miss the chaos?"

"A little."

"Liar – you missed it *a lot.*"

He laughed.

Yeah. It was good to be home.

~\*~

"Ouch!"

"Hold still."

"I am."

"You moved."

"You pinned my boob!"

"Because you *moved.*"

Oh, god, this was chaos – they were going to be late, and the flower arrangers had phoned not ten minutes ago telling them they had now finished arranging the *wrong fucking flowers.* "When's the hairdresser getting here?"

"Five minutes!" answered her mum from the kitchen, somehow able to hear her question from the living room – she'd always had selective hearing.

Candy eyed her cautiously. "You still breathing?"

"Barely. My chest is tight, but I can control it because I know what's coming – this is how weddings are. I'll be fine."

Her mum floated into the living room with her still-not-greying blonde hair pulled up in an intricate French plait, wearing a silk Mata dress and holding a plate of cous-cous as she ate from it.

Michael was going to have a heart attack.

"Is that really what you're wearing to my wedding?"

"It's the best dress I own. And it's Fairtrade."

Merri bit her tongue. It *was* actually the best dress her mum owned, and no way was she ever going to get her into anything remotely High Street or designer unless it could be proven that children didn't starve to death to make it. It was admirable – she didn't mind. But Michael was still going to have a heart attack.

Then, as if reading her mind, "Have you heard from Michael?"

She shook her head. "I won't hear from him now. You know how traditional he is – no contact with the bride before the wedding. It's why the hen-do was last night and not weeks before, speaking of which," she frowned at the feel of her tired, dry eyes and turned to Candy, "*why* did you let me drink so much?"

Her friend grinned. "So you wouldn't start stripping."

"You were stripping?" asked her mum.

"No!"

"Oh, shame, darling – you've always had a nice figure."

Candy burst into laughter.

"Mum!"

"What? It's true. Let your hair down a bit."

"We all know how that ends."

"There's an ending? Did I miss it? Your life's not over yet, darling."

Rick had walked out on them three years after they'd moved to London, and six months after her mum had been diagnosed with the tumour. His departure had never broken her mother's spirit, perhaps because it wasn't the first time a man had walked out on her, or perhaps because meeting your mortality gave you a better perspective on things. But it had been all Merri could do to hold it together and *not* hunt him down where he worked and give him hell on earth; after all, *he* had been the reason they'd moved here in the first place. Since then, and perhaps because of her health, her mum had chosen more casual relationships over serious ones, putting her focus into being the breadwinner. She'd landed the Clairvoyant job in the New Age store and hadn't really looked back. They'd had to move to smaller dwellings in a cheaper part of the city, but a few years later saw Merri's studies pay off when she got offered a job with a small, independent accountancy firm which had links with the Bank of England. It didn't take her long to realise she had a natural knack with money. Money was reliable for the most part – it always worked to a pattern, and if you could see the pattern, you knew which way it would or wouldn't flow. Her talent had been spotted and she'd been trained in Investments, Stocks and Shares. She had moved from the small firm, to the bank and now she was heading into a big firm.

No, her life wasn't over, but it had a definite pattern to it, much like money did, and sometimes, next to her mum, she felt like the old-timer laying down a solid foundation while her mum enjoyed living more carelessly – maybe 'carefree' was a better word. Without care. Normally, Merri didn't mind. Today, however, it got to her.

The buzzer on the intercom went off, signalling the arrival of someone downstairs.

"That's the hairdresser!" shouted Merri.

"Okay, calm down, I've got it." And her mother swanned away to let her in.

Candy frowned as she concentrated on the last few pins and laces. "Almost there."

"I wanted you to be my Matron of Honour."

She looked up, surprised, but clearly delighted. "Really?"

"Yes, but Michael's only got one sister – who'd better hurry the fuck up and get here – and he really wanted her to be involved, and you and I hadn't seen each other in so long, plus, Michael's traditional, like I said, and the Matron of Honour's supposed to be married which you're not, and his sister is—"

"Merri, it's fine – you know I don't mind. There." Candy took in a deep breath and stepped away from her. Her eyes watered as she took her in. "Bloody hell, Merri, you look like Cinderella at the ball."

"Really? Thanks a million for helping me into this."

She waggled her eyebrows. "Let's hope Michael's good at getting you out of it."

"Candy, really..."

But the next thing she knew, Candy was taking her into a careful embrace and staring at her intently. "You *do* love him, don't you?"

"What? Michael? Of course I do. Why would you think otherwise?"

"Honestly? I don't know how things are with you – I haven't seen you in years – but ... in the past twelve hours I feel like I've learnt more about the first boy you ever slept with than the man you're marrying in two hours. You've barely said a word about him."

"That's not true."

"Yes, it is. Okay ... tell me how you met Michael."

"Um ... well, it was two years ago; he was already there when I started working for the bank and he was in one of my weekly meetings. We sort of always caught each other's eye, but never really did anything about it, and then, eventually – I can't remember exactly when – we started a conversation that wasn't work related and one thing led to another, and we had our first date."

Candy stared at her in contemplation.

"What?"

"What did you do on your first date?"

"We went for dinner and then wine at our local wine bar."

"And did you sleep with him that night?"

"Wha—Candy, I'm not telling you that!"

"Why not? You told me about Jamie."

"That was different."

"Why?"

"I was drunk!"

"Exactly. You let go of your inhibitions and I learnt nothing about your fiancé and everything about your first fuck."

Merri cringed. Candace could be blunt sometimes, but thinking of Jamie as her 'first fuck' seemed wrong, even though she supposed that's what it was.

"I just want to know that you're happy. Maybe it's not what a friend should ask on the day of your wedding, but I'd feel like a shittier friend if you ended up miserable and I'd said nothing at all, and you don't *seem* a hundred percent happy."

"Look ... I know I used to be this wild, crazy girl, but that was when we were kids. It was time to grow up and I did. Compared to back then, I can see how my life might look a little bland to you—"

"It doesn't look bland, it looks ... safe. Really safe. You've picked a traditional man – who's wonderful, I'm sure – and he likes things a certain way and you always know where you are with him, and you both know exactly where you're going 'cause you have it all planned out—"

"Is that such a bad thing?"

"If you were anyone else, Merri, then I'd say no, but you're *you*. And this isn't about your recklessness – there were nights I wouldn't sleep worrying about what you were up to, and I hated that you were like that; so fucking angry with yourself all the time and blaming yourself for... No. This isn't about 'reckless Merri', this is about a girl I knew who lived life like she was the wind. That was the core of your personality. I get that events can colour a person, but they can't change who you are deep down – they can't change your soul."

Merri hid her exasperation. Candy was *such* a dreamer – no wonder she and her mum had always gotten on so well. "You know the problem with living life like the wind? It's really hard to stop when you're on a collision course with badness, and you have no say where you land."

"Merri—"

"I'm happy, Candy." Annoyingly, her throat suddenly felt dry and the words didn't come out sounding as sure as they should have. *That's what you get for drinking half a bottle of Baileys.* She took her friend's hands and squeezed them. "Thank you for looking out for me; I'm glad that you are. But I'm *happy*, Candy."

She didn't look convinced. "Promise?"

"Promise."

She sighed and then smiled. "Okay. Then, I believe you. I shall forever hold my peace."

Merri returned the smile. "Thank you."

Her front door opened and her mum came in looking rosy-cheeked and slightly dishevelled. Sarah, the hairdresser, was right behind her, also flushed.

"You pick your days, Merri – the wind outside is something else! I hope your dress is weighted down or we'll all be seeing your Long-Johns."

"Ha ha."

"Luckily, Sarah's brought a mountain of hairspray."

Sarah dropped her bag of paraphernalia with a heavy clunk.

Her mother approached her, taking her in from head to toe. Her eyes grew wet. "You look sensational."

A lump nestled in her dry throat. "Thanks, Mum."

"Okay," piped up Sarah with a grin. "Now let's make you look sensational for eight hours straight."

~*~

"Well," announced his dad as they pulled up into the driveway. "That didn't take as long as we thought it would through the Saturday traffic."

"Home, sweet home," said Pippa, patting him on the arm.

Her kids were all asleep.

"Dad, can I drive The Beast back to mine? I don't want to wake them yet."

He turned the ignition off, and then handed the keys to her. "Go easy on the clutch."

"I always do."

He grunted.

"Jamie, darling," began his mum in that quiet voice of hers, "I was using your room as my crafts room, but I've moved most things to one side for now. And I've changed the bedsheets."

"Crafts room?"

"Mum does knitting now," stated Pippa. And then she leaned in closer and whispered, "There's a lot of wool."

He raised his eyebrows at her in question. Mum was notorious for her 'obsessive projects'. They generally lasted about three years before she moved on to something else. "Wool?"

Pip nodded, stifling a laugh.

He turned back to his mum and took her hand. "Thanks. It's just for two or three months until I figure out what I'm going to do."

"I can't believe your job left your position open for you for three months," said Pip. "You must be their golden child."

"I am," he grinned. "I've taken very few days off in eight years, and my last research project gave them some good exposure in the public eye. We're calling this my sabbatical."

"Ooooo!" sang his sister, pulling a face. "You always were a boffin."

"Grow up, or I'll give you a wedgie."

Her laughter was precious. Two years his senior, she'd protected him fiercely his whole life from anything she'd deemed a threat, comforted him when Mum hadn't been able to, and brought him out of the occasional slump with relentless determination. She'd taken a huge blow last winter when her husband had had a fatal accident. One good thing about coming home was that he could now be here for her when she needed him most.

They all piled through the front door, except for Pip who stopped at the porch. "I'm going to head back to mine now, but we'll all be here for dinner tonight to welcome you home."

"I'm making a roast," added his mum. "Beef – your favourite – with Yorkshire pudding."

His stomach growled.

She heard it and smiled. "Or maybe an early lunch first?"

"Thanks, Mum. I think I'll hit the sack for a few hours. The jet lag..."

"Of course. You know where your room is."

His mum shuffled off into the kitchen, and Pippa leant in for a final hug. "See you later," she whispered. "Oh, and try not to step on the wool."

Bloody hell.

He shut the door behind her, shaking his head at the craziest month of his life. A dull thrum in his skull announced the stirrings of a headache, most probably brought on by the flight and the fact that he hadn't slept a wink last night at the hotel – time zones were not exhaustion's friend.

He made his way upstairs with his luggage, and into his old room, and then fell about laughing when *hundreds* of rows of balls of yarn, along with knitting ... *stuff* ... decorated three bookcases from top to bottom. That wasn't all of it – there were also two, huge, bin bags full of wool on the floor.

Good god, the entire room smelled like a knitting shop.

Dumping his bags, he walked over to the window and pushed it all the way open. The wind had picked up and the beautiful, Cornish air filled the bedroom with its glorious, salted scent. It made him think of one particular windy summer night about thirteen years ago, and one particular girl – the second time in twelve hours she'd entered his mind.

Oh, to be a kid again – things had been so easy. At least,

with hindsight they had been. At the time he was pretty sure he was wishing himself into adulthood so things would be more simple.

Leaving the window open, he collapsed onto his old single bed, grateful his mum hadn't tossed it out with the rest of his abandoned furniture to make room for her new obsession.

*Ooooh, lying down is goooood...*

His heart panged as he thought of Claire and some of their final words to each other – hurtful things, words could be...

And then it wasn't a strong breeze, but a huge gust that flew through his window, carrying leaves and dust with it. *Fuck.*

He flinched as some grit pelted his cheek, but he was too far gone, his eyes already closed – no way was he getting up, because he was sure he had become bonded with his bed somehow.

Instead, green eyes from his past met his. *She'd* been like the wind, hadn't she? Strong and carefree, and so damn defensive, but in a way that had gotten under his skin and had made him want to find a way into the fortress she wrapped around herself as she went blazing trails to new heights.

He mentally chortled at his description of her, and in his head, she replied, *"You should be a fucking poet."*

She'd said that to him that night, laughing softly as she'd rested her head on his chest.

Drifting off to sleep, he smiled. Yeah, he should have been a poet – then he wouldn't have met Evil Monster Claire.

Thankfully, Claire failed to make her way into his thoughts just then. There was just the smell of home on the wind, and the single word he uttered on his last exhalation before sleep took him over... *"Merri..."*

# V

## Vows

"What?" Meredith asked sharply as she bolted upright and regathered her wits. She was in the back seat of the wedding car.

Candace, her mother and Judy, Michael's sister, all stared at her like she was insane. "What?" replied Candy.

"Er..." she frowned. "What?" she repeated. Why was everyone saying 'what'?

"Don't *tell* me you just fell asleep twenty minutes before your wedding."

"No!" Fuck – she hadn't, had she? *How* much had she drunk last night? "It's just so warm in here after battling the wind to get in that I must have zoned out until you said my name."

"I didn't say your name."

"Yes, you did."

"No, Merri, I didn't."

She looked at the others.

They shook their heads.

"Oh."

"Wedding nerves?"

"I guess ... just a little."

"Well, good," smiled Candy, "you're *supposed* to be nervous."

The car pulled up outside the registry office, and *what* an office this was. The building was a Civic Hall – old and architecturally masterful. Neither Michael or herself had wanted a church wedding since neither of them were particularly religious, but this building ... wow. This was as good as any church.

Butterflies catapulted around her stomach, and her chest restricted, familiar anxiety rising, but it was okay. This wasn't unexpected, so it was fine – she could deal.

"Ladies," addressed the chauffeur, "I'll let you out – hold onto your dresses."

Merri had always loved the wind, but today, it niggled her, and it wasn't because of the mess it could potentially make of her hair and make-up. She couldn't quite put her finger on it, suffice to say that when she stepped out into it, she almost felt as if it was pulling her in the opposite direction to which she wanted to go. It was a stupid thing to let bother her – *that's what the wind does, Merri* – nevertheless, she was bothered.

She gathered the hem of her dress and followed the three women out of the car. Candy and Judy both shielded her on the right, while her mum, downwind of her, took up the left. "I can't believe I'm walking my baby girl down the aisle," she said.

*That* had taken some convincing with Michael, but Merri had put her foot down. There was no dad to give her away and she'd wanted no one other than her mum to do it.

London grit smacked her shins under her dress. Damn. It had better not nick her tights, and she really didn't want small stones in her shoes – bad enough trying to walk in these heels on a good day. "Maybe there's a storm coming in or something."

"Mmmm – the wind does feel ... unusual."

She looked up at her mum's statement. Was that supposed to be a reference to something metaphysical that she never fully understood? *Mum, just for one day, please be normal ... please.*

The doorman opened the glass double doors to the Civic Hall and they all hurried into the huge reception area. The other three bridesmaids – all friends from work – had made it five minutes earlier in the other car. Laura was one of them.

She shuffled towards them in her outfit, beaming. "Everyone's here – you're the last to arrive. We're all ready to start."

*Shit. Shit-oh-shit – I'm doing this. I'm really doing this!*

Candy gave Merri a hug. "I'll go take my seat. Thanks for letting me ride here in the car with you, gorgeous. Good luck."

"Candy..." she began, but lost all words.

"You'll be fine. I'll be with your mum near the front – right there if you need me for moral support. I promise not to cry ... loudly." And she was off down the hall towards the ceremonial room with one of the ushers.

Judy was the next to hug her. "Can't wait to call you sis. We'll wait by the door – give you a minute with your mum."

"Thanks," she squeaked. *I'm squeaking now?* Holy crap, how was she going to say her vows with no voice?

A warm hand lay on her arm and she turned to her mum.

She brushed a loose strand of her hair behind her shoulder.

Uh-oh. "Is that strand supposed to be loose?"

Her mum laughed. "Leave it be, honey. You look beautiful. Sleek and hair-sprayed doesn't suit you as well as wild and carefree." A strange look passed over her eyes. "I love you, Merri – you know that, right? I don't mean just as a mother – I mean, I love who you are. Every single bit of you."

Merri blinked back the surge of tears before they could surface. "Now, you promised you wouldn't make me cry."

Another laugh, and there was that odd look again, but it quickly disappeared, replaced by a beaming smile as she brought her in for a hug. So much hugging and she wasn't even married yet! "I'm so glad you've found happiness."

The niggle was back – small but annoyingly noticeable.

Another couple stepped into the foyer through the front doors, bringing the persistent wind in with them, before the doors shut behind them.

*"I'm happy, Candy."*

*"Promise?"*

*"Promise."*

She pushed away the earlier conversation, right along with the lump that had risen in her throat, and hugged her mum tighter. Yes, she was happy. She *did* love Michael and of course she was happy – it was just that happiness had varying degrees. She'd talked to her therapist about this. It was hard for her to feel delirious joy, just as it was hard for her to feel seething anger or deep pain. It amounted to a whole load of crap about her dad leaving and then dying, and her relationship with drugs, and then her mum almost dying, not to mention... No – she couldn't even *think* about that, suffice to say that her and the grim reaper seemed to have formed a sort of bond the past decade. Nothing was permanent. To feel so much led to the inevitable 'crash and burn'.

There was a term for it in Chinese Medicine: too much joy. Her therapist had been the one to mention it to her and she'd been fascinated by the idea. The heart could hold 'too much joy' and that led to sorrow, draining the heart of its energy, or Qi, or whatever. She had delighted her mum by discussing the concept with her – this kind of thing was right up her mum's street.

But, the point was, *this* was her happy. It didn't have to be dancing-on-the-hilltops-singing kind of happy; it could just be ... relaxing, safe happy. And Michael did make her feel relaxed and safe.

She pulled out of the embrace and gave her mum a smile. "I am happy."

The windows in the building rattled with the mini-gale outside. Merri wondered how old they were. She hoped they'd been reinforced somehow.

"Come on," said her mum, offering her arm to her.

Merri took it and linked it through her own.

They approached the ceremony room, her bridesmaids got in position behind her, and the doors opened.

~*~

Jamie's eyes flew open as he bolted half-upright in bed. "What the fuck...?"

It took him a couple of seconds to remember where he was: home.

He looked at the small clock on his bedside table. For Christ's sake, he hadn't even been asleep half an hour. "Give me a fucking break," he called out to absolutely no one. He felt drained and he sorely needed sleep.

What had woken him?

He had no idea, but the wind was now going bananas and the edges of the open windows were banging against the frame.

He hauled himself out of bed and wandered over to shut

it ... and hesitated. Fatigue washed over him – the fresh air actually felt quite nice, even if it was on the wrong side of cold for summer. Maybe a storm was coming in.

"Shit!" he cursed as a small stone whacked him in the brow, and as sharply as if it had happened yesterday, the image of Merri squealing as she turned away from a similar gust of sharp wind, hit him bright and clear.

It had been their last few minutes together, hadn't it?

Why the hell was he thinking about her now?

Because she was a point of reference for his life, that was why; because she had been his first – the girl he had lost his virginity to.

*'Cause your ten year relationship's just ended and you're up shit-creek with no idea which way to go. What happens next? If you count your first, then you've only been with two women in thirty years, and for once in your life that thought stinks. Maybe you should go sow your wild oats ... or do you wait for Miss Third Time Lucky?*

*Once times thrice...*

He paused, half way to shutting the windows as they played tug-of-war with him against the crazy English climate.

*Once times thrice...* What were those words? The ones Merri had said... He had replayed them in his head over and over, a decade ago, until time had allowed them to slip away from him. They had meant so much to her; so much that he'd never once repeated them out loud, feeling it would somehow ruin the absolute perfection of that emotional moment. It would be nice to feel that kind of meaning again, even if it only belonged in a memory. He said them out loud now as he tried to grasp at the words coming back to him.

"Once times thrice, I bind thine heart..." *yes, that was*

*it...* "to mine, to hold, to never part."

He stupidly grinned in triumph for remembering them.

The wind stopped dead.

The windows slammed shut in his hands because he'd all at once won the tug-of-war, and he almost went flying backwards as he let go of them with a small yelp. "Bloody hell," he muttered, "freaky British weather. Give me a bush fire any day."

He stood there for a second, not quite knowing what to do. Where he'd been sleepy on waking, he now felt bright and alert.

Rummaging through his suitcase, he found his towel.

Shower, then lunch.

~*~

The windows flew open with a bang.

Ha! She'd *known* they were old and rickety!

The guests all gasped as 'London' hurtled in through them, and it was the most bizarre thing, that for a split second she was back at the top of that cliff, right on the edge, feeling like she might fall, and this time, she wasn't sure she could be saved.

The scent of beach and ocean encircled her; seeped into her and it was so bloody *real* that for a moment, she lost her head, completely forgetting where she was.

"Merri," whispered Michael.

For some reason it didn't sound like him calling her name.

*"Merri."*

A scramble to shut the windows.

A cough.

"Er ... Miss Goodwill?" The registrar looked at her in

earnest.

Michael looked at her with slight trepidation as they both stood in the front of the room and makeshift altar before their friends and family.

"Huh?"

The registrar coughed again. "You need to repeat after me, dear."

*Fuck!* "Oh, of course." She could see Candy's scrunched face out of the corner of her eye and her mother's raised eyebrows. Heat crept up her cheeks. "Sorry."

"Very good – once more then. *I, Meredith, take thee Michael...*"

"I, Meredith, take thee, Michael..."

There was another loud, collective gasp.

Michael's face went instantly red, and... Everyone was *staring* at her. What the hell...?

Candace's face was now unscrunched; her eyes as wide as saucers.

"What is it?" she whispered, not actually able to speak any louder. She was uncomfortably aware that her chest could tighten at any moment. She *definitely* didn't want a panic attack on her wedding day.

Michael looked like he had just as much difficulty talking. "My name's Michael," he said tightly.

*Am I missing something?* "Yes," she replied, confused. "I know that."

He went redder and looked highly embarrassed and honest-to-god, she had no idea what she'd done wrong. "You just called me Jamie."

You could have heard a pin drop.

And then two more.

Her crazy-sounding laughter broke the silence and filled the room. "No, I didn't."

If only Candace hadn't been sitting there, in the corner of her eye, nodding her head.

*No... Noooooo! Oh, fuck, no!*

Her gaze landed on Judy who was giving her the most murderous of looks.

*I, Meredith, take thee ... Jamie...*

*Oh-fuck-oh-fuck-oh-fuck...* She turned to the registrar. "Say it again ... let me say it again."

He looked uncertainly at Michael who was standing as still as a statue and Meredith's heart dove towards her feet as her eyes filled with tears. Oh, god, she'd just hurt him ... and this was *bad*. "I swear, Michael..." and *everything* sounded like the wrong thing to say, even if it was the truth. "There is *no* Jamie. Er ... well, there *is* a Jamie, but from thirteen years ago, and Candy and I were talking about him last night and the conversation must have got stuck in my mind somehow..."

Candy was now shaking her head, her face scrunched up again, making sawing motions with her hand against her neck.

*Damn it!*

*Breathe...*

"It's not what you think, and it's not what it sounds like." Her voice rising, she practically shouted at the registrar. "Let me say it again!"

The registrar looked at Michael for confirmation.

There was a deafening pause as the entire room waited for his answer, the only sound in it the slight wheezing to her breathing already announcing itself. *No – just hold it together...*

Michael swallowed, his eyes softened, and then he nodded.

Okay ... everything was still okay...

"All right, Miss Goodwill, repeat after me – *carefully...*"

*Smart arse.*

"I, Meredith, take thee, *Michael...*"

"I, Meredith, take thee—"

There was an almighty BANG, she was pulled into Michael's chest and tucked under his body as calamity ensued over the sound of shattering glass.

The third window on the left – thankfully nowhere near anyone – had come off its hinges and smashed onto the floor.

~*~

Tea was a godsend, and that's what everyone was drinking now as they sat in the bar of the Civic Hall awaiting news of the repair to the room, and ultimately, the repair to her marriage – or near-marriage.

Candy wasn't drinking tea. She'd gone and ordered a double shot of vodka on ice.

Michael was talking to the staff as they tried to organise the rest of their day and Judy looked like she was about to rip Merri's liver out and eat it in front of her.

"Well," said her mum as she sat next to her with her cup of loose, floating Chamomile flowers – she always carried some with her in her bag along with her rune stones and some oils. She preferred the loose dried flowers to the powdered stuff you got in the sachets. "That was certainly the most *interesting* wedding I've been to. This is for you." She pushed the Chamomile in front of her.

"Oh, I don't—"

"Drink it. And here..." She took hold of Merri's hands, turned them, palms up, and proceeded to place a drop of whatever oil it was onto each wrist before rubbing it in.

"It'll calm you."

"I don't need calming," she snapped.

"You're still wheezing, dear."

Oh, damn it – she was. She mentally congratulated herself for not collapsing into a hot mess on the floor in front of everyone, although saying the wrong name at the altar constituted a description far worse than 'hot mess', she was sure.

But yeah, she was wheezing and her chest kinda hurt right now, and it felt bizarre to realise she couldn't figure out if it was from the suppressed panic attack, or from hurting Michael. In her mind, it seemed obvious which it should be.

She frowned and then stood.

"Where are you going?"

"I need to speak to Michael and sort this whole thing out. I need to explain."

"Wait until he's ready, darling."

"But—"

"Wait until he's in the right place to hear it. Come on, Merri – sit." Her tone was gentle and her hand, warm.

Michael was wrapped up in a conversation with the registrar, and his family were pointedly ignoring her. In fact, most people were ignoring her, save for the odd sympathetic glance, or the it'll-be-all-right grin.

She sighed in defeat and took her seat once more. "I don't understand what happened."

"You said 'Jamie'," Candy stated, and her mum's lip twitched.

"Yes, thank you, I understand *that*, I just don't get *how*. In my head I said, Michael – how could 'Jamie' come out instead?"

"Who *is* Jamie?" asked her mum.

Candy answered for her. "The boy she lost her virginity to the night before you both left Cornwall."

Merri glared at her. Was nothing sacred? There were things her mum could do with *not* knowing ... *ever*.

Her temperature rose along with the prickling sensation across her arms and chest. "Oh..." Her hand went to the base of her throat in a bid to calm her system down.

"Drink your tea, Merri," said her mum, softly, and for the first time in a long time, she did as her mum asked. The sweet, light flavour of the flowers was welcome.

"This tastes a bit lemony."

"I added some Lemon Balm leaves, too."

"Oh, it's nice."

"Good. Now," her mum's tone altered from soft, to matter-of-fact, "tell me about that night with Jamie."

Merri looked up, aghast. So not going there.

"Was it windy then, too?"

This day was getting weirder, but it's not like her mum never asked weird questions – regularly. "What are you talking about?"

A slight shadow fell over their table and Merri glanced up and met Michael's eyes. They were guarded – he looked so distant, which wasn't unusual, but this time, the distance had a cold edge to it. It wasn't what she was used to, although he did always carry himself with a certain amount of decorum and that was no different today. She'd fucked up big time and he'd kept his cool and sorted it all out.

She abruptly stood. "Michael, I want to explain—"

He held his hand up to still her, and for a brief second, laid it on her arm before pulling it away.

She wanted to lunge forward, grab that hand, and glue it to her limb.

"The venue staff are endlessly apologetic about the window, so much so, that they are letting us have the hall two months from today, for free, to complete the ceremony. It's the earliest date they have it available."

"Two months? Er..." Did that mean the wedding was on? Did he forgive her? Two months was enough time to iron out this crap she'd created, wasn't it? Hope lit her up. "That's great! We can do that, can't we?" She looked down at her mum and Candy, both of whom nodded enthusiastically. "Fantastic."

"Yes," said Michael, and then he paused as he looked straight at her. "I've booked it out of practicality – in case we decide to use it."

"In case we..." An ache rose within her from her gut, swallowing up the hope.

"I'd like us to take some time apart – maybe a month ... to reflect."

Apart? A whole month?

Her face grew hot as tears rushed to her eyes. "But we need to talk about this. I need to explain to you that there is *no one* else. I'm a klutz and I don't even know why—"

"You called me another man's name in front of every single member of my family."

Her entire being shrank. His family owned *Fortune Airs*. The not-too-small global enterprise owned an airline, a chain of hotels and a portion of the media. Michael had gone all out to ensure the media wouldn't be here, against his parents' wishes, as they had both wanted a small(ish), private wedding. That was one small mercy in this fiasco. She felt five years old again and completely powerless. "I'm so sorry."

Candy cleared her throat. "Talking is always a good idea though ... erm ... look, I know this is none of my business, but—"

"That's right, this is none of your business." He cut her down, just like he was so good at doing in those work meetings.

Candy bit her tongue and Merri's anger sparked – it wasn't Candy's fault and she was just trying to help.

But the anger fuelled her panic and she quickly pushed it back down and allowed the guilt of the reality to put the flame out: this was all *her own* fault.

He returned his attention to Merri. "I need some time, Meredith – apart from you – to clear my head."

Apart. She hadn't misheard: he wanted at least a whole month apart. She felt crushed.

Touché.

"Are we ... is this us breaking up?"

"I need to *think* about all this." His anger went up a notch. "You called me by someone else's name on our *wedding* day. I don't know what the hell this is, but I know I don't feel like marrying you right now and can you blame me?"

She winced.

"I need to calm down; I need to calm my family down... Maybe we can talk in a couple of weeks. Until then, we have email and texts."

Yes, they did. Emails and text messages were how they thrashed out arguments: they debated them non-verbally, reached an agreement in a civilised manner via digital communication, and then met up again with everything sorted out. It was perhaps a little unconventional, but it had worked for them. This way, their anger could be channelled accordingly over a set space of time, and she didn't have to worry about losing it in person because she couldn't cope with feeling emotions too strongly, after all, it was hard to put her point of view across properly when in the middle of a panic attack. Their strange way of arguing via text and email was right for them.

Only, this time, it felt somehow wrong. *Really* wrong. How could something that had worked so well in the past seem so strange now?

*You want to have it out. You* want *to see his face when he's angry and you want him to see yours. You need to fight, face to face. The way your parents fought.*

Oh, god! She sucked in a breath with difficulty. What was *wrong* with her? Who the hell *wants* to fight?

*Don't lose it!*

She swallowed the anxiety back, her breathing now more laboured. "Yes, we have email – of course we do."

"I'll email you first when I'm ready and we'll take it from there."

*But I'm ready now...* Except she'd called him another man's name at the altar, so she really had no right to protest. Instead, she nodded. "I'll wait for your message."

Sadness seeped through his formal exterior for a moment, overriding the anger, and then he leaned in and pecked her on the cheek, before turning to leave.

"Michael..." his name broke on her tongue.

He glanced back at her.

*If you go, you stay gone.*

She shook away the memory. She tried damn hard never to let her past overlap with her present.

"I really, *really* am sorry."

"I know," he gave her a small smile. "Me too."

He turned away from her, raised his voice and addressed their guests. "Thank you, everyone, for coming. Unfortunately, we cannot continue with the ceremony at this time..."

*Oh, god, we've just separated...*

"You are all free to take your leave whenever you like – the reception has offered to call cabs for anyone who needs them."

Candy tugged at her hand, and Merri sank back down into her chair. "Emails and texts, Merri?" she muttered, still obviously annoyed at Michael's rebuttal of her. "Seriously?"

"Don't start, okay?" She clasped her hands together to stop them from shaking and hid them under the table.

Candy chewed on the side of her cheek. It was what she did when she *really* wanted to say something but knew she shouldn't, and Merri didn't have the energy for anything else. Her eyes burned hot and she leaned down and pressed her forehead onto the table top. *Do. Not. Cry.*

She felt suffocated ... and like her relationship had just ended. A slip of the tongue – that was all it had taken: one second and one stupid mistake. "I need to get out of this dress."

"Do you want to go back to yours?"

Fuck. She had no idea. She had no idea what to do.

A hand rubbed her back. "Breathe, honey." Her mum.

She took her other hand and held it like a lifeline, some-how hoping it would better enable her intakes of breath. "Thanks." And she *was* thankful right now – for her mum's tea and her oils and the fact that she was just *her*, because she suddenly no longer knew who *she* was. Who was Meredith Goodwill? The old, emotionally-reckless Merri, and the current, emotionally-suppressed Merri, stood side by side, merging, and she was having difficulty *un*-merging them.

Really ... what the fuck had just happened? One hour ago felt like one year ago; a lifetime ago ... she felt herself unravelling, and she had no idea what would happen when the last thread came undone, but visions of hospitals and drips came to mind, and death ... and blood between her—

*No, no, no, don't think about that.*

Her mum's voice came from far away. "Candy, call a cab for Merri's flat."

Candy left the table and her mum leant into her ear. "We're going to get you home, out of that dress, and into a hot shower, and then we're going to sort out what happens next, okay? But you're safe, Merri." She squeezed her hand. "You're safe."

Sparks floated in front of her eyes and she had to force air into her lungs.

Her mum had no idea how wrong she was. She wasn't safe. And she couldn't keep anyone else safe either.

The journey back home happened in silence.

Every five minutes, Merri looked at her phone to see if Michael had emailed.

She could *feel* Candy's jaw twitching, not just see it, and she knew it was a matter of time before her friend exploded. "You're going to have to explain the 'emailing your fight' thing to me because I just don't get it."

Her mum placed a hand on her knee and squeezed. In moral support? Or because she wanted an explanation too?

"Look, it just works for us, okay? I'm really bad at controlling my emotions when someone's shouting in my face – this way, we can have a reasonable discussion, even though we're angry and then we meet up when most of it has simmered down."

"It's an *argument*. You're *supposed* to be uncontrolled and ranty!"

"Which almost always leads to a panic attack. This way Michael doesn't have to feel bad for—"

"Oh, my god, will you *please* stop apologising for yourself. You're not this meek, mild, *safe* person – who are you and what have you done with my friend?"

"Candy..." Her stupid face crumpled and there came the tears.

"Fuck! Fuck, Merri ... shit, I'm sorry." She sidled up next to her, tugging the seat belt as far as it would go. "I may be a bit pissy about the fact that he verbally smacked me down."

"I know, I'm sorry," she sobbed.

"*Don't* say sorry anymore, okay? Just don't. Do *not* apologise for him. You said another guy's name at the altar – boo-hoo. If he loves you, he'll get over it."

"Are you kidding me? Did you hear what he said to me? He *broke up* with me. I've just ruined our relationship forever."

"If that's really true, then he's a dick and he doesn't deserve you. Apart from having a clumsy tongue, you haven't done anything wrong. There are people out there having affairs left, right and centre and their partners always forgive them – he'll come around, especially when he understands there's nothing between you and Jamie."

"I don't even really know who he is."

"I know."

"I don't even know *where* he is."

"I know, but he's your fiancé – he's not going to leave you over one thing, no matter how—"

"I'm talking about Jamie."

"Oh."

"Maybe you *should* find out where Jamie is."

All eyes landed on her mother and her ludicrous suggestion. So ludicrous, she was pretty sure she hadn't heard her right. "Did you just say—"

"Merri, I want you to think... Did anything happen

between you and Jamie that was, you know ... magical?"

Oh, for fuck's sake... "Is that a metaphor for losing my virginity?"

"No, although ... but no. I'm talking about real magic."

"Real magic? Mum, real magic doesn't—"

"Don't tell a witch magic doesn't exist unless you're prepared to announce that you don't believe in fairies."

She huffed, annoyed. Ever since she'd first read Peter Pan at the age of eight, she hadn't been able to say that, even though it was just a story, and her mother damn well knew it. "That's so not fair, using Peter Pan against me," she muttered between sniffs.

"Whether you believe in magic or not, I have people who *pay* for my spiritual guidance and spells – I'm actually being serious here. Did you do or say anything magical while you were with him?"

"No. We went bird-watching, and star-gazing, and..." Her voice faltered as a white, worn-looking scooter weaved in and out of the traffic as it passed the cab.

*Soft lips...*

*The dawn...*

*Fingers laced...*

"Wait..."

They waited.

"No ... it couldn't be..."

Candy shoved her with her elbow. "Are you trying to kill us with suspense?"

She looked at her friend, and then at her mum. She struggled to say what she wanted to – it sounded so ridiculous. "I said the words."

"Words?" frowned Candy.

"Which words, exactly?" pressed her mother.

She blushed and squirmed inside, and pushed away that

dull ache she'd first known when she was five. "The words I heard you say when Dad left."

Her mother furrowed her brow, and then ... "Oh..."

"Once times thrice—"

"Sssshhh."

"It's a spell, right?"

"You heard me say that?" She turned to stare at her, a deep sadness in her eyes. "I didn't know – you never told me."

Merri shrugged. "I heard the whole argument. I saw him leave; saw you go into your magic box and say the words while you wrote them down and then you—"

"Oh, Merri." Her voice was thick with tears. "Why didn't you tell me?"

"I didn't want to upset you further, and then time just did its thing and it didn't matter anymore."

"Jesus Christ," she whispered, and sunk her head into her hand.

Merri shuffled, feeling uncomfortable. "So ... it's a spell?" she repeated, hoping to get her mum out of the past.

She gathered herself, bringing her head back up. "Sort of."

"Sort of?"

"Well, *anything* can be a spell. Magic is created from will, intent and desire. Put those three things together and words aren't even needed if the *want* is strong enough."

Impatience ate at her. "What does that even mean? Did I do a spell, or not?"

"It was him you said the words to?"

She nodded, hesitantly.

"Did you mean them when you said them?"

Another nod.

"And what happened after you said them?"

"Nothing."

"Nothing?"

"Well, I don't know, it was thirteen years ago. Erm ... nothing, and then ... wind. There was a big gust of wind."

"Like today?" she asked, wryly.

"Yes ... oh, god, it *was* a spell, wasn't it?"

"It appears you're a very gifted witch," she smiled.

Merri didn't even have the energy to glare at her.

"Huh," chimed in Candy. "All those times we played around doing spells and you *actually* made one work without me. I don't know how I feel about that."

"Damn it, this is serious!"

"Oh, starting to believe in magic now, are we?"

"Mum," she warned, and her mother sighed.

"Those words were part of your father's and my wedding vows; they were the last couple of lines that sealed everything together."

Candy whistled.

Merri sat, stunned, as the cab pulled up outside her apartment.

"That's fifteen pound, love," said the driver.

She stared at the man behind the wheel, not seeing him at all. *Wedding vows?*

Her mum paid him and both her and Candy dragged her out of the car, still numb. "Wedding vows?"

"Let's get inside."

She followed them both like a robot, stating, rather stupidly, "The wind has stopped."

Her mother nodded, knowingly, which increased that really bad feeling she had – the one that said her world was about to topple over.

Once inside her flat, she sat on the nearest chair and stayed there. "Wedding vows?"

"What greater spell is there than the one weaved between two consenting hearts? What greater magic?"

"Consenting... Wait, no. I said the words – Jamie never did."

"He must have done."

"No."

"For things to play out the way they did today? I'm ninety percent certain he did."

"No, he ... hang on!" A small amount of anger lit a flame and she rose with it from her seat. "Are we really having this discussion? For things to 'play out the way they did'? Today was all about bad luck, or coincidence, or whatever you want to call it."

"No such thing as coincidence."

"Bad luck, then! Hardly surprising with my background, is it?"

"We make our own luck, Merri."

"What happened today wasn't magic."

"How do you know?"

"Because Dad never came back!"

She froze, as did her mum, both of them staring at each other as her exclamation rang through the air. She'd just gone and blurted that right out, hadn't she?

The silence grew – it practically shrieked.

Candy cleared her throat. "I'm gonna go put the kettle on," and she hurried away.

Her mother finally dropped her eyes and turned to put her handbag down. "You know, you're very much like your father, Merri. He had this free spirit that couldn't be tempered. It was why I fell in love with him, but even then, I knew... I knew he couldn't be bound to anything, or anyone. I often joked that the reason he chose to help ghosts was because he would see himself in them – their entrap-

ment in the land of the living mirrored his own restric-
tions."

"And you think I'm like that?" she asked, flatly.

Her mum turned back and stared straight at her, fierce
pride in her eyes. "No. I think you're braver than he ever
was, because you face your fears – every day I see you facing
them. But where he refused to acknowledge his fears and ignored them to his detriment, you rein them in so tightly
they have no room to transform into anything else – maybe
hope; maybe your wishes, your dreams...

"Your father didn't come back because he *chose* not to,
and because I *chose* to set him free. That is all."

She bit her lip and tasted salt on them. She'd had no
idea she'd started crying again. "We weren't enough ... I
wasn't enough for him—"

"You were *everything* to him, Merri, *everything* and
*that* is what scared the shit out him. *That* was his fear – that
the tremendous amount of love he felt for you would keep
him bound – he couldn't face that and that has *nothing* to
do with you and everything to do with his cowardice."

She lowered her head, but couldn't stop the flow of
tears now it had started, right along with this conversation.

Her mother's hands came around her arms, her own
eyes shimmering. "Why haven't you ever been back to
Cornwall in all these years? Not even for a weekend?"

She shook her head, but her stubborn head answered
her silently in a slightly scolding fashion: *Because you loved
it there so much, you didn't want to be reminded of it.*

And yes, she got the point.

"Merri, I want you to listen to me for once, and this
isn't about magic – forget magic. You already have these two
weeks off work for the honeymoon – go back home to
Cornwall. Go back home and remember *who you are* before

you decide to get married. For some reason, you've been given extra time – use it wisely."

"Even if Michael forgives me, it didn't sound very much like he wants to tie the knot anymore."

"It's all still so raw – give him time, and use yours to re-discover yourself."

"I'm not the same person I was then."

"You don't have to be. But you do need to know who you are now, before giving yourself to someone else, or that really isn't fair on him now, is it?"

Regret churned in her. "I really hurt Michael."

"Because you've been hurting yourself. Things happen for a reason. Maybe today happened the way it did so that your wedding can take place *properly* in two months, with you *whole*."

A cough sounded to her left, and there stood Candy with a tray of mugs. "I was going to drive back home to-night – you're welcome to come with me. Stay at mine – we'll go visit our old haunts," she smiled. Then she frowned, "No climbing allowed, though."

"Climbing?" asked her mum.

Merri threw Candy her shut-up stare.

"Er, ladders," said Candy. "Old, rusty ones that are likely to fall apart."

"Sounds like something I'm better off not knowing about."

"Might be best, Mrs Goodwill," she grinned.

"Oh, please, Candace, you're old enough to call me Penny now."

Merri's mind churned. Well, what was she going to do? Michael would be keeping his distance and she would be sitting at home feeling stupid and watching her phone or laptop for his email. This way, she could at least feel stupid whilst doing something semi-useful and in someone else's company. "Are you sure it's no bother?" she asked Candy.

"God, no. It'll be nice to have some company at mine for a change. Catching up last night was awesome – I'd love to do it for longer."

Merri attempted a smile. "Okay then ... I guess ... and I'm pretty much all packed anyway." Her smile faded as she pictured her suitcase in the bedroom, all ready for the honeymoon. "I feel like such a fucking idiot."

"We all make mistakes. The only way is up."

Merri took a steaming cup of tea from the tray Candy offered while her mum retrieved her handbag. "Honey, I'm going to head home and give you some breathing space, but let me know what you decide. I've got a full day with clients tomorrow – the weekends are always so busy, but if I can manage to come down to the coast with you during the week, I will."

"Okay, Mum." A bout of exhaustion hit her. "Thanks – for everything today."

"No need to say thanks, and this isn't as astronomical as you think – nothing is." She smiled and then gave her a last hug. "I'll let myself out."

Candy sipped her own tea as the front door opened and shut. "So ... looks like *I'm* the lucky one to get you out of that dress."

She tried and failed to find Candy's joke funny. "Go for it. I can barely breathe in this thing now, and there's no limit to my embarrassment. It's my twenty-ninth birthday next week – we were going to celebrate it on our honeymoon." Fresh tears rushed to her eyes, but she blinked them away. "Instead, I feel like some clumsy teenager turning sixteen all over again with no idea how to live my life."

"*We'll* celebrate your birthday and it'll be so fucking

amazing you'll wish you were thirty already."

This time, she did manage a laugh, albeit a weak one.

"That's better. There's nothing that can't be fixed some-how."

"That's what my counsellor tells me: nothing's perman-ent. It's sort of become my mantra."

"Does the mantra work?"

"It calms me down when something's gone wrong and I feel the anxiety come on."

"Well, good. Let's get your non-permanent arse out of that gown, so you can get ready for the most non-perman-ent next few days of your life."

She glared at Candy. "And are you going to be laborious for that whole time?"

"Oh, no," she smirked. "Unmanageability is your depart-ment, sweetie – not mine.

# VI

## Home, Sweet Home

Unmanageable. Completely unmanageable.

Having since lost all fear around him, Rebecca was doing her best to climb up his clothes as he sat in his chair trying to let that *amazing* roast go down.

Samuel was trying to drag Liam away from the television so they could play in the garden, but the final instalment of whatever series containing aliens or monsters (he wasn't sure which) was proving too enticing, much to Sammy's annoyance. It was fast turning into Liam's annoyance because Sammy wasn't letting him go. The fists would come out real soon, he was sure.

"Christ, Pip, how the fu—er..." He glanced down at Rebecca who was staring at him, wide-eyed and half way up his torso, just waiting for him to finish that swear word. "How the frig do you cope with these lot?"

"I might have to let you in on my secret identity, Jamie," she replied, dryly, as she cleared the plates.

"Uncle Jamie?"

"Hmmm?" He looked down at his far-too-adorable niece.

"Were you going to say 'fuck'?"

"Rebecca!" exclaimed her mother in horror. "*Where* did you learn that word?"

She went red and cast her eyes downwards for exactly three seconds and then stuck her chin out in timid defiance. "Sammy says it."

Pip's mouth dropped open, and then she snapped it shut, muttering as she left the dining area with her hands full, "Right ... I'll be having words with that boy."

"Uncle Jamie?"

"Hmmm?"

She had resumed her attempt to mount him. "Can you climb up people?"

"Er ... can't say it would be well received, munchkin."

"What does that mean?"

"It means, no."

"Oh. I like climbing."

"I can see that. And feel that," he winced as a knee dug into him where he'd rather it wouldn't.

"Sammy says that girls don't like climbing and only boys like climbing, but I like climbing and I'm a girl."

He made a non-committal sound, distracted by that drool-worthy aroma wafting in from the kitchen. *Mmmm ... that apple pie smells delicious. No one makes apple pie like Mum.* "Mum? When's dessert ready?" He wondered if he needed to pee enough to bother getting up ... he didn't want to have to take the little mountaineer with him.

"Ten minutes!" she called back from the other room.

"Uncle Jamie?" Rebecca's feet were now balanced on the crease of his elbows. He placed his hands where he could on her legs so she wouldn't do herself damage.

"Yes?"

"Do you know any girls that like climbing?"

"There was one girl I knew once who liked climbing."

"Did she climb any mountains?"

A crash and a scream came from the living room, followed by Pippa's scolding tone. "Liam, let go! Sammy, you too!"

"It's always bloody like this," grumbled his dad as he came back into the room.

"Geoff – language," said his mum disapprovingly, appearing from behind him. She placed dessert spoons on the table.

"Bloody isn't a swear word."

"Yes, it is!"

"Sammy says 'bloody' as well," his niece informed them.

His mum frowned at his dad. "Now look what you've done."

"What? What have I done?"

Jamie laughed and stood, taking Rebecca with him. She let out a squeal at being so high up, and then he promptly dropped her on the huge bean bag in the corner of the room, which earned him giggles of delight. "Again! Again!"

"Later, pipsqueak. I'm gonna catch some fresh air before apple pie. Be good."

But she was already running into the living room. "Yeeeeey! Apple piiiie, apple piiiie!"

"You all right, Jamie?" asked his mum with concern.

"Right as rain. Just fancy taking in the smell of the ocean."

"You've spent your whole life by the ocean."

"And every ocean smells different," he grinned.

"They do? Well, you know best."

He dropped a kiss on her head. "Back in ten."


A five minute walk only took him to the top of his road, but his road was on a slope and the top of it offered a view of both the sea and part of the coastline.

He breathed in deep.

The salty air swirled in his lungs with the warmth of family and home, but it didn't quite alleviate the ache in his chest. Part of him longed for the hot Australian sun he'd fallen in love with, not that it was particularly hot there this time of the year.

He also longed for Claire.

He didn't bother blinking his tears away, but let the breeze dry them on his skin instead. He didn't want to miss Claire. After what she'd done to him, missing her felt like a demoralising kick in the gut, but there it was.

He needed to get his mind off her. Maybe tomorrow, he'd go to The Boat Shop down by the beach, if it hadn't closed down, and see if they still hired out yachts and scuba gear. Getting lost under the waves he cherished would be the perfect distraction. And it was the summer holidays, so maybe Pip and the kids could come with him. It'd be good to talk to Pip alone for a bit – it seemed like she'd been struggling and, unusually for them given their close connection, he had no sense of how his sister was *really* feeling about the situation with David.

Headlights flashed far off in the distance through the settling dusk as a car took a corner on the winding road, but his attention was called just to the left of them; to the top of *that* small cliff overlooking the sea, where one of the best nights of his life had begun – he'd never forgotten it. A niggling 'what-if' entered his field of thought and he quickly pushed it away. 'What-ifs' were useless things and he'd always been a believer in looking to the future and not the past. But following this philosophy was proving excruciatingly difficult this time around.

They said time healed all wounds.

He turned away from his view and headed back down

the road towards the promise of home-baked apple pie.

He was trying hard to believe in that saying, but...

*Ten years of love – gone in a second.*

He couldn't help wondering if time was also a trickster who was bloody good at his game.

~\*~

Meredith tore her eyes away from the slope which she knew led to the top of the cliff she'd scaled a lifetime ago. The car turned right and the slope disappeared behind her.

"We're just ten minutes away from where I live," said Candy, a note of excitement audible in her voice, and despite the shitty day she'd had, she had to admit Candace's happiness was catching. A part of her was overjoyed to be back here, if somewhat anxious at the overwhelm of it.

"Of all the places you could live, why did you stay in Cornwall?"

Candy shrugged over the steering wheel. "I saw lots of places backpacking in my Gap Year before uni. Every place is special in its own way, and here's as good as any. I didn't really know what I wanted to do with my life – ended up taking a degree that hasn't really gotten me as far as I'd like – so might as well stay somewhere that I know and love."

Candy had gone to university to study Journalism. She'd always loved writing and there was a bit of the detective about her, but the practicalities of the job had proven harsher than she was prepared for, with uncompromising deadlines and cut-throat, ambitious peers who'd do anything possible to steal recognition from anyone too mellow to fight for it.

Candace was mellow.

She'd slipped away from the commercial side of it all,

and currently had a job with a small publisher that brought out a handful of country life magazines a year. On the side, she had taken up photography as a hobby, but it was fast growing into a nice little earner for her since she'd started a blog and had gained some interest. Merri had only learned these things about her in the past two hours, and for the first time in years, it hit her hard just how much she'd missed this – just *this*. Catching up, talking, getting along with, sharing ... all the things that made up friendship.

In a small way, Candy was right: her current friends were lovely people, but she didn't have anywhere near the same rapport with them as she had with Candace, or even some of her childhood friends before she had left. She'd been so work-focused; so geared on rescuing her ruined life. Time had passed, and she had forgotten.

"Tell me more about Michael."

She turned towards Candy, surprised. "You really want to know?"

"Of course I do – he's a huge part of your life. I'd like to know him better and I can't really picture sitting down with him over lunch and getting all chatty, you know?"

Merri laughed. "Yeah, he's a bit reserved. He's not had it easy. A lot of expectations were placed on him as a child by his parents, and they still do expect a lot from him." Her guilt resurfaced. "It's partly why he was so cut up about what happened at the wedding – for me to say what I did in front of his parents..." She swallowed the lump in her throat that had come up with the guilt. "I know you think he'll forgive me, but ... there's a history there I'm not sure I can break through."

"History?"

"With his family ... he hasn't told me everything; just bits and pieces. Also..." She hesitated, but Candy wasn't the type to go gossiping. "He's got these scars. I mean physical ones ... on the backs of his thighs." And she couldn't carry on. However distant Michael and herself could be with each other, there was still a mutual respect for each other's hidden turmoil. He didn't ask about hers and she didn't ask about his. But, once, when they had been making love, she'd run a finger down one of those scars. He'd flinched under her touch, and she'd expected him to emotionally withdraw and pull himself out of her. Instead, he'd lost it – bucked like some wild thing, climaxing so hard, all his usual control gone.

When they had finished, she'd met his eyes and had seen something stripped from him that she ached to put back. She'd also seen herself reflected in them – her and all her demons. Memories she could do with burying for good.

They had stared at each other in the dark, he'd finally lifted himself off her and retreated into the bathroom, and that had been that. Neither of them ever spoke of it, and she had never touched any of his scars again.

Candy stared at her a beat through the darkening night. "Have you told him everything about what happened to you?"

She shuffled in her seat, uncomfortable. She hadn't even told Candace everything that had happened to her. "Some."

Pause.

"And does that work for you both? Living as you are, about to get married and *not* knowing the most important aspects of each other's lives? And I'm *not* picking, before you start on me; I'm just interested. Different relationships work in different ways – I'm not judging."

The ball of anxiety in her gut grew, but, thankfully, her chest wasn't as tight as it usually got with the apprehension. Maybe it was the fresh sea air. "I respect the parts of his life that are too painful for him to talk about, and he respects mine – there's love in that. Do you have to know every dark thing about a person to be with them? If the dark stuff doesn't matter when it comes to love, then there's no need to know."

"Maybe not; like I said, every relationship's different ... as long as *not* divulging those painful dark bits is for a reason other than fearing reproach from your partner. I mean, love is supposed to be unconditional, isn't it? If you really love someone, you love all their dark bits too. Hard to do that if you don't know what they are."

She couldn't tell whether that was Candy being all judgy again, even though she said she wouldn't be, but it annoyed her that what she said sort of made sense. Before she could think of a fitting reply, the car was pulling up into the driveway of a small cottage.

Candace turned to her in her seat and grinned as she put the car into park. "Home, sweet home."

The alarm on her phone went off. Damn – she'd forgotten to take it off work setting, which meant it must be only seven in the morning. On a Sunday.

Merri groaned and rolled over, eyes still closed, until she remembered she hadn't checked her phone for hours.

Her eyes snapped open and she reached for it, silencing the alarm and unlocking it to see her emails and messages.

Nothing from Michael.

Her heart sank low and heavy.

She rolled onto her back again, and took in her surroundings. Candy's guest room was simple and cosy, and probably the neatest room in the house. She wasn't messy, but she wasn't exactly tidy either. "Artistically casual," she called it.

The summer sun streamed through the half-closed slats of the wooden blinds, and it was too pleasant, too beautiful, to ignore. She got out of bed and pulled the blinds up, enjoying the warm rays through the glass pane.

The smell of coffee wafted up from downstairs. Candy was awake? Already? She remembered her to be atrocious in the mornings.

In her vest and boy-shorts – sleepwear Michael hated with a passion, but the ones she felt most comfy in – Merri made her way downstairs to find Candy on her laptop.

"Morning!" she beamed.

"Morning ... and you're a morning person since when?"

"Oh, I'm definitely not – this is an anomaly. I haven't been sleeping so well lately, usually waking up with the sun, so I thought I'd pop out into the garden and try get some shots of the sunrise with one of my new lenses. I'm just uploading the pics. Coffee?"

"Yeah – I'll help myself. Why are you not sleeping?"

"Who knows. Hormones? Early menopause?"

"Candy! I hope you're joking!"

She smiled. "Well, yeah – I'm only twenty-nine. Not unheard of though, and I haven't had sex for so fucking long I reckon my ovaries might start to shrivel up soon... By the way, do you know what you'd like to do for your birthday?"

That was a swift change of subject.

Ugh. Her birthday. "Nope."

"There will be no moping allowed. I thought we'd go see if we can hire a boat and have a picnic lunch and champagne on deck – the weather's supposed to be good on Wednesday."

Her heart lightened at the thought – as teens, they used to take boats out regularly over the summers. It had been *such* a long time... "You know, I don't know if I brought any sun lotion with me."

"I wondered – you're as pale as a ghost. Ever catch any sun in the city? Or are you permanently glued to your office chair?"

She pulled a face and went for the coffee jug ... because the answer was the latter.

"We'll buy sun lotion – no biggie. If you want, we can head down the beach around eleven and have lunch there."

"Will shops be open on a Sunday?"

"The ones around the beach will, as well as the cafés and it's looking like it's gonna be an awesome, hot day."

"I do have my bikini." Her voice dropped. "Was saving it for the honeymoon in Bali."

"Oi – no moping! We don't need Bali!" She stuck her tongue out at her. "Who the fuck needs the warm, crystal clear waters of Bali when we've got the freezing cold, North Atlantic Ocean on our doorstep?"

Merri smiled into her coffee mug, Candy's droll humour lifting her out of her gloom just enough. "Sold."

~*~

"Mummy, I want to stay out here and look at the toys," whined Rebecca, as she clutched the photograph of her and her dad in her hand. She'd woken up sad today, and Pip had informed him that photo was the equivalent of a doll or safety blanket for her. She wasn't about to let it go, not even for the promise of sand castles and bathing.

Pippa sighed.

"They'll be fine, Pip. We can see them from inside and Liam will look after them, won't you, Liam?"

His oldest nephew nodded in earnest.

Pippa frowned.

Jamie noted she was in a bit of a stroppy mood this morning – probably owing to her daughter's sadness.

He'd been on the receiving end of quite a few of those moods in their youth, and it usually took an hour or two of complete disengagement with her surroundings, coupled with a heart-to-heart, to bring her out of it. Unfortunately, that wasn't so easy with kids to watch over – he'd have to work miracles in five minutes.

"You know I hate leaving them."

"We're not leaving them – they're on the shop's property looking at all the beach toys out front – we'll still be able to see them, and the minute we can't I'll run outside in panic and start shouting, okay?"

Pippa's lip twitched, and he knew it was because he was generally so laid back that the idea of him doing anything in panic was practically comical. He'd even taken the news of Claire's infidelity with a slow (but not unpainful) contemplation that had annoyed the hell out of her.

*Huh ... annoyed* her.

It had then taken him another week to decide what to do about it.

Liam rolled his eyes, managing to look exactly like his mother when she did the same thing. "Mum, I'm ten. I can look after Sammy and Rebecca for five minutes."

And Jamie was pretty sure he could – he was damn sensible for his age, having had to grow up extremely fast in the past seven months, poor kid.

Pippa let out another sigh, this one resigned. "All right, but *scream* if anything happens, okay? And *don't* go off with anyone, or talk to them, or even look at them."

"Mum, we know *everyone* around here."

"That's beside the point!" she snapped.

"Come on," pressed Jamie, "we'll just be five minutes. One of us can come out if we need to." And he really wanted those five minutes to chat.

He steered her in by the elbow, guiding her over to the hire counter, and when she almost stumbled because she was looking backwards, he slung an arm around her shoulder and pulled her a few steps into the corner of the shop. "Pip, talk to me."

"What? About what?"

"About you. About David ... about how you're coping."

She all but scowled at him. "You're not usually so direct."

"I've got five minutes before your mothering instincts take over your genetic blueprint again – I have to be direct."

This time, the lip twitch gave way to half a smile.

"That's better."

But her eyes filled with tears. "Shit. You'd think it would be a bit easier by now; you'd think I could just make myself numb to it, but when one of the kids say they're missing him so much—"

"Christ ... are you kidding? You love him – you shouldn't be making yourself numb."

"For the kids..."

"The kids also love their dad. Would you ask *them* to grow numb to it?"

Her face collapsed and she shook her head.

He pulled her into his chest for a hug, which she accepted for all of two seconds before pushing herself away and swiping furiously at her eyes.

Jamie squeezed her shoulders. "These months were never going to be easy. I just wish I could have come home earlier for a bit—"

"No. We're not your responsibility."

He didn't get angry often – it just wasn't in him – but anger did stir at that statement. "No, you're not my responsibility, you're my sister and bloody-minded, too, I might add. I'm not asking how you're doing because I want to step into his role, I'm asking because I fucking care about you."

Her eyes widened.

No, he didn't often show anger and it always seemed to surprise people when he did.

"That's not what I meant – I'm sorry. Jamie, I'm sorry." She fell back into his chest for that hug.

His anger faded as quickly as it had risen. "Hey..."

"I'm fine – really, I am. It's just that some days are harder than others. What do you do when the father of your children ends up in a home for the disabled, unable to do anything for himself when he had once done *everything* for his kids and family. He *doted* on us – he was such an active person. How do I explain to his four-year-old daughter that he can't play with her when we visit – that he might not even recognise her straight away, if at all." Her voice had gone high-pitched, the words stumbling over each other. "I don't even know if it's right to take them in to see him anymore, but then I think, how can I not? They love him, they miss him," and then, her voice broke, "and most of the time, I don't know if I'm making anything better, or everything just ten times worse..."

"It's okay ... it's okay..."

"Fuck, Jamie," she squirmed out of his arms again and put herself back together. "*This* is why I don't want to talk about it, okay? It can't change any of it and I need to be strong for my children."

Shit. He needed more than five minutes and he felt as useless as she did. "Look, why don't you go back outside to them. I'll sort out the boat hire and everything here. I'm sorry – I just wanted to know how you really are, but I'm clearly crap at timing."

"No," she gave him a grateful smile, "you're not – there's no good time, not with three kids around. Thanks."

"Well, if it isn't Mr James Corbin."

They both turned to the blond man, of slightly dishevelled appearance, who'd just walked in behind the hire counter. He nodded at Pip. "You're looking dashing, Mrs Fellows."

"Oh, for fuck's sake, Jimmy..."

"Jimmy!" exclaimed Jamie, his smile widening.

Jamie and Jimmy.

They had been inseparable until around fourteen when attending separate schools had forced them apart. But they had remained the best of friends, and certainly the best swimming and boating buds, both of them having a great love of the big, wet divide. Pip had told him he now owned The Boat Shop. He'd always had a thing for Pip and had never bothered to hide it, preferring the more blatant, honest approach to life. Unfortunately for him, his attraction had never been reciprocated.

Shaking Jimmy's outstretched hand, Jamie was brought in for an easy hug and a clap on the back. "Ya don't call, ya don't text ... you here to stay, or just passing through?"

"I'm here for three months and then, who knows. Guess I'll see where the wind takes me."

Pippa's nails dug into the flesh of his arm, making him wince. "Ouch, Pip..."

"The kids..."

He looked from his sister's paling face to where her stricken gaze led, outside the shop window.

They were gone.

~*~

The beach was *just* as she'd remembered it, as if some bubble encased this part of the world while time changed everything else.

"Do you remember The Boat Shop?" asked Candace.

"Only vaguely – I never really went in there."

"Well, since Wave Riders shut down – about seven years ago now – that's been the only place around here to hire boats and other gear, so that's where we're heading. And you can get your sun lotion there, too."

Merri held her loose hair back with one hand against a sudden strong flurry of wind. "I thought the forecast said hot and sunny today."

"It did. Hopefully, it's a passing breeze that won't bring in the clouds – surely you remember there's always a *bit* of wind around here, I mean, we're right by the sea. Look, the sky's totally blue over there."

She followed Candy along the pavement, still clutching her hair. She hadn't bothered to straighten it this morning and was starting to regret it. It was already beginning to feel coarse and wiry under her palm with the sea salt in the air.

Having said that, there was something about the delicious scent of sea, sun and sand that had her simultaneously awakening and relaxing. A thousand memories stirred within her. She felt more alive being here for just half a day than she had for too long to remember. It wasn't an altogether comfortable feeling, as she knew it wouldn't be. Which was why she'd never come back.

Automatically – it was second nature, really – she let her mind wander around her body in search of signs of anxiety. Not a minute over the last twenty-two hours had been planned.

There was nothing – not a trace. Not even the general unease that came from constantly pre-empting a potential panic attack. She'd lived with that foreboding apprehension day in and day out for ten years, so much so, she'd kind of gotten used to it, and that's when it hit her – what her sense of discomfort was: it was that there was no discomfort.

*Wow ... talk about wrecked. You're jonesing to feel anxious 'cause it makes you feel safe – soooo screwed up!*

Something flew into her face.

With a small squeal, her hand came up at lightning speed to grasp it, but she didn't quite manage it. The breeze was too quick and it lifted whatever it was – a piece of paper or something – over her head, and took it sailing up into the branches of the nearest tree.

Another squeal sounded, and this one wasn't from her. It was the pained cry of a child.

Just a few feet behind them, a small, brown-haired, brown-eyed girl – too cute for words – was bawling her eyes out as she chased the paper. Two boys were trying to calm her down. Well ... *one* of them was trying to calm her down. The other one looked like he was having way too much fun trying to catch the lost item.

"Becca, it's okay ... we need to go back..."

And the girl screamed.

*Screamed.*

Not just a sound, but a single word that pierced through Merri as if it were a blade. *"Daaaaaadddddyyyy!!!"*

"Bloody hell," mumbled Candy.

"It's there!" yelled the other, younger boy, bouncing up and down by the trunk of the tree and pointing upwards. "I can see it – it's stuck up there!"

The older boy looked like this was completely out of his

depth. "We have to go back *now*," he hissed, "or we're going to get grounded for the rest of our lives!"

The girl was now sobbing uncontrollably, still calling for her daddy between blubbering gasps, and something inside Merri ... didn't quite snap – it sort of clicked into place. "What did you lose?" she asked the older boy.

For a second, she thought he wasn't going to say anything, and so he shouldn't – they were strangers – but it was obvious his ... sister? ... was in a state and that he had no idea what to do. "It's a photo of our dad – he's ill and we don't get to see him very much. She misses him."

"It's there! It's there!" The other boy with the seemingly never-ending supply of energy was still jumping up and down.

She walked over to the tree.

"Er ... Merri? What are you doing?"

She shrugged Candace off.

"See?" said the uber-boy when she approached the trunk of what was a Horse Chestnut tree. It was a big, old thing, with firm, wide branches for the most part, and right there, about fifteen feet up, was the photograph. It had gotten wedged between some leafy branches. She guessed the wind couldn't reach it, nestled between those bunches of overlapping leaves.

Her gaze switched from the tree to the girl, and the girl's pain bloomed inside Merri.

*I can reach it.*

And she knew she could – it was like riding a bicycle.

She bit her lip and took a peek at Candy who raised her eyebrows at her in question.

She should be getting the shakes roundabout now. She should be feeling like her chest was so tight she wouldn't be able to hold herself upright.

Instead, what she felt was a strange sense of hope. She could fix this, and after the hash she'd made of her wedding and her inability to fix *that*, she didn't want anything else ruined if it could be helped. Her eyes went back to the girl.

This was worth it.

She dropped her bag by the bounding boy's feet. "I can get it," she announced, and Candy's mouth dropped open. She ignored it. "Look after my bag for me, okay? You're in charge of that."

He nodded in wide-eyed admiration. "You're going to climb up there?"

"Yep," she stated. And then she couldn't help it – she grinned. Whatever that thing that had clicked into place, it had her feeling certainty over fear, no matter how bizarre the situation, and it was damn nice – more than nice.

"You *promised*," accused Candy, albeit more quietly than she would without the kids right there. "Merri—"

"You want to leave this poor girl like that? Look at her."

Candy's face reddened and Merri knew it was a cheap shot, but it was too late, because she *had* to get that photograph. And it wasn't just for the girl.

Before anyone else could protest, she took a small run up to the tree, leapt, dug her left foot into the bark of the trunk, grateful she'd worn her trainers and not her sandals, and brought her right leg straight up towards the lowest branch as she reached for the ones above with her hands.

*YES! On the first try!*

That had been the hardest bit – the rest was just easy calculation and a bit of legwork. As long as the wind didn't get to it before she did, she'd have that photograph back in the girl's hands within five minutes.

She could hear Candy mutter something under her breath – something along the lines of her doing grown women a disservice – but she knew she wouldn't let rip in front of the kids. "You'd better not have a panic attack, 'cause no way am I going up there to rescue you," she grumbled more loudly.

But Candy didn't understand – not this time. This wasn't like thirteen years ago. Back then, she'd been climbing to mask her anger, her recklessness fuelling the thrill of danger which overpowered her frustration with the world, making everything so much easier to cope with. This time, she was climbing because ... she didn't know exactly why, but she knew it was different. Yeah, the 'thrill' was still there, but it *felt* different. She could heal the girl's pain.

She'd stopped climbing after moving to London. This was the first time she'd climbed anything in ages, and it felt unbelievably wonderful to stretch her limbs in this way. And maybe it was that old and familiar sense of excitement filling her mind with illusion, but with every branch she climbed, she was sure she felt an age-old pain of her own, healing too.

# VII
## *Blast from the Past*

"My kids!" Pippa all but sent an elderly woman stumbling with her panic – the third passer-by she'd accosted in ten seconds flat. "Have you seen three children? A girl and two boys? Dark hair—"

"Pippa..." He tried to sound calming, but what did you say to a mother who thought she'd lost her kids?

"Oh, yes, dear..."

"Yes? Where? *Where?*"

"The girl was having a tantrum or such." The old woman tutted in disapproval, and Jamie saw a deep crimson rise up his sister's neck.

He took hold of her arm and pulled her back a step. Not even little old ladies were safe now. "Did you see which way they went?"

"Up that way," she pointed along the pavement towards the beach, "chasing some litter or something that the wind took from them."

Pippa gasped. "The photo?"

"Well, I don't know what it was. I thought they taught kids to put rubbish in bins nowadays."

"Oookay, then!" announced Jamie. 'Thirty-two Year Old Mother of Three Attacks Pensioner' would *not* be a great headline to wake up to tomorrow. "Thank you so much for your help." He dragged Pip in the direction she'd pointed. "Let's go find them."

He could see her close to exploding, but the threat to her children's safety outweighed her need to lay into the woman, thank god. They hurried towards the beach, until the sound of crying caught their attention.

"That's Becca! Oh, god..." Distress radiated from her.

Jamie followed the noise with his gaze until it landed on four figures in the distance all standing around a tree. "There, look." He pointed them out to her, and then Pippa was sprinting, and he was cursing as he followed her.

"Liam!" She shrieked as they neared.

Liam turned, fright and the child's equivalent of 'oh, fuck' in his eyes. His arms were protectively slung around Rebecca's shoulders.

"Liam ... Sammy! *What* is going on?" But it was the wo-man with the short, dyed-blue hair she was staring at in warning, not Liam or Sammy, and Jamie felt sorry for her because she looked like a deer caught in headlights. She didn't *look* like she'd done anything wrong and the kids were obviously not scared of her.

"Erm..."

It was Rebecca who saved the woman. "Mummy," her bottom lip trembled on her dirty, tear-streaked, slightly snotty face, "I lost Daddy."

"Oh, honey, come here."

She ran into her mother's arms and buried her face in her neck. "He's stuck in the tree and the super-hero lady's gone to get him down."

The blue-haired woman snorted.

Jamie raised his eyebrows at her. "Super-hero lady?"

"Not a super-hero," she finally spoke up. "Just insane. Likes to give her friends heart attacks."

"Woohoo! I've goooot it!" came the holler of triumph from somewhere up in the tree.

"See?" said Becca, whose lip had stopped quivering now that her face was lit up with renewed hope. "Super-hero. *And* she likes climbing, like me." Rebecca jumped off her mum's lap before she could stop her and ran until she was directly under the tree, standing next to Sammy, looking up. "Be careful!" she called up to her saviour.

"It's okay, I know what I'm doing," came the reply, and something intangible ran through Jamie. He broke out in goosebumps. Maybe he'd been more worried about the kids than he'd thought.

He looked at Pip. "Are you all right?"

She nodded, her face pinched, a hint of anger still shading her countenance. "You shouldn't have run off, Liam," she said, sternly, addressing her eldest.

"I know, Mum, I'm sorry, but Becca ran off before I could stop her, and I couldn't leave her—"

"We'll talk about it later."

And that was that.

Jamie caught Liam's worried eye and gave him his best reassuring smile, before turning back to the tree where he could now see one trainer-clad foot and most of a leg, in cropped trousers, stretching down to feel for the best place to land.

That weird sensation came over him again, the hairs on his arms rising, and out of nowhere, the craziest idea in the world entered his mind: *It's her.*

Ha!

No way.

No. Way.

But he was now stepping closer, that thought not letting go, taking in the shape of her legs and thighs with more concentration as they appeared into view, followed by an undeniably gorgeous backside – pert, smallish, but definitely rounded – almost *exactly* as he remembered it, albeit more ... womanly.

*It can't be...*

Whether it could or it couldn't, that goosebumpy sensation had transformed into a warmth that cascaded through him as her hips came into view. He'd liked to have been a gentleman and say the rush of warmth was all centred around his heart, his chest, his mind and memories, but no ... there was definite heat elsewhere too. *Exactly* like that night he'd first seen her.

*It can't be her.*

As she came down a bit more, a branch snagged the sleeveless, white top she was wearing and it rode up her torso a couple of inches. The small birthmark just below her belly button on the left, told him it was her.

*"What's this?"*

*"What's what?"*

*He kissed it, loving the way her skin pimpled under his lips.*

*She giggled. "It's just a birthmark."*

*"No it's not."*

*"It's not?"*

*"It looks like Africa, and look – here's Europe." He traced his tongue along it and her giggles got louder, turning into squeals when he nipped it with his teeth. She pushed his head away.*

*He bit his lip to keep from laughing, instead putting on the most serious voice he could muster. "No, keep still. I want to see – I'm behind on Geography."*

*"You doof!" she said, but she couldn't stop her own*

*laughter which had her shaking uncontrollably.*

*So, he kissed it again, and again, and all around it, and higher, and lower, and lower, until her laughter turned to gasps.*

Holy fuck.

It *was* her.

"Stand back, I'm jumping down!"

Dutifully, six pairs of feet took a step back and the woman jumped, landing with a small 'oomph', her dark blonde hair – no longer coloured pink at the ends, and straighter than he remembered – falling over her face as she clutched Rebecca's photo in her hand.

Becca was unstoppable. She flew at her, grabbed the photograph, then flung her arms around her neck, almost dragging her down to the ground. "Thank you!"

"Pleasure," she replied, somewhat out of breath, and Jamie couldn't drag his eyes away.

Pippa went to pull Rebecca off her. "Sweetie, let her up. Yes, thank you – that photograph means a lot to us."

She stood and waved her off. "Really – not a problem at all."

And Jamie stared.

Her green eyes sparkled with exhilaration; the smile on her face was pure contentment.

It was god-damned gorgeous.

*She* was god-damned gorgeous.

She didn't recognise him straight away. She turned to look for her friend, her eyes skimming past him; their lids fluttered for a second and her gaze shot straight back to him.

Disbelief turned into astonishment, coupled with some emotion he couldn't quite place, but that fucking adorable blush he'd had so much fun with thirteen years ago bloomed into her cheeks, her lips parted as a small gasp came out, and never in a million years would he understand what possessed him to do what he did next.

He blamed her defensiveness, already morphing around her like an invisible, yet tangible, armour; he blamed the way her chin jutted out slightly in that stubborn way time clearly hadn't changed... Or maybe it was his name on her lips, just before her armour took over – his frigging *name* which she remembered.

Her armour was a silent challenge for him as it always had been. He'd been underneath it. He knew how soft it was under there. And no matter how stupidly out-of-character and primal it was – how fucking 'caveman' and completely unlike his laid-back self – he was led by one persistent, forceful thought: *I know you – like hell are you shutting me out.*

It took two steps, that was all, before he had her face cupped in one hand, the small of her back against his other, and her mouth under his.

~*~

She couldn't breathe.

And for the first time in a while, she found she didn't really need to.

Her brain was fucked – that much was obvious. She couldn't process exactly what was happening at this precise moment, so her mind went into shutdown, and all that was left was reaction.

Somewhere in between the past and the present, confident lips found hers in a kiss that was alarmingly familiar, yet excitingly new, and she *reacted.*

The hands that she'd laid on him to balance herself – that should now be pushing him away – clutched at his T-shirt instead and she kissed him back. Her tongue tingled at its tip where it brushed against his and she let out a little moan, which only encouraged this madness – his madness ... or was it her that was mad?

His hold on her tightened, bringing her closer to him and she almost collapsed at the feel of his growing arousal against her hip.

Her entire body responded, a startling heat surging through her. *It's him. It's him!*

His tongue swept over hers, deeper, as if seeking out the last decade plus three years and—

"EEEEEEWWW! GROSS!"

Out of the mouths of babes.

"YUCK. Mum, can we go to the beach now?"

*Holy. Crap.*

Jamie wrenched his head away from hers, looking just as bewildered as she felt.

Merri landed back in her body from wherever the hell she'd floated off to and her mind scrambled to gather sense.

Behind her, she heard the little girl giggle as her brother kept sounding his disgust. God only knew what Candy and that other woman were thinking.

Other woman?

Oh, fuck! Please don't let that be his—

"Mummy, is that Uncle Jamie's girlfriend?"

Uncle Jamie ... Uncle. *That's his sister!*

She had no right to feel relieved about that.

"Er..." he stuttered at her, seemingly unable to look away. She was having the same problem. Instead, he stared down at his T-shirt still bunched up in her hands because she now realised she hadn't let him go when he'd pulled back.

A look of mortification crossed his eyes.

*What...?*

She followed his gaze, only for it to land on the engage-ment ring on her finger. *Engagement ... Jesus Christ! What have I done?*

He dropped her like a lead balloon the same second she finally managed to let go of his top, and she *sure* as fuck had no right to feel the sense of loss she did over that.

"I'm sorry," he muttered, still having trouble speaking. "I don't know what ... er ... I shouldn't have ... I didn't know you were—"

"It's fine," she squeaked out, even though it shouldn't be fine and wasn't fine ... really it wasn't. It *wasn't.*

The breeze whipped her hair across her face.

He went to move it automatically, then abruptly froze mid-movement, and dropped his hand.

She swept her own hair back into place, tucking the strands behind her ears.

"Christ, I have no idea what came over me, I swear. I saw you, I recognised you and ... all the memories just ... and the rest is a bit of a blur."

"And it kinda looked like a blur, too," quipped Candy from her left.

Merri's face flamed.

She approached them with the hugest grin – the kind that always had Merri wary – and an outstretched hand. "Jamie, I presume?"

He took her hand, probably because he didn't know what else to do.

"I'm Candy. I've heard a lot about—"

"Candy!" interrupted Merri. "Er ... used to live here. I mean, she still lives here. I mean, she used to live here back then." *What the fuck...? Brain – work.* "As well. As me. But she still does now. And I ... don't. Live here."

She decided to shut up.

Candy was biting her lip signalling some thought process going on in her head, and Merri wasn't sure she liked the idea of that.

"Merri's down visiting me for a bit because her and her fiancé have just separated."

*Candy!* What in god's name was she *doing*? Yeah, they were separated, but they weren't *separated.* She was still waiting for his call for them to iron things out.

She turned to Jamie to correct her friend's badly phrased statement, but that look of mortification on his face was now fading at Candy's words, relief taking over, and that familiar light of amusement in his *gorgeous* brown eyes – *bad, Merri; very bad* – was returning. She stalled.

"I'm sorry to hear that," he said. He did sound genuinely sorry; he didn't *look* completely sorry.

Jamie's sister sidled up beside him, bemused confusion – if there was such a thing – evident in her half-smile. She looked at Jamie questioningly, and then at her, also holding her hand out in greeting.

Of course, she took it.

"So ... *you're* Merri."

Jamie coughed.

"The beach! Mum, please can we go now?"

"In a minute, Sammy."

"Ooo, ooo!" Rebecca jumped up and down clutching herself between her legs, looking alarmed. "I need a wee-wee, Mummy!"

"Oh, god, here we go ... right. Kids, we head that way – off to the beach – sweetie, you can pee in the sea. Jamie, are you still coming down with us?"

"Erm—"

"We were heading that way ourselves," announced Candy, "let's all go."

Merri glared at her, and she thought she caught Jamie's lip twitch out of the corner of her eye.

"Muuuummmmyyyyy! Weee-weee!"

"Okay, let's go – now, now, now!" She marched her kids off down the path towards the sand, not that they needed much encouragement. Sammy whooped and ran down the path, with a more quiet Liam sprinting after him, and Rebecca was going as fast she could with her legs as crossed as possible. Candy stepped in behind them.

Jamie and herself didn't move.

He gestured with his arm. "Ladies first."

"So not a lady," she blurted out, without thinking.

Her cheeks burned when she remembered those were the exact words she'd spoken to him as he'd dropped her off after their night together. She also remembered his reply.

A sudden, intense heat briefly flashed through his eyes, before he let out a breath and looked down. "I really am sorry – about the kiss. I'm not usually so impulsive," and then, he grinned, "nowadays, anyway."

*Oh ... that smile...*

She found herself smiling back. "It's really all right." *But it really shouldn't be.*

A shadow of guilt about kissing him back stirred inside her. Could that be considered cheating? God, she hoped not – it's not like she'd instigated it. *Yeah, but you kissed him back – a lot.*

But was it cheating if they were separated, but not 'separated'?

She found herself internally assessing her breathing and emotional levels – she was fine. No wheezing; no rising panic... *Of course there isn't – this is Jamie.*

That seemed to make more sense to some alien part of her than it did to the 'normal' her. The simple fact that it was *him* shouldn't make everything okay.

*Unless this is the result of a spell after all?*

She brushed that daft thought right out.

"It's good to see you, Merri."

She didn't know what that was – that, right *there*, hidden in the depths of his very sincere eyes – but she found herself drawn into it, just as she had been thirteen years ago, when the thought of not knowing his secrets had gutted her. He looked older, wiser...

*Hotter,* teased her mind.

She mentally gave it a slap, but she couldn't deny the thought it had conjured. He'd filled out in all the right ways and worked outdoors a lot judging by his tan. The ponytail was gone, but his dark brown hair was still longish, and tousled, and all 'hey, why don't you run your fingers through me?'.

*Fuck. Think about something else... His accent.*

The Australian tilt to his accent was intriguing – had he gone and studied abroad after all?

The need to know was like a slow burn – to know *him* all over again; who he was now. And the thought of not knowing... She had to force her throat to work and tried to keep her tone as light as possible. "It's good to see you too, Jamie."

She didn't miss the way his questioning gaze fell back onto her ring finger before she turned and followed the others down the path. Nor did she miss the very uncomfortable realisation that, at this very second, she wished the diamond-tipped band wasn't there.

Most of the talking took place between Candy and Pippa over the next two hours. They got on like a house on fire. Great.

Jamie would often wander off and play at the edge of the sea with Rebecca while the boys tackled each other in the water, and sometimes, he'd tackle them in the water too, which made Merri want to jump right in and join in the fun. She hadn't swum in the sea since the panic attacks had started as the freezing water had a tendency to bring them on.

Instead, she sat on her beach towel trying not to turn as red as a lobster, cursing that their trip to the shops never happened – she was using Candy's factor eight sun cream, when what she needed was factor twenty. But she still had her trousers and top on and this was good, not just because she would fry under the afternoon sun, but because she was wearing the new bikini intended for use on a private area of a hotel beach in Bali.

Jamie did *not* need to see her in that.

Guilt washed over her again, although she must still be too shell-shocked to really absorb it, because she was trying her damnedest to think about Michael, yet all she could see was Jamie. She supposed it didn't help that he was *right there* in her line of vision, with his nephew under his arm in a head-lock, while the beating sun showed off every contour of his torso, skin glistening with drops of the ocean.

Thirteen years ... why the hell couldn't he have grown a flabby beer belly?

Merri tore her eyes away and abruptly dived into her bag and pulled out her phone, forcing her gaze to remain on the screen. Nothing from Michael. Sod the waiting – this was an emergency.

She pressed the key for his number and waited for the ring tone.

The ring tone was all she got ... not even an answering machine.

Confusion clouded her reason. She was angry he hadn't answered, but also, not angry enough; also relieved. She missed Michael, but she only missed him a little because total independence was the way they had built their relationship. They were apart fairly regularly because of his business trips. That had always been the way from the very beginning, and it wasn't every day they got the chance to speak when that happened, but that was normal, wasn't it? That's how some relationships were; some relationships thrived on distance and she'd always been grateful she never missed him that much – it was why they worked as a couple. She had never wanted to pine for a partner; it only led to angsty feelings and she hated angst and so did Michael. She'd never *wanted* to feel that kind of longing.

Except for now.

"Hi."

She looked up to find a dripping, wet Jamie looming over her, the sun to his left.

"You coming in?"

"Oh ... you mean into the sea? Um—"

"I was going to ask you the same thing," called out Candy from three feet away as she spread more lotion on her. "I recall rarely being able to get you out of the sea."

"Er..."

"Come on," he pressed. "You're missing out. It's wonderfully icy."

She laughed. "Well..."

"I dare you."

*Oh, no fair!* She narrowed her eyes at him. That self-assured grin on his face told her he knew exactly what he was doing with those words – he hadn't forgotten, and fuck, that buzz, low in her belly responded to the challenge. God damn it! Surely by now she should have outgrown something so childish – and in her case, *dangerous* – as the thrill of the dare.

"I double-dare you," said Candy.

She aimed her death-glare at her. Panic attacks aside, did she not know how a seemingly harmless dare could be so perilous to her and those she cared about?

*No ... no one knows...*

In alarm, she pushed away the crude memory that threatened to surface, but it was too late – there it was, the first hint of panic since she'd gotten here, rising ... but just as she thought she was going to have to excuse herself, Jamie sank to his knees in front of her, warmth radiating from his sun-kissed skin. "You need sun block – you're so pale."

Wonderful. So sexy.

*No, you don't want to be sexy, remember? Remember Michael?*

Right. Good. Pale was good. "I forgot to pack any."

"Why didn't you say?" He reached across her to his bag and the scent of sun, sea, lotion and *him*, wafted around her, causing all manner of metaphorical winged things to collide in her abdomen ... and lower. At least they chased away the panic.

"It's okay, I've been using the one that Candy—"

"Here." He dumped a bottle of factor thirty right in her lap.

"Um ... thanks. You don't look like you need protection this high."

*Very good, Merri – let him know you've been looking at*

*his body.*

He shrugged. "It's become second nature. Down under, the sun gets blazing hot, and quickly too. If you don't screen yourself properly it can be hazardous."

"So, you did go to Australia. To study the ocean?"

This time, his smile was slow, but wide. It was like watching chocolate melt – as mesmerising as always, complete with that dimple that now nestled in a grown man's shaven cheek. "Yep. And what did you do after we parted ways?"

She wished she had something exotic to say, something that resembled her having followed her dreams and that didn't sound like 'I moved to London, fell into light drug use, fucked up myself and the people I love, finally dragging myself out of it when my mother almost died'.

Unfortunately, she didn't.

And she didn't want to talk about it.

"Come on, let's go swim." She pushed herself up to standing, ignoring his puzzled expression.

She didn't know where the hurt had come from; old hurt she was usually good at dispelling when it arose. How revealing her stupid bikini was suddenly seemed unimportant ... or maybe very important if it got her mind off the past. *Er ... and what about the imminent panic attack when that cold water reaches your chest?*

"Mum!" Sammy shouted as three pairs of legs ran up the beach towards them.

"Sammy, Liam, waaaiit!" whined Rebecca, a few metres behind her brothers.

"Mum," he gasped as he plonked down on her towel, spraying her with sand.

She glared at him in disapproval. "For god's sake, Sammy..."

"Is it lunch time yet? We're hungry."

"Mmmm, I'm kinda peckish, too." Candy turned to look at Merri. "You?"

"Not overly, but I guess I could eat."

"Well," said Pippa. "I'm going to take the kids up to the café for lunch. We could either all go, or," she directed at Jamie, "you could stay, keep our places, and I'll bring you something back?"

"Pip, was that you asking, or dictating?"

Pippa pulled a face at him. "You know I hate moving all our stuff if I don't have to."

"Merri and I will stay." He looked up at Merri for confirmation. "And you both go with the kids."

Candy rose to her feet, brushing the sand off her. "Sounds good to me."

Merri tried to look like it made no difference to her; that the thought of being alone with Jamie, after all this time didn't cause her heart to speed up a fraction. They hadn't exactly talked yet.

*Just kissed,* her head reminded her, as if she could forget. Maybe that wouldn't matter if she couldn't still taste that kiss on her lips. She sneaked a glance at her open bag, her phone resting on the top. She willed it to come alive with Michael's ring tone.

Of course it bloody didn't.

After a lot of dusting down, dressing, and trying to keep the kids together, Candy and Pippa were off towards the café at the top of the beach.

"They seem to be getting on well," said Jamie.

"Yeah."

"I'm glad. Pip's had it rough for the best part of a year, she could do with a break; some good friends..."

Should she ask? He'd been the one to bring it up, hadn't

he? "What happened to her?"

"Her husband was in a car accident seven months ago, just before Christmas. It's left him disabled, physically and mentally. He's in a care home because she needs to both work and look after the kids, and she feels she wouldn't be able to care for him properly if he stayed at the house – it cut her up making that decision. I don't completely know how she's fairing to be honest, but I'd hazard a guess it's been a long time since she's been as relaxed as she is this afternoon."

Merri felt a little dumbfounded, both at Pippa's circumstances and at the fact that Jamie had been so open with her about it considering she didn't know his sister at all. "That's horrendous. I'm so sorry."

"Yeah, it's shitty all right, but shit happens to good people. So ... swim?"

Shit happened to good people. Wasn't that the truth – her mum, Pippa – and she felt like crap, because all the shit that had happened to her, she had done to herself.

"Hey..." Jamie's concerned voice... "Are you all right?" He stepped in closer and laid a hand on her arm, making her skin tingle where he touched.

Her world teetered for a moment, an overwhelming sadness sweeping her off her feet – almost – and then she pulled herself back together. "Yeah."

She reached down for the hem of her top and pulled it over her head, pretending not to notice dark brown eyes fall to her barely covered chest before they were hastily averted.

Her life was fast becoming a heated mess after years of her getting it all together, and the mess had started when she'd said 'Jamie' at the altar.

The freezing cold of the sea would be good roundabout now; make her numb...

*And the panic attacks?* reminded her sensible self for the second time.

Shit. Maybe she could make herself numb to those too.

# VIII

## *From a Distance*

Holy fuck, that was *not* swimwear.

*'Let's go for a swim.'* Yey! Great idea.

Why exactly had he thought it would be okay? What part of his slowly deteriorating brain thought, for one second, that seeing her practically naked wouldn't conjure up every minute of that life changing night he'd spent with her?

It was ridiculous, actually, how drawn he felt to her, but then, he had thirteen years ago too. However, this time he was far too wary of the fact that he'd just come out of a ten year relationship, and even though he was the kind of guy who'd always known his own mind, he couldn't deny the possibility that he was rebounding. The only thing that had his mind whispering *'this is not a rebound'* was the fact that he had *already* known Merri. He'd already had feelings for her way before Claire came on the scene; granted, those feelings had never been allowed to flourish because of the circumstances they had found themselves in, but he had entertained the notion, more than once in the months following their night together, that he could have easily fallen in love with her. He'd gone so far as to wondering if he actually *had* fallen, just a little, 'cause god knows, he'd thought about her a hell of a lot after that. He'd also fallen in love with Claire easily. He hated to admit that he found it incredibly easy to fall in love – he was just open like that; he found people interesting and Pippa had often said he was way too trusting for his own good. It hadn't been a problem until Evil Monster Claire.

The fact that Merri was here, now, blew his mind in delicious and worrying ways – ways his heart wasn't ready for.

That didn't seem to stop his mouth from blurting out all kinds of inappropriate things though. Bugger.

"Could you pop some of this on my back?" asked Merri, holding out the bottle of sun lotion he'd lent her.

*Don't tell me you didn't see that one coming.*

Shit – he was an idiot. He actually hadn't. If he had bothered to think about it at all, he'd most probably have assumed she'd have gotten her friend to do it.

Fighting every image possible of running his hands under the barely-there pieces of her not-swimwear, he took the bottle from her. "Sure."

She turned to face the other way and – *dear god, that's a semi-thong!* – held her hair up, away from the nape of her neck.

What was her game?

He squirted cream onto the palm of his left hand.

One minute she was distant, the next she was ... doing *this*. One minute she was cold, the next she was all volatile heat. If she were anyone else he'd have been turned off – he didn't do games and he'd suffered enough of them from Claire to last a lifetime, thank you very much – but he *knew* Merri, and behind her prickliness there was something important going on. It had been that way when he'd first met her too. Back then, her haughtiness had been hiding stuff about her dad and her having to leave home. He'd gotten through all those layers to the vulnerability beneath and had discovered beautiful secrets – beautiful because she had entrusted them to him. It's what he did every single day of his life: he dove fathoms deep to uncover hidden treasure, and when the ocean chose to divulge, it was a high like no other. He *loved* it, he *lived* for it, and perhaps that was why he simply couldn't turn away now despite all signs indicating he should run in the other direction.

She let out a little gasp as the cold cream met her back and he wondered how he was going to hide the erection that had just sprung to life inside his trunks. "Sorry. Should have warned you first."

"It's fine."

It was *too* fine. "So ... what happened between you and your fiancé?"

She tensed right under his palms and he almost wished he'd said nothing, but his Claire-damaged heart needed to know before things went any further.

*Oh, you're thinking of taking things further?*

Fuck it, he was. He really was. Who was he kidding? As soon as he'd known it was Merri climbing down that tree, some part of him had been unable to turn away just like thirteen years ago. That same part, he already knew, would put up a fight before it allowed him to let her go twice. It was illogical, but when it came to this woman, he'd always broken all his own rules. He should *never* have slept with her really, when she had only just turned sixteen and he knew he'd never see her again. He'd been seventeen – about eighteen months older than her if memory served him right – he should have known better. Any outsider looking in would have seen some nearly-man taking advantage of an innocent girl because he'd never have to take responsibility for it, no matter how far from the truth that was.

But, somehow, Meredith Goodwill managed to seep inside him, throwing all caution out the window in favour of 'the moment'. She made him impetuous and he'd loved every second of it. The only other time he felt that same sense of spontaneity and freedom was when studying the ocean. He knew the ocean like the back of his hand – could predict its patterns with spooky accuracy: its tides, the length of a wave base and pretty much exactly where it would disrupt the sea bed ... his peers, funnily enough, had coined him 'the sea whisperer'. He didn't bother telling them he'd fantasised being exactly that as a kid. He knew the ocean inside out – he wanted to know Merri inside out.

"We were ... um ... supposed to get married yesterday. I ruined it all."

*Yesterday?* Holy fuck.

He quickly finished rubbing the lotion into her back and capped the bottle with finality. This is the part where he needed to turn away.

She turned first, a world of confusion in her eyes. God, she looked completely lost, but also, somewhere under there was some iron strength that kept her upright. What had she been through the past thirteen years?

*Turn away.*

"Candy seems to think he'll forgive me, but I'm not so sure. I'm suddenly not sure I know him as well as I thought I did." That green gaze locked on his. "I'm not even sure I know myself."

*Yesterday ... this happened fucking yesterday! You can not go there!*

He took a step back. "Time heals all wounds."

"Does it? 'Cause I'm still waiting." She'd blurted that out and now looked slightly embarrassed at her admission.

He stepped back towards her. "So I'm told, anyway. I've just come out of a ten year relationship myself. It's why I came home – I flew in Friday night."

Her eyes widened. "Friday?"

"Spooky, huh?"

"You were together for ten years? Wow ... I'm sorry."

"I'm not. She ... Claire ... turned out she'd been seeing some guy behind my back. For the best part of three years."

For a second there, he thought a flash of anger crossed her face, but if that's what it was, it was gone in a heartbeat and something that looked like guilt fell over it instead. "I'm sure I should feel more upset, you know? About everything that happened with Michael, I mean."

He assumed 'Michael' – and his inner-voice snarled his name in an unseemly fashion – was her fiancé.

"But maybe it makes sense in a messed up kind of way that I don't; after all, I said someone else's name at the altar."

"You said..." *Whoa...*

"I know." She deliberately avoided his gaze. "It wasn't intentional. It wasn't someone I was seeing – I've *never* cheated on him; I'd never even thought about being with anyone else. I don't know why it happened – although my mum has an outlandish theory which is, rather scarily, starting to look reasonable – but I wouldn't forgive me either."

"So, what happened next? You said someone else's name and ... he broke up with you?"

"Maybe? I think so? I'm not really sure. He said he needed some time away from me to think, but this is also kinda how we have arguments: away from each other. The registry office has been rebooked for two months, but he indicated we may not have the wedding at all and I haven't heard from him since."

"You have arguments *away* from each other?"

She went a bright shade of crimson and he wished he hadn't homed in on that.

"I know it sounds stupid, but ... it works for us."

"Wait, I'm sorry – that didn't come out sounding like it was supposed to. I can completely see you as someone who'd prefer to argue from a distance."

Her eyebrows rose in surprise. "You can?"

He laughed. "With the mile wide moat you've put around your fortress, yeah – I can."

And now she looked pissed off. "I don't have a moat."

Aaaah – *that* look. He couldn't help digging in, even though he knew he shouldn't. "Like hell you don't. You have a moat, a barbed wire fence, a fifty foot wall, and a whole battalion of armed men."

The most beautiful scowl, coupled with an adorable glower, painted her features.

It was all he could do not to lean in and kiss it right off her face. His feet reacted without consent and took him another step closer to her; so close, he could feel the heat of her skin meet his. "And it makes me want to break in all over again."

He hadn't actually meant to say that last bit out loud, but apparently his mind was no longer connected to the rest of him.

She exhaled, sharply, that gorgeous red colour tinting her skin all the way down to the tops of her breasts.

Yeah, he was looking.

Shame on him, but really ... that was *not* swimwear. What lit his fuse though, was that she was clearly as aroused as him. Whatever he was feeling about seeing her again, she was feeling it too and that took every single part of him to new places filled with salacious and torturous possibilities he had no right thinking about when both their lives were in such tangled states.

*But it's her ... of all people. She's come back into your life, somehow.* And *that* was extremely difficult to turn away from – like snubbing fate or something, not that he necessarily believed in fate, but heck, maybe he'd give it a go.

"Shit," she cursed under her breath, her glower a fraction less glowery and now filled with a need she failed to hide that went straight to his obstinate cock.

She abruptly turned and strode down to the sea.

Fuck. Was that a rebuff? He was trying to be his calm self, but it seemed the more he tried, the more tempestuous he became. This was not him. He wasn't this no-thought, quick-action guy.

*Correction: you're not this guy with anyone else. With her...* She'd always taken him that little bit out of his depth.

"Hey!" she yelled at him from near the water, her silhouette, against the sun, in that poor excuse for a bikini, making him feel light-headed. He'd been standing there like a lemon, not moving. "You coming, or what?"

Not a rebuff, then.

He let out a slow breath.

He should yell back, 'no'. He should sit on his towel and refuse to go anywhere with her because everything needed to end right here.

A brief wind smacked his bare back and peppered his legs with sand.

And like a moth to a flame, he followed.

~*~

Candace could just make out the tiny outlines of Merri and Jamie if she squinted against the sun. They were heading into the sea, and it was about bloody time. If she'd had to watch her best friend sitting on her beach towel, stiff as a statue, when what she clearly wanted to do was throw her metaphorical shackles off, she'd have lost the plot. She was aware that Merri was potentially walking into a mess – what, with Michael and everything – which she clearly needed to sort out and *not* by fucking email. But as far as she was concerned, walking into a mess was better than sitting still and watching everything you really want slip away.

Candy had wanted more than anything to watch Merri fulfil the happiest day of her life. What she'd found was a lack of 'happy' that had bugged her more and more over the few hours after she'd arrived to greet the person she'd not seen in ten years ... the person she still knew too well. Merri had always held joy – *real* joy; the kind that warms your heart and makes you vulnerable – at arms length, compensating for its lack with wild, daring ventures that had allowed her to feel whatever she'd needed to, but had gotten her into a shit-load of trouble. When she'd heard she was getting married, she'd assumed her friend had found her way out of that maze. Turned out, she'd traded one maze for another; this one, thankfully, more sedate than the last, but still just an excuse to avoid the path that would lead to her goal: happiness. In fact, the only time she had really conveyed a deep happiness to Candy was when she'd been recounting her night with Jamie.

*And then he conveniently shows up out of the blue.*

Candy *did* believe in fate, despite her own circumstances, which she really didn't want to think about right now, and it was Mrs Goodwill who had taught her to believe – something that seemed to have skipped her daughter by, although Candy knew Merri was simply too afraid to believe in ... what? 'Magic', she supposed. Most people thought of magic as some external force with a mind of its own, but Mrs Goodwill had told them when they'd been much younger, that magic was entwined in everything and was connected to your will – like a string attached to your thoughts that you could pull in any direction with the correct amount of force and the right intent. Of course, magic couldn't make everything come true, but it was a step towards taking charge of your life and facing your responsibilities, for that is what the force of intent actually offered: personal power.

Candy had latched onto the lesson; had used it unsparingly over the past few years when she'd needed it the most, using everything Merri's mother had been through as her own inspiration – even what Merri had been through to some extent.

And Jamie was here. He was actually *here*.

She knew she was being a bit pushy with the two of them, but Merri needed to break out of the safety net she'd placed around her life, and this was as good a place to start as any. She wanted to see Merri happy ... she *needed* to see Merri happy before...

She blinked back unexpected tears – *not going there today* – and returned her focus to Pippa who was at the food counter and her kids who were at the back of the café in the play area, Sam already causing mild havoc.

She grinned to herself, perhaps more acerbically than she'd intended. Kids knew how to live, didn't they?

"Candy!" called out Pippa across people's heads, holding up red sachets. "Ketchup?"

She replied with two thumbs up and then moved the used mugs from the previous occupants of the table she'd claimed – clearly there was an under-staffing issue going on here on a Sunday.

Before too long, a tray piled with fish and chips was dropped onto the table top. "Mmmm, smells good."

"Can't beat fish and chips at the beach. Also, there's always enough of it so the kids are never hungry thirty minutes later. Kids!" she yelled in their general direction. "Lunch!" Then she looked back at Candy. "You all right? You look tired."

"Oh, you know – it's the afternoon lull," she lied. "I'll almost definitely fall asleep on the full belly I'll have after eating this lot, so kick me awake if I start snoring."

Pippa smiled. "David used to snore."

Candy stared at her as she separated the plates and piled the food on them. This woman was strong, even though she was falling apart – *must* have fallen apart after the accident.

Why exactly Pippa had decided to tell her about her husband was a mystery to her – perhaps she just needed someone to talk to – but they'd hit it off really well, and Candy was no stranger to bad news or needing someone to talk to, so she had responded in a casual, yet meaningful way, allowing Pip the space to say more if she wanted. Sometimes, that was all someone needed: the space to allow them to be. If only Merri would jump into hers...

"Do you still hear phantom snoring that wakes you up?"

Now, she laughed. "Funnily enough, I did in the beginning, but not so much in recent months."

Three small bodies jostled into view as three hungry mouths verbally fought over the biggest portion.

"Oi!" Pippa softly slapped creeping hands away. "There's plenty – quit acting like beggars. Liam, can you sort out Becca on her chair? Sammy – sit!"

Like soldiers they followed their mother's orders. Food

was obviously akin to gold doubloons.

"Mummy, where's Uncle Jamie?" asked Becca.

"He and Merri stayed at the beach to look after our things – you know that."

"What about their lunch? Do they have any lunch? What are they eating?"

"Uncle Jamie's eating Merri's face," shot out her brother.

"Sammy! For god's sake!"

He made fish lips then aimed for Becca's cheek with slurpy, kissing noises.

Becca squealed, and Liam caved in and sounded out his laughter while Candy failed to hide hers.

"I doubt Uncle Jamie's going to want to buy anyone making fun of him any ice-creams after lunch, do you?"

And that was that. Ice cream was *better* than gold doubloons.

The topic changed to something about why crabs pinch toes as tomato sauce and salt went flying over batter and fried potato.

"So..." Pippa eyed Candy cautiously. "What exactly happened at the wedding?"

Candy filled her in while Liam pretended not to listen, Becca tried to understand the complicated sentences, and Sammy couldn't give a hoot as he pulled the batter off the cod to eat that before anything else. She told Pippa about Merri saying Jamie's name at the altar, much to her bemusement. After a moment of hesitation, she also decided to tell her about how Merri, the night before the wedding, had recounted her and Jamie's one time together.

"Oh, my god," Pippa looked to the heavens in exasperation, "I swear, I had *never* seen a guy swoon until after that night, and for weeks later Jamie was all 'sighing' – *literally* – all over the damn place like some love-struck girl! I finally got what had happened out of him; learnt my little brother had lost his ... er..." she glanced at Liam, then away again, "you know – before *I* even had. I was almost twenty and considering a nunnery."

Candy laughed.

"What's a nunnery?" piped up Becca.

"Somewhere you go where you're not allowed to have any fun," came Pippa's slightly sarcastic, adult reply. Clearly, her mum-switch had been temporarily turned off for this discussion.

Becca frowned in thought as Pip turned back to Candy. "So, is this thing with her fiancé on or off?"

Candy shrugged. "Your guess is as good as mine. The big whoops happened, he buggered off, said he'd email her and he hasn't yet."

"Email her?"

"Apparently they don't discuss things face-to-face like normal people."

There was a momentary pause while Pippa simultaneously chewed and contemplated things. "Jamie's been through a lot in the past few weeks. He was in a relationship for ten years when—"

"Evil Monster Claire," mumbled Sammy with his mouth full.

"Yes, thank you for the input, second child of mine... When," she continued, "he discovered that Claire had been cheating on him for three years."

"Ouch."

"Yeah. My point is, that my little brother is a sweetheart, and I don't mean that in a pet name kind of way – I mean, he has an actual sweet heart. He's open and giving and I don't want to see him get hurt again."

Aaah ... overprotective, big-bear sister. Yep, she'd seen

this coming. It only upped her respect for the woman. "Merri's like a sister to me. I don't want her to get hurt either."

"Sounds like she was the one doing the hurting at the altar."

"Or maybe she was being honest with herself, even if it happened in an accidental way... if you believe in accidents."

"Kind of hard for me not to."

Shit! Her stupid mouth! "Oh, Pippa, I didn't mean—"

"I get what you're saying – that things happen for a reason, or because of fate or whatever – but every time I've told myself that over the past seven months it just makes me feel powerless and kinda sick to my stomach."

Fuck it. "I'm sorry."

"No." Pip dropped her fork and sighed.

Liam and Sammy exchanged looks.

"I'm the one who's sorry – it's just me being a negative bit—er ... a bit negative."

Sammy's cutlery fell onto his plate with a loud clatter. "Finished! Can I go play?"

"NO!" pouted Becca. "I wanna go too – I've finished too!"

"Really? That's all you're having?"

Her pout grew bigger.

"Fine. I'll box it up for you so you can eat the rest for dinner."

The pout miraculously transformed into a wide grin. "Thanks, Mummy!"

They both scrambled off the table, leaving Liam to finish up at his own pace.

Pippa looked at Candy. "Jamie and Merri are both adults – they know what's what and they can do what they like; you'd have to be blind not to see there's something there... I just can't help thinking they should take some time to sort out their own lives first before tumbling into each other's."

"Agreed. Except..."

"Except?"

She squinted back at the couple out the café window. They hadn't moved much further out into the ocean. The sun looked gorgeous shimmering on the water. She ignored the way her throat closed up. "Except sometimes, time's the last thing you've got ... you know?"

Pip fumbled with a chip in retrospective silence before sticking it into her mouth. Candy didn't miss the sheen to her eyes which she quickly blinked away. "Yeah. I know."

She looked back out the window.

This had been a whirlwind of a day. It was as if they'd all been unwittingly picked up by some invisible cyclone and set down again in each other's tumultuous paths. She'd only just met Jamie and Pippa, but she felt like she'd known Pippa all her life. Maybe it was down to who they were and what they'd been through – bonds didn't need to be seen to exist. They also didn't need to make sense. That was something she knew too well.

The small figure that looked like Merri suddenly scooped up a load of water and threw it at Jamie.

Candy tore her eyes away before she saw whatever the retaliation was. She didn't need to see it. Just as it felt like she'd known Pippa since forever, she couldn't shake the feeling that Merri and Jamie had already waited thirteen years. Yeah, okay, Merri was right – she *was* a hopeless romantic. But she'd never had a problem with that aspect of herself, even if romance had never really worked for her ... at least not in the conventional way.

Whatever had brought them all together today, be it a

spell like Mrs Goodwill had implied, or not, it was nothing short of a miracle as far as she was concerned. And if she couldn't have her own miracle, she'd bask in her friend's. Whatever the logic, for Merri and Jamie to 'wait until the right time' seemed the wrong move to her, when it was so obvious that the right time had already arrived, albeit in an unseemly fashion complete with baggage. But sometimes, life did that to you.

*The right time...*

She had to tell Merri about what she'd been through.

And she would, but she needed to see her friend happy first – truly happy. It was the goal she had set herself, unknowingly, the minute she had seen her in that wedding dress. It was partly selfish: she needed a reason to believe in a happily ever after.

Merri's happiness was suddenly more important than anything else in the world.

# IX

## Above the Surface

She should have told him about the panic attacks, god damn it.

She was an idiot, because here she was, neck deep in the Atlantic Ocean with her frozen chest burning (as was ever the contradiction) with the need to expand and take in air.

All because she wanted to forget her past for a second.

Mission accomplished. Her past was the last thing on her mind right now. "Jamie," she stuttered, barely audible.

She was good at hiding rising anxiety – could win a bloody Academy Award for it.

Despite her excellent performance, Jamie had been throwing her odd looks as if he sensed something was wrong. Then he'd quickly glance away and keep his eyes averted – more often than not – probably due to the sodding inappropriate bikini she was wearing.

"Jamie," she threw out again, louder this time, forcing her throat to work.

Ahead of her by a few metres, he stopped and turned her way. "Are you all right?"

She had larked about, playing down her doubt in her body's ability to do as it was told for once. She had pretended she was fine and acted the part of the capable person, forcing out a laugh and impulsively splashing Jamie with water, to which he'd looked at her confused 'cause, yeah, she was behaving a bit like a loon to mask her worry.

It was only the sea.

She'd thought she'd be able to do it – she'd done all kinds of crazy things when younger and now she couldn't even swim in the fucking ocean. Tears stung her eyes and they were ones of disappointment in herself. What the hell had happened to her? She'd been doing well, hadn't she? It had been so immeasurably hard at first, ten years ago, when she'd started seeing her therapist and had come off the drugs – she'd practically gone cold turkey because the thought of putting any of that junk in her, after finding her mum almost dead, turned her stomach. Not to mention that other thing that had happened just weeks before... But she *had* done it; had blocked out all those thoughts of everything she was losing – or thought she was losing – and concentrated on getting better one day at a time. It had involved a huge reality check, an endless amount of frustration and a colossal amount of boredom. Because life *was* boring when you weren't allowed to smoke it or snort it; when you weren't allowed to live in your head, or live it to extremes.

Correction: *it was boring if you never found anything to be passionate about.*

With the slightly-larger-than-she'd-predicted waves hitting her, came that niggle that had made itself known yesterday as she'd walked into the Civic Hall – the niggle was more persistent this time, and, rather annoyingly, seemed intent on forming song lyrics in her head and
playing them on repeat, even though she couldn't grasp at what the frigging song was ... *Where is the passion when you need it the most? ... Where is the passion when you need it the most? ... Where is the passion when you need it*

*the most?*

Argh! Something about kicking leaves and losing magic, but she couldn't remember the damn song.

"Merri?"

Okay, so she was rambling in her head to try and stave off the clawing fear... She brought herself back to the here and now, and ultimately, back into her cold, nearly-hyper-ventilating body.

She shook her head, feeling like the moron she was. "I'm sorry. I get panic attacks. I can usually control them, but the cold water's brought them on."

He seemed stunned for a second, and then a flash of anger crossed his face, making her feel worse. "Why the hell didn't you say anything?"

The reply froze inside her, just like the rest of her was frozen, and a wheeze came out instead.

Jamie's anger fell away in an instant, replaced by concern as he made his way towards her through the water. "It's okay." He placed his hand on her left arm, slid it down to her wrist, then brought her own hand up, palm facing her, and laid it below her ribcage. "We're going to try and breathe, okay? We can do it together. You'll know when you're breathing right 'cause you'll feel it here, under your hand – your diaphragm moving up and down."

Another wheeze.

She might have nodded – she wasn't sure because a dizzy spell took over her, and she didn't know if she was moving or if the world was moving...

His arm slipped around her waist, firmly supporting her at the small of her back and keeping her above the surface. His warm hand remained over hers. How his hand managed to feel warm in the freezing water was anyone's guess.

"Everything's fine," he said, sounding ridiculously

chilled out. "I've had to do this with a couple of divers after they lied on their application forms to get their licence. It's harder when you're underwater with scuba gear on, believe me. This is nothing." He squeezed her hand. "I want you to think about breathing, Merri – okay? Right here..." He squeezed her hand again. "Up and down."

And she did.

It wasn't a new thing – she'd had to bring herself back more than once in the past few years. To have someone helping her through it, though, was a small kind of wonder.

She concentrated on wiggling her toes. She couldn't feel them at all, but she was expecting that, and she kept on wiggling them until she finally *could* feel them, right there on the ocean bed; sand between her toes. Once that happened, the edge of her panic went and the colours around her came back into focus.

"That's it ... just relax."

His eyes were really brown. *Really* brown, like they had only depth and nothing else; like they were the universe and could go on forever...

"You need to keep on breathing."

Had she stopped? "Er ... right..." She tore her eyes away from his, 'cause what they did to her was nothing short of confusing, but the sudden loss of his gaze was too much, seeming to bring that anxiety up all over again. Before she knew it, she'd locked onto those dark irises again. For better or worse, he didn't look away.

Her breathing evened out as her body relaxed into arms that still held her. "Thank you. I should have said something – I'm sorry. I thought I had a handle on it, but it's been such a long time since I've been in the sea."

"It has?" he asked, surprised, as if he couldn't fathom such a thing, and maybe he couldn't, ocean-lover that he was.

"Yeah. I've missed it, but with the anxiety..." There were lots of things she missed, but most of the time, she just blocked it all out and got on with it. Better than the alternative. Better than wreaking havoc to find the joy, then escaping it by tripping out. She couldn't go back there.

His stare burned into her, complete with a small frown of deliberation. Whatever deep thing he was thinking, her mind wasn't privy to it, but her body clearly was because that burn traversed her from head to toe.

"We'll have to remedy that then, won't we?"

She took in a sharp breath that had nothing to do with panic. The way he'd *said* that ... as if he was planning on being around for a while; on having her around; on not letting her go...

As if he could somehow fix every part of herself she'd damaged.

She wriggled out of his embrace before it swallowed her up with the waves that seemed to be getting bigger. "We should go back to shore."

He nodded, eyes still fixed on hers – she turned away first and pulled herself along against the weight of the water with her legs, walking in slow motion.

"Wait..." He grabbed her arm and she halted. "Look." He pointed out to the right. "See that patch of calm water there? About twenty metres away? Where there aren't any waves?"

"Yes."

"That's a rip current. We need to stay this side of it and not venture into its channel."

"Oh." Having grown up around the coast, she knew some of the bigger beaches favoured by the surfers were prone to rip currents; that the more experienced surfers sometimes used those currents to propel them offshore – but she'd never been a surfer. She'd never seen a rip current, or heard of them in smaller bays before, but then again, she had lived two towns over – this hadn't been her local beach. "Thanks. I wouldn't have noticed."

"If you ever get caught up in one, try not to flail; try to relax and let it take you where it wants to. When you feel the pull lessen, you can then try to swim across it and off to the side so you can go around it. To be honest, if you suffer from panic attacks, you're best just knowing how to spot them and avoiding them altogether. They can be a killer if you lose it and thrash about. I pointed it out to the boys earlier."

He was still holding her arm.

She didn't mind, because the thought of getting caught up in a rip current suddenly called to her thrill-seeker self, and right there on its tail, was that good old friend, anxiety. It never truly went away: the craving for the thrill. She might have won her battle against taking drugs years ago, but the more abstract drug that had led to her downward spiral in the first place had never really left. It was the story of addiction: the original cause – the real wound – needed healing.

His grip on her arm tightened a little, and she looked away from the rip current and back at him – who in turned penetrated her with that stare in a way that suggested he knew *exactly* what she was thinking; that he knew all of her deepest secrets...

*So, why isn't he running? Any sane person would.*

God, it was just like that summer, thirteen years ago: he hadn't run then, either.

She found her voice. It had a touch of the defensiveness about it which, annoyingly, only ever seemed to encourage him rather than repel him. "You do this often? Go around saving lives?"

A small smile turned the corner of his mouth upwards. "No. Just yours for some reason."

The smile was contagious. "What am I going to do with you?" she muttered, and then she heated up all over again when she realised what that sounded like: exactly how *he* had sounded – as if whatever this was, was more than a one-day thing; as if she was planning on sticking around … with *him*.

His gaze grew hot, and for one, intense second, she thought he was going to kiss her again.

The second ended on the shriek of a child, towards which they both turned, and sure enough, far in the distance she was sure that must be Candy, Pippa and the kids causing some kind of chaos around an ice cream van. Maybe Becca had dropped her ice cream. Christ, that girl had a good set of lungs on her.

"Come on," said Jamie. He took the lead, his hand clasping hers as he pulled her along.

"What's the hurry?"

He raised an eyebrow, then let his gaze fall to her skimpily clad breasts as they emerged from the water. "If Pippa's boys see you in that, you and I will both be in deep shit."

"Oh."

"You don't want to see my sister in 'mama bear' mode."

"I guess not…"

There was a pause, and she swore she felt his thumb caress hers under the surface of the sea. "I'd like her to like you, Merri, and vice versa."

She had no idea what to say to that. Her heart hammered in her chest as the implication of his statement seeped into her fully. Unlike all other implications passed between them the past hour, this one was not accidental – he'd said it with intent.

*He wants me in his life.*

That thought astounded her.

*He wants me in his—*How? Why? *Why?* He didn't even know her.

*He knows you better than any other man because you let him in. You. Let. Him. In.*

It was true. Since that one and only night with Jamie, no one else had even come close to...

*Hurting you. No one's come close to hurting you.*

And here he was, holding her hand, leading her to shore and he *wanted her in his life.* She felt overwhelmed, yet powerless to walk away, and perhaps that was the most mind-blowing thing of all: walking *out* of his life was something she wasn't sure she could do yet, even though she knew she should.

~*~

Panic attacks.

He hadn't seen that coming.

The girl who climbed up cliffs with no safety harnesses suffered from panic attacks.

Except, she never used to, did she? At least, she'd never told him she did, and he suspected she hadn't. They must have begun after they'd parted.

Just like thirteen years ago, everything that was Merri screamed, HAZARDOUS: KEEP AWAY. And just like thirteen years ago, he was pulled towards the danger, metaphorically travelling the rip current he had warned her about.

Her sleeveless top went over her head, finally pulled

down over her non-swimwear, and he let out a sigh of relief, even though the way it clung to the wet triangular patches barely covering brown, did nothing to ease the ache that had been steadily growing around his crotch.

Holding her in the water had been a torturous combination of forbidden and blissful.

The sun peeked out again from behind a moving cloud and bounced off the diamond on her finger.

He frowned and also decided to get dressed, pulling his beach shorts over his trunks as well as donning his T-shirt, just to convince himself he was doing everything he could to fight the mounting attraction between them.

*Mounting? That's an understatement. It came in mid-explosion and the show's not fucking over.*

The one good thing to come from it was that he hadn't thought about Claire for the best part of an hour.

At all.

An empty, Claire-shaped space in his brain hadn't happened for weeks, if not months.

Well, if anyone could do it...

He realised he was staring at her again, as she ran a large comb through her hair – hair that should be knotted and tousled, not straight and neat. All at once, he got the distinct impression this is what her life was: her, trying to get the knots out.

"Want a hand?" he asked, before he could stop himself.

Her green eyes widened a little and her cheeks flushed, also just a little, but she had no time to reply.

"Uncle Jamie! Look what I've got!" squealed his approaching little niece – the whole crew behind her – delight shining from her eyes at the colossal, spiral-shaped ice lolly that was almost half her size.

"Wow! That's ... er ... huge. You gonna finish all that?"

Becca nodded enthusiastically, not a trace of doubt evident, that he couldn't help but laugh.

The boys were already to the bottom of their ice cream cones.

A dripping one was held in front of his face. "For you," said Pippa.

He eyed her suspiciously. "Is that supposed to be ice cream? It looks like it's been eaten."

"Me," butted in Becca, voice muffled by her lolly. She slurped her way free of it. "It was my ice cream, but a big, fat wasp attacked it."

"Aaaah... The screaming?"

His sister nodded while Candy let out a low whistle signifying that the memory of the tantrum was just a little too much to bear.

"It was a really big wasp, Uncle Jamie. I think it was trying to sting the ice cream."

"So, I get a half-eaten, wasp-stung ice cream for lunch?"

Merri laughed.

A *real* laugh that sort of tinkled out of her – not that insane crap she'd pulled earlier in the ocean – and it was the first time he'd heard her laugh today. No ... for over a decade. It sort of threw him.

It also made him want to make her laugh more, and he was so completely fucked. So much for getting his life back together.

Candy held up a bulging paper bag. "Never fear – fish and chips is here!"

Drool! Aussies ruled the barbies, but no one did fish and chips like the Brits.

A stomach growled – not his. Everyone stared at Merri and Sammy let out a chuckle. Jamie expected her to go red in the face like she so often did with her pale skin; instead she grinned and dove for the bag. "Anyone mind if I use my hands?"

"Hell no," he replied, pleased at her show of spontaneity. "Hey, don't take the biggest piece!"

"It's not!"

"That's definitely bigger – you're the size of a shrimp. That's mine."

She slapped his hand away. "You can have more chips."

"I want the fish."

"You like eating your friends, the sea life, that much?"

Liam found that hilarious, while Pippa threw Candy a look. "Don't they remind you of the kids? Some things don't change."

Their hands brushed together as they rummaged in the bag. The hairs rose on his arms at her touch, and he spotted her skin break out in goosebumps.

No – some things didn't change.

Candy sat herself down on her towel, resting her shades on her head as she straightened it. She looked a little tired around the eyes, but then, the kids were a handful to anyone not used to them.

"Merri," she said, "we stopped at The Boat Shop after eating at the café and hired a boat for Wednesday, and I've managed to get that day off work – my boss just texted me back and okayed it."

*Wednesday? What's Wednesday?*

Merri licked grease off her fingers. "Your boss texted you on a Sunday?"

"It's a small, family-run business – we have each other's numbers. I told him it was your birthday and I hadn't seen you in ten years."

*Her birthday!* Shit – of course it was! It was almost *exactly* thirteen years ago since—

"Okay, great." Then he saw her stiffen slightly. "When you say, 'we'..."

"I mean, 'we'. Pippa paid for half of it."

She glanced at Pip, startled. "Goodness... thank you – you really didn't have to—"

His sister shrugged her off. "We were about to hire a boat ourselves this morning before the kids went running off and all hell broke loose. Just works out cheaper for us," she smiled.

"And this way," continued Candy, with a grin, "you can have a proper, on-board birthday party."

Was she pleased? Annoyed he would be there? Hurt that her silent fiancé (ex-fiancé?) wouldn't be? He couldn't tell.

"Er ... I don't know what to say... Thank you so much. You've all got the day off work?"

"I teach, so I'm off over the summer anyway, and Jamie can apparently do no wrong and has somehow wrangled three paid months off work."

"Pip, I *earnt* them."

"Uh-huh."

"Mummy?" said Becca licking sticky lolly off her hands, not quite as quickly as it was melting. "Is Liam and Sammy and me going to the party too?"

"'Are' Liam, Sammy and 'I' going too... And yes, as long as it's okay with Merri."

Becca looked imploringly at Merri.

As if anyone found it easy saying no to *those* brown eyes.

Merri looked helplessly at Candy.

Candy's grin widened impossibly.

"Well, of course it is! The more, the merrier."

"Yey! Paaaarrrttyyyyy!" And then her focus went back to her ice lolly.

"Excellent." Pip looked at her watch. "I'd best get the kids back home."

"Mum!" protested both of the boys. "We don't need to go back yet."

"Yes, we do. You both still have homework over the holidays. Do it now, early on, and you can enjoy the rest of the weeks, homework-free." She turned to Candy who had her shades back down. "Are you guys staying, or going?"

"It might be nice to head back too – what do you think, Merri? Enjoy a chilled out rest of the afternoon before dinner?" Something in her tone – only slight, but definitely there – held what sounded like a small plea.

Whether Merri noticed it or not, Jamie couldn't tell, but she nodded anyway as she finished off the last of her lunch. "Sounds good to me."

"I'll head back with you and the kids, then," he said to Pip, wiping his hands clean on one of the paper towels at the bottom of the fish and chip bag. A perplexing mix of relief and loss came over him. A part of him wanted more time with Merri, alone, but another part of him needed some breathing space, because his chest felt achy, as if his heart still remembered the way Claire had punched through it, even though his head was all Merri-focused.

*Yeah – your groin's kinda focused in that direction, too...*

Unhelpful inner voice.

They all collected their things, dusting everything down as best as they could.

He turned to Merri. "So ... I'll see you Wednesday. For your birthday."

*Now* her face tinted red and he knew exactly why: her birthday meant something to them. The day after it was the anniversary of ... well ... *them*.

She raised her hand in a tense, half-wave of goodbye – a stark contrast to the way he'd greeted her. (Although, maybe that hadn't been his brightest moment.) "See you Wednesday."

It was only three days away, but as they all parted further up the path near where they'd met earlier by the tree, he couldn't ignore the fact that walking away from her felt *just* like it had leaving her all that time ago: too bloody difficult.

*But this time, you don't have to leave her, do you?*

Didn't he?

Back then, they'd been kids, unable to change the course of things. Now, they were adults who could.

*But she's engaged. She nearly got married.*

But she *hadn't* gotten married. She'd ended up here with him. Again.

"Hello? Earth to Jamie..."

"What?"

Pip held open the door of her car for him. "Are you getting in?"

"Oh, sorry." He ducked his head and got into the passenger seat. The kids, for once, were quiet in the back.

The door slammed shut and as Pippa made her way to the other side, he couldn't resist turning in his seat to catch a glimpse of the woman who had him at an unexpected crossroads.

There she was further down the path, some distance away, her hair flying about around her in the rising afternoon breeze, like he'd always remembered.

*She's mine.*

That thought came from the same, unfamiliar, caveman urge that had led to him kissing her.

But it was fucking true, he thought with a silent growl,

suddenly one hundred percent sure of the fact: She. Was. His.

The only problem, was the ring on her finger.

*So, what are you gonna do, Jamie-boy? Are you going to walk away? Or are you going to stay and fight?*

Fighting for Claire had been a waste of time.

*Because she didn't want you to.*

And Merri did?

Hope flared his pummelled heart. She was clearly as drawn to him as he was to her, that *had* to mean something.

Pip's door slammed shut and she started the engine. Its whirr took him back to the roar that beloved scooter of his had made as he'd left Merri on the side of the road. That had been one of the hardest rides to take, knowing he'd never see her again...

He settled into his seat as Pippa reversed.

He was a glutton for punishment.

He was going to fight for her.

# X
## *Not Forgotten*

Her phone sounded its text tone and she held herself back from leaping at it across the dining table. Instead, she kept her face as straight as possible and calmly picked it up. *See? I don't care if Michael contacts me ... or not...*

She unlocked her screen, looked at the message and her heart skipped a beat.

> **Thanks for a great day. Stay out of**
> **trouble until Wednesday ;)**
> **J x**

Merri stared at the 'unknown number' of the text-sender as she chewed on her evening salad across from Candy. The soon-to-set sun fell in through the patio doors of the dining room that led out into the garden. Candy's home might be small, but it certainly was nice, making up for a lack of space, with a whole load of cosiness. "Candy?"

"Mmm?"

"Did you give my mobile number to Jamie?"

"Aaah ... yeah – I exchanged all our numbers. Sorry. Figured you'd be okay with that since we're all meeting up in a couple of days anyway."

"I see." Was it okay? She supposed it was practical, but... "What's going on?"

"Huh?" She looked up from her home magazine, fork half-way up to her mouth and blue eyes questioning, but not questioning enough – she damn well knew what she was referring to.

"What's with the 'assertiveness' where Jamie and I are concerned?"

She stuffed the fork in her mouth. "Assertiveness?"

Merri frowned. "Yeah – the pushiness."

"I'm not being pushy."

"Yeah, you are."

"What's the problem? You're totally into each other."

"What's the problem? Did you just say that? Does the name 'Michael' ring any bells?"

"The name you didn't say at the altar? Sure."

"Candy..." she warned, and her friend prodded the side of her cheek with her tongue and lowered her cutlery.

"Look, it's *really* no big deal, is it? I mean, if there's nothing between you and Jamie, you can keep in touch as friends – we're all meeting up as *friends* on Wednesday."

Friends.

Merri's brain erupted into sardonic laughter.

"And if you can't be friends because you're *just that into* each other, then maybe you shouldn't be with Michael anyway."

"It's not okay to just—"

"And *now* is the perfect time to find out which it is, because Michael left of his own accord, giving you the room to figure things out. He could have stayed and worked things out, you know."

Irritation trickled up her spine. "He *will* call. He just needs some room himself."

"I know he'll call. And don't you want to be sure of what you're feeling when he does?"

Fuck.

She let out a sharp exhalation of annoyance and continued with her dinner. Candy was pissing her off with the way she was butting in, but she was sort of right – Merri *didn't* want to talk to Michael without knowing what the hell she was going to say.

Yesterday, she'd known. When she'd woken up *this morning* she'd known. It had gone something along the lines of *grovel, grovel, "I'm so incredibly sorry", grovel, grovel, "I'm such a fuck-wit", grovel, grovel, "I'll do anything to make it up to you".*

Unfortunately, her plan had gone all pear-shaped the moment she'd climbed back down that tree and laid eyes on Jamie. Who had kissed her. Who she had kissed back and wanted to kiss again.

But it was just nostalgia, wasn't it? It was because he took her back to the best night of her life. How could she possibly *not* want more of that?

"Why don't you phone your mum?"

"What?" she asked, startled, Candy pulling her out of her train of thought.

"You talked to me about Jamie the night before your wedding, you blurted out his name at the altar, and then you literally bumped into him the next day after unprecedented events had played out. Your mum said it was a spell. Maybe it's true. Give her a call and see what she makes of it."

That actually didn't sound like a bad idea. She didn't 'believe' in spells the way her mum did, but her mum was right: she *did* have plenty of clients who paid her for that sort of thing, so *some* people believed in them. Maybe that was enough to make it possible. If it was a spell, then there had to be a way to break the spell, didn't there? So, she could ask her mum what it was, break it, and voilà! No more Jamie, and her life could go back to the stable, non-surprising way it had been.

*And I can't believe I'm thinking this crap ... this isn't a fucking Disney cartoon. I can't just make Jamie disappear...*

No more Jamie.

Her chest ached at the thought, which she abruptly ignored.

*There was no Jamie for thirteen years, and some nights you wished so much there had been – remember?*

Christ – *go away!* Some things needed to be forgotten. Jamie and her had been a one-night thing – *one night!* They'd both known it would never be more. It was perfect the way it was and she needed to let it go.

*Maybe it's everything else you need to let go of – everything* except *Jamie...*

Great. Her head was throbbing with all this yo-yoing.

"Merri?"

"Yeah? Oh ... yes, good idea – I'll phone her tomorrow."

Candy gave her a thumbs-up, and then cleared both their empty plates. "I'm at work tomorrow and Tuesday, so won't see you much, but you can have my spare key. Still remember the bus routes?"

"Not really."

Candy smiled. "Well, there's a bus timetable in the drawer under the landline. I'd lend you my car, but my office is out in the sticks and takes half an hour to drive to."

"No, this is great," she reassured her. "I'll be fine – looking forward to revisiting some places."

"Good." She gave the table a wipe down, and then loaded the dishwasher. "Erm ... do you mind if I call it a night?"

Merri looked at her, surprised. "Now? It's only eight o'clock."

"I know – sorry. I guess 'cause I didn't sleep well last night, coupled with the drive to London and back ... I'm sorta pooped."

Merri studied her friend carefully. She did look whacked, and her eyes were guarded which was generally quite un-Candy-like, but she hadn't seen her in so long ... people changed. She had.

*Have you? Do they really change that much?*

She recalled what Candy had said to her after getting her into her wedding dress – stuff about the core of a person remaining the same. "Of course I don't mind, but ... are you sure you're okay?"

"Yeah," she shrugged. "I'll be happier when you're happy," she grinned, rubbing moisturiser on her hands while Merri churned over that odd comment about her being happy. Why was Candy so obsessed with her happiness?

"I am happy," she replied, automatically, without thinking, and then internally reeled at how fake that sounded. It hadn't yesterday when she'd said she was happy, standing there in her gown ... had it? It seemed like a lifetime ago. Jesus, *what* was going on? That weird 'merging' thing seemed to be happening again. She was *definitely* phoning her mum.

Candy's reply was a snort, which said it all. "I'll be happier when you're doing cartwheels across the sand, then. Hey," her tired eyes suddenly brightened, "remember when we used to take that long walk down the promenade, from the old church to that crappy fun fair that was never busy?"

Merri smiled.

"We used to take it in turns piggy-backing each other all the way there as we sang every single Beatles track we could think of."

"We turned quite a few heads," said Merri, fondly.

"That's because we were two, hot teen girls!"

She laughed. "And a good thing too, 'cause our singing sucked."

Candace laid a hand on her shoulder where she sat, and squeezed gently. "Some things shouldn't be forgotten." That came out with a slight quiver, as if she was on the verge of tears.

Merri looked up at her, surprised, but she'd already moved on. "The spare front door key's in the cutlery drawer – don't forget to lock up before you hit the hay."

"All right. Good night," she replied, softly.

Her friend retreated to the bathroom leaving Merri still a little confused as to what exactly was going on with her.

*She's lonely. She's missed you.*

An old hurt caressed her heart. She'd been a crap friend the past ten years. Yeah, she'd been through a lot – had had to put all her strength into healing herself, without distractions – but was that really an excuse for having shut out those she loved? Candy had always been like the sister she'd never had.

She was going to make it up to her. Her days down here were going to include a massive amount of Candy time. They'd been six years old when they'd first met. Candy had been shuffled into her classroom, led by the head teacher, and announced as the 'new girl' to her mortification. She'd been seated next to Merri, and Merri had taken in her crushed face and immediately wanted to make it all better. So, at break time, she'd gone into her bag, pulled out Blue, had approached Candy sitting alone in the far corner of the playground and offered her her most treasured possession...

*"Her name's Blue. You can play with her every day as long as you give her back. She looks after me when I'm sad."*

Candace gave her a trembling, ghost of a smile. *"Thanks,"* she whispered. She tentatively reached out and gently took her rag doll. *"Why is her name Blue?"*

*"Because blue is my favourite colour."* Merri sat down next to her, and she seemed nervous over the action. *"You don't have to be scared,"* she assured her new friend. *"My mum says everything always works out the way it's supposed to."*

The girl stared at her with enormous, blue eyes; her almost black, unbrushed hair, slightly matted to the side of her face. *"My mummy doesn't say that."*

*"Oh."*

*"She's sad quite a lot. And she worries about everything."*

*"My mum doesn't worry about anything ... but I have seen her sad. I've seen her crying."*

*"I've seen mine cry too."*

Merri reached out and held her hand. Candace held hers back. *"Your name sounds funny."*

*"It does? Everyone calls me Candy."*

Merri grinned. *"That sounds like sweets. My name's Meredith, but everyone calls me Merri."*

Her smile was returned. *"Does that mean you're really happy?"*

She giggled. *"Maybe."*

Candy's smile was getting wider, her shyness slowly falling away. *"How can you always be happy?"*

Merri shrugged. *"Because Blue looks after me, and because Mum says everything always works out, which means my dad's coming back."*

*"Where did he go?"*

*"Chasing ghosts."*

*There was a pause, and then Candy laughed. So did Merri. And a bond was forged.*

Her eyes shimmered at the memory. No – some things shouldn't be forgotten. She'd tried so hard to forget the horrible, painful bits that she'd forgotten the important bits. She would make Candy dinner tomorrow and get to know everything she'd been through the past decade. There was a lot of lost time to make up for.

She picked up her phone, and stared again at Jamie's text. Hitting reply, she sent him a smiley face and left it at that. She could bury her head in the sand and pretend seeing him again meant nothing, but what was the point in lying to herself?

There were other things, however, that needed sorting out first, and for the first time in quite a while, she felt like meeting those problems head on. For some reason she couldn't fathom, everything suddenly felt urgent – that same urgency that came with that weird sense of 'time merging' ... that illogical feeling that there wasn't much time left. Maybe it came from avoidance. She was good at avoiding things; had spent years trying to avoid anything that would send her panic metre rising.

She found Michael's number and dialled it.

It rang out.

She muttered under her breath and tried again.

*Answer, damn it...*

Nothing.

She sighed. *What now?*

Her phone beeped.

It was Jamie, replying to her smiley with an 'x'.

She put her phone lock on and set it down, her heart thumping away because that's what Jamie did to her, even if he wasn't physically here. In the days and nights following their one night together, her heart had done the same thing just thinking about him. It had been months before he'd started to fade from her thoughts. Thinking about him every day had turned into once a week, then once a month, and then only occasionally until she hadn't thought about him in years – at all – until the night before her wedding.

Her eyes landed back on her phone, now silent, that 'x' burning into her mind as strongly as his impetuous kiss had burnt every other inch of her.

Everything was getting more complicated by the minute.

~*~

Thirteen missed calls.

Michael pushed away the twinge of guilt he felt and left his phone on silent, before slipping it back inside his jacket. He'd always been bloody awful at multi-tasking. For the first time in his life he had a plan – he *saw* a plan – and it didn't involve being groomed into a duplicate of his father. But he needed to do things in the right order – Meredith would have to wait. Now that he knew, without a shadow of doubt, how he wanted to proceed, there was a sudden urgency to everything.

Long, familiar legs, in stockings and heels and an A-lined skirt that belied the flirtatious nature of its owner, stopped in front of where he sat on the bench, in the park outside the offices of his last meeting. The Gulmohar trees that could be found around the small park shed some of their flowers' petals, colouring the brown-green grass red and orange, the slight breeze making it look like some rippling magical carpet. Hong Kong had its pretty seasons.

"What are you doing here?"

Michael smiled up at his long-time 'friend' ... all right – *more* than friend ... who had also been his business competitor more than once. "I've just come out of a meeting trying to secure an important new account you might be interested in."

"No – I mean, what are you doing *here*, when rumour has it you should be waking up to honeymoon sex and a spectacular sunrise across the Indian Ocean. Or is this your honeymoon? Always were a bit of the workaholic, weren't you."

"As dry as ever, Lesley?"

She sat herself down next to him. "You're lucky I never had any interest in your gold band dressing my finger; I always preferred the other packages you had to offer – both business and personal," she smiled.

Her smiles were always fraught with sex and danger, but he'd learnt how to read them a long time ago, using them to his advantage when he'd needed her intense nature to bring him relief, or take him away from reality... until Meredith had come along.

His parents had never approved of Lesley. When he had shown an interest in Meredith, as mild as it had been, they had swarmed all over it like flies on shit. Meredith was safe. Lesley, however, was always a step away from poisoning him in his sleep and taking his family's empire from under his feet – that's what they thought, anyway.

He knew better.

Lesley was a viper, but her desires lay in creating her *own* empire, under her own name. Yes, she'd tear him apart for her gain if he was stupid enough to lay himself bare for her – which he never had been – but his family name was not a thing she was interested in, which is exactly why he had to see her face-to-face to make this offer.

She'd come far in an industry dominated by men. He admired her ruthlessness, because it was something he sorely lacked. It was why he'd remained on the financial side of *Fortune Airs*, rather than move into enterprise like his parents wanted.

He hadn't 'loved' Merri at first – not at all. In fact, he'd resented her presence in his life once his parents had insisted she be in it. But that wasn't her fault, so, over their first few months together he'd been civil, if distant; polite, if perhaps somewhat dispassionate...

However, she was an interesting woman, hiding a host of pain that reflected his. He didn't know what all of it was about, but resonating with her on that level had been easy, as had his acceptance of her hidden, silent turmoil. He'd understood and sympathised, and had finally felt like he wasn't quite as alone as he'd thought. It was her pain that had led him to eventually accept her into his life as a girlfriend, much to his parents' delight.

The most astounding thing for him, though, was that she had also accepted him, just the way he was; no questions, no probing ... just acceptance. For the first time he could remember, he'd discovered peace in the arms of another. The fact that it was the peace of friendship rather than some soul-shattering love was a moot point when acceptance was something he'd never before received from anyone.

Ever.

His parents had always dominated every aspect of his life, from where he'd studied, to who his friends were. Even now, at thirty-five, he hadn't escaped them. If he were able to be more like Lesley, he very well might have, but he didn't have it in him ... until now. Meredith and Lesley were the only two people who had looked at him and seen *him,* rather than the man his parents wished them to see.

That was his real hurt in all this: he'd lost a true friend. It was a shame he'd never told Meredith how much her friendship meant to him. He'd assumed it would have been wrong to say such a thing – after all, he was supposed to tell her how much he loved her, not how much he valued her allowance of his extremely heavy, family-induced, emotional baggage.

It had fucking hurt when she'd said whoever else's name at the wedding – he couldn't even remember what bloody name it was right now – but not because he loved her; it was because he'd just lost the sanctuary she'd made for him.

No, he didn't think she had said what she did on purpose; nor did he think she was cheating on him, although it had certainly crossed his mind in the first few hours after her clumsy slip. But the whole palaver had been like an arrow through his brow. Not his heart – his brow.

When that window had shattered, he'd suddenly seen Merri shattered in some future he'd ruined for her because he had never been honest with himself, and ultimately, with her. He wasn't in love with her and he'd been too selfish to tell her because he had needed her asylum; her quiet recognition of him. If he had told her he wasn't in love with her, she'd have walked away ... maybe. He'd always suspected she wasn't really in love with him either, but selfishly hoped that what he offered in return was a similar kind of hideaway for her; that their odd relationship was mutually beneficial.

When that window shattered, it hadn't mattered anymore, because he'd seen, with clarity, her happiness stripped away. Because of *him*. She didn't deserve a life without love. She didn't deserve *his* life.

No – he sorely failed at being ruthless. "I'm here because I need your input."

"Hmmm ... you going to input me in return?"

He ignored Lesley's wicked smile at the double entendre. "As a wedding present, my parents signed over half of *Fortune Airs* to me – the division that is *Fortune Airlines* to be exact."

Her eyes widened.

"And as you know, they've been wanting to do that for quite a few years despite my ... unresponsive ... attitude to it. Since I was marrying Meredith, they saw me as finally having settled down; as 'safe'."

"Jesus..."

"Judy has always shown an interest in becoming more involved with *Fortune Airs*, but you know my mother and father: tradition before sense. Only their eldest son would do."

"I can't believe you finally have it," she whispered, awed.

"In an unusually careless moment, however, common sense evaded them, and they signed *Fortune Airlines* over to me thirty minutes before the wedding was due to commence, probably owing to the fact that we were jetting straight off to our honeymoon and I wouldn't have been around for the transaction if they'd waited. Unfortunately, for them, the wedding never took place and has since been cancelled."

She stared at him, stunned.

"Careful, Les. If the wind changes you'll look like that forever."

She consciously relaxed her face, a small scowl quickly

passing over it, then fading away again as she processed what he'd said. "What on earth happened at your wedding?"

"I'd rather not talk about it, suffice to say that I'm relieved."

"You are?"

He nodded. "Meredith doesn't need my life; she doesn't deserve the fucking train wreck that it is."

"Michael Fortune, are you telling me you're putting a woman before yourself? Many more shocks to my system this morning and I'll be needing defibrillators."

The laugh didn't quite make it past his wry smile. "Yes, Lesley, I am putting a woman before myself ... two women, in fact."

She furrowed her brows. "What do you mean?"

"There's no retrievement clause to my acquiring *Fortune Airlines*; nothing in the contract to say that the transaction is annulled if the marriage is over ... or if it never happens in the first place."

She waited, not understanding where he was going.

He brought the point home. "I want *you* to have it."

"You want ... you want..."

He'd never seen her so flushed with surprised excitement before... Wait, no – he had. Often. But the reason for her current state was so much better than any other he'd given her, because he wasn't just helping her, he was helping himself in the process. His family were his shackles and he'd long wanted to throw them off, but had never known how without losing his entire inheritance. The thought of having no money wasn't as much of a problem for him as his peers might think, but he was realistic enough to know that going from riches to rags was an added struggle he could do without if he could help it.

"There are some conditions: I want to be a primary

shareholder in your half of the business, and I want to sit on the board of directors. I'd also like to man your accounts. If you genuinely feel someone else can do a better job of them, I at least demand that the accounts remain open to me at all times so that I can advise on any difficult transactions. By owning the airline division, however, you will also in effect be sharing *Fortune Airs* with my father and he hates your guts. He'll do anything he can to get rid of you."

Her brown eyes glittered with the challenge. Of course they did. Obstacles were food to her – she fed on them like Popeye fed on spinach. "I can take him."

"Oh, I know. I wouldn't be making you this offer if I had any doubt. You're shrewd, talented and as ruthless as they wish I was. I'll remain loyal in my investment of you, because I know you can do a better job of the business than I ever could."

In a rare display of vulnerability he doubted any other colleague of hers had ever seen, that glittering of her eyes seemed to melt into a shimmer. She looked away, composed herself silently, not a trace of the sudden show of emotion evident when she turned back. "Why are you doing this? You *do* know I can't afford to buy the airline from you, so why—"

"That's why I'm giving it to you. There's no catch, Les. See it as me hiring you. Except, instead of me hiring you to run the business, I'm hiring you to own it. My returns will be evident when my shares in *Fortune Airlines* grow. I've known you for near-as-dammit fifteen years, and I've seen you go from working class student to business mogul on nothing but persistence and tenacity. You're more deserving of *Fortune Airlines* than I am, and you'll take care of it better than me. I'm also sick of this game I've been expected to play since I could walk," he muttered with disdain. "I'm flying back home tomorrow to make it back in time for Meredith's birthday. I need to explain things to her properly and say goodbye. And then..." He smiled. "I don't know. I've always fancied taking an expedition through South America and writing crime novels."

She let out a stunted laugh, still looking bewildered at everything he'd just laid at her feet.

A strange silence followed.

She shook her head at him.

"You don't think it's a good idea? Should I try writing science-fiction instead? Or maybe family sagas are more up my street," he scoffed.

Her voice came out softer than he'd ever heard it. "I think it's a great idea. If I didn't know you, I'd say you were having a mid-life crisis, but ever since I met you in college, all I've ever seen is you struggle against who you want to be; seen how you'd put this armour on for your parents and almost everyone you knew. I was so frickin' jealous of what you had and aggravated at how you never seemed to appreciate it; as much frustrated about your charmed life, as you were about being forced to live it, when you never wanted it in the first place."

Another retrospective silence filled the air. A few metres away on the grassy area, a small group of men went through their Tai Chi routine. The way they moved reminded him of a flock of birds flying in perfect synchronicity. Total flow without words. "So, do you accept my offer?"

"Pending the terms of the contract, which I will need my solicitor to view, yes." She grinned, broadly. "Yes, I accept."

An odd, but beautiful peace invaded him as they shook on it. Breathing became easier; the air smelled fresher.

"Your parents are going to flay you alive."

"Yes," he smiled, "they are. And Judy's going to blow a gasket, which I'm a little sorry for, but you've been a good friend, Les, and if I signed over the business to Judy, my parents would still have influence over it, meaning they would still have influence over me. I want you to have it – it's the only way that makes sense."

"You're happy being under *my* influence?" she asked, her teasing tone making a reappearance.

He smirked. "You, I can handle. It's my family that have never been able to handle you," he turned his head towards her and met her eyes, "and that's what I'm counting on."

She tucked her legs up under her on the bench and rested her head on his shoulder – another show of femininity that was just for him and their friendship alone. "Are you sure you want to say goodbye to Meredith? I mean, I didn't know her too well, but you seemed to really like her. Given your sexual history..." Her voice faded, because they both knew he hated going back to that particular area of his past. "I just figured, since you don't find relationships easy, maybe stick this one out if she can offer you something that's even half way easy."

"Something about her does make it easy, but that's just not enough for a marriage – not for me. It might be enough for you, for my parents ... but there are a thousand things I want to do with my life before I can know whether it's enough for me. And it's also not exactly fair on her, is it."

She pressed her head further into him in affection. "I always saw this person in you – I never thought you'd set him free though."

Neither had he.

"I think I've been building up to it, without knowing it, and then..." his mind replayed the sound of shattering glass.

He'd grabbed Meredith to him in that second – tucked her under his chin and against his chest, partly to protect her against flying shards, but also, he realised later, in an apology ... *I'm sorry that I'm breaking you...* "And then something happens – it only takes a second; a fraction of a second – and everything changes. A door opens, or a window, and you just know: *it's now, or never.*"

She placed her hand on his and squeezed it in silent pride. They'd been through a lot together. In some ways, it was a shame he didn't love her either, but Lesley understood more than anyone that 'love' came with too many scars for him. Their sometimes-physical relationship had worked easily in the past, because love wasn't in her life plan either. At least with her, it was by choice.

"Now it is, then," she said.

He squeezed her back and nodded. "Now it is."

They sat there in silence for a few minutes, letting the 'swish' of blossoms against leaves in the breeze, lull them into relaxation. And then, she squeezed his hand once more. "So, you're flying back tomorrow."

He opened his eyes against the morning sun and glanced at her.

Her wicked smile was back, complete with extra 'oomph'. "Where are you staying tonight?"

# XI
## *Climbing Mountains*

"Er ... now?"

Merri frowned in impatience. "Yes, now."

A long sigh... "Okay, hold on." There was a clack and then a rustle as the phone was put down while the shop assistant went to find her mother.

Jesus Christ, she loved her mum, but she worked with some totally bizarre people who always spoke to Merri like she was some kind of outsider. She wanted to speak to her *mum* for god's sake – was that a crime?

More rustling... "Merri?"

"Mum? Hi. I swear, everyone you work with hates me."

"Darling, don't be ridiculous, they love you. We're on a tight schedule here, that's all. It's Monday morning and we're busy and I have a client in for a reading in five minutes."

"Okay, well, I never know when's best to catch you ... I only need to ask a quick question."

"Yes?"

"Let's say, in theory, that the whole thing that happened on Saturday with my saying the wrong name *was* the result of a spell ... is there a counter-spell?"

"A what?"

"You know – another spell that will override this one, or

undo it, or something."

"Good grief, Merri, are you in Cornwall? What on earth is going on?"

She muttered under her breath – no way to get out of telling the whole story if her mum was going to offer any advice that made any kind of sense to her non-witchy brain. "I bumped into Jamie. There was a photograph, there was wind, it took the photo from this little girl, I climbed a tree to get the photo from where it had gotten stuck, and it turned out the little girl was Jamie's niece, okay? Probably just the strangest coincidence ever, but for argument's sake, let's say that I believe you about it being all magical woo-woo whatever ... how do I change it? How do I get rid of the spell?"

There was a heavy pause.

She held her breath, assuming her mum was processing everything she'd just told her at the break-neck speed she had, and then, her mother's voice came through her phone's earpiece a little clearer, as if she was pressing her mouth closer to the receiver so she would listen. "Merri, why would you want to change it?"

"Did you hear what I said? Why *wouldn't* I want to change it? I don't want to be under the influence of a spell."

"Merri, listen. I want you, in your mind, to go back over this entire conversation – everything you said to me – and replace the word 'spell' with 'desire'. Because that's one of the most important ingredients in any magical working: desire. You have to *want* it for the magic to work so well, and assuming this is your *desire* playing out, then why would you want to change it?"

Argh! Why couldn't her mother *ever* give her a straight answer to *anything*? "I don't desire Jamie!" she snapped, stubbornly ignoring the tell-tale tug in her gut that told her otherwise.

Fuck.

"Look, forget Jamie. What about Michael? I don't desire what I did to Michael – hurting him the way I did. I didn't want that."

"Of course, you didn't, honey. That happened the way it did because you've been *ignoring* your desires for so long. Desires are like our dreams – they're the secret key to our goals. It's a mark of a good witch that the universe cares so much about you, it'll do whatever it can to set you on the right path again," she added, proudly.

If Merri were a camel, her back would've just broken. "I'm not a witch!"

"We're all witches and wizards inside. Oh, honey, I've got to go – my client's just walked in."

"Counter-spell! Mum – is there one?"

"*You're* the witch – *you* make the spell. Or, 'desire', which is how I asked you to think of it. If you *truly* have the desire to make this thing with Jamie go away, then the words of the spell will matter less than the intent. You could write gibberish down and say it, and it would still work – if the *desire* is there."

"So – what? I just 'make up' a counter-spell?"

"Gotta go. Merri, don't fuck up your life because you're scared, honey. Don't go chasing ghosts. Use the fear to climb mountains – like you used to."

The line went dead.

Mountains? *Did Candy tell her about me scaling that cliff? Or was she referring to all that time I used to spend at the indoor climbing centre?*

She wondered if the centre was still there.

She dropped her phone on the bed and stared at it, try-ing to form words to some abstract spell in her head. Did the words have to rhyme?

But it was visions of ropes and walls that invaded her mind. Up until thirty seconds ago, she hadn't known what she was going to do with her day all on her own.

With a quiver of excitement, she smiled.

She was going climbing.

~*~

"Are you sure it's okay?"

Jimmy unlocked the back door of The Boat Shop and switched the alarm off. "Yeah, course it is – I own it."

The shop closed at 5 p.m. – half an hour ago. Having phoned Jimmy first thing this morning to see if they could catch up, he'd been in luck – he had Monday's off. Catching up had been a bit of an understatement, though. Almost eight hours later and they were up to speed on each other's lives, and Jamie had to grudgingly admit he wasn't half as good at surfing as he used to be. In recent years, his focus had been on scuba diving and work, and the surfing he had regularly done during his first years in Australia had fallen away to occasional rides for fun, rather than a hefty work-out, or for training.

"Let's go clean these boards up. We need to stay in the back so we don't get sand on the floor."

"Fine by me."

Jimmy grinned. "There's a stocked fridge back here."

"Stocked with what?"

"That would be beer."

He laughed.

Ten minutes later, having rinsed and dried the boards, they were both sat, with wetsuits unzipped and half off, propped up against the wall at the back of the shop; chilled beers in hand.

Hell, this was nice. If he could just get Merri off his mind for more than five minutes, it would be awesome. It was ridiculous that he was actually getting pangs from missing her. Couple that with a fab day chillin' with Jimmy – just like they used to – and it was like he was seventeen all over again. Maybe no one ever grew up. Maybe everyone just went through the motions, year after year, doing shit they were supposed to, *thinking* all their days equalled big achievements when really, they were just waiting for that big crack in the path that changed everything.

"So, how's Pip really doing? You know ... since the accident."

He glanced at his friend. "Not sure, in all honesty. She doesn't talk about it much, and I don't want to force her to. I guess she's doing okay ... the kids keep her busy."

"Those kids keep everyone busy."

Jamie smiled.

"Nah, I'm kidding – they're good kids."

"They are. And brave to go through what they've had to – especially Liam."

"He the eldest?"

"Yeah, and the quietest, but he sees and hears everything. Probably feels it all the most, too."

"How long's it been now?"

"Since the accident? Seven months."

"That's tough. And he's showing no signs of recovering?"

"He's recovered a lot, but no signs of anything more. I think they told her a couple of months back that this is as good as he's going to get now."

"Fuck."

Two more swigs of beer helped process that a little easier. He hated thinking about how David used to be, compared to what he was now.

"He's er ... gone, isn't he? I mean, mentally ... in the head?"

"Yeah." His throat constricted at what that meant for Pip. "I think that sometimes, there's like a glimmer of recognition or something, but he's mostly gone. Not just mentally, Jimmy – he can't function physically the way we can. He needs daily care. He's permanently disabled."

A pause, and another swig.

"You seen him?"

"Not yet. I'd like to, but I haven't brought it up with Pip – haven't found the right opening."

"Do you know what she's gonna do with the rest of her life now? I mean, she can't just ... *stay* with him ... right?"

Jamie sucked in a breath. "Dangerous territory here, Jimmy. Sure, that's crossed my mind, but again, I haven't mentioned it and I don't even know if I should. She *loves* him. They were together for almost as long as me and Claire; how the fuck do I even bring up the mere possibility of other men? Pippa's the poster child for duty and loyalty and it's not just her, you know? It's her kids. He's their dad. Who's gonna fill those shoes?"

He shrugged and muttered, "I would."

"Yeah, and she's very not into you, so that's never gonna happen."

"Had to go drive that stake through, didn't ya." But it was said jovially and perhaps that wasn't a bad thing if it lightened the mood of the conversation.

"In all seriousness, Jimmy, why the heck are you still single? If you wanna be, that's cool, but do you? Is there no special lady waiting in the wings?"

"Are you fucking kidding me? Tell you what, you trade me your brains, your looks and your charm, for this shop, and you won't see me for the dust rising from the heat of a romantic sunset – James Bond-style."

"Come on!"

"No joke, mate. You know what women see when they look at me? Some geezer who ain't goin' any further. They don't want some no-hoper with an independent seaside shop that screams 'no plans to move on, out and up'." He shrugged. "Whatever. That's cool. 'Cause you know what? I'm happy. I've got the surf and I've got an income and a bed to sleep in, and sure, there are flings – the occasional hot bod wanting me to teach them to ride a board..."

Jamie snorted.

Jimmy chose to ignore it. "What about you? What if Claire turned up right here, right now, and said she'd made a stupid mistake and that she wanted you back and would never hurt you again?"

"A stupid mistake for three years?"

"Forget the technicalities – it's a serious question. What would you do?"

The doorbell rang, chiming throughout the whole shop.

They both raised their brows.

Jimmy jumped to his feet. "Fuck it, the part-timer forgot to put the 'Closed' sign up."

"If that's Claire, the answer's no."

It was Jimmy who now snorted as he made his way to the door, leaving Jamie where he sat.

*And what if it is Claire...?*

That was a stupid thought.

But yesterday, he'd bumped into Merri, which had been way more unlikely than Claire hopping on a plane and following him to the UK, so...

To hell with it. He got up and followed Jimmy into the front of the shop and caught his breath at the voice he heard. "I didn't know you were closed – sorry. I saw the lights on and..."

The voice trailed off as Merri's eyes met his, and a very male pride filled his chest as her gaze wandered down it, all the way to the V of his abdomen where his unzipped wet-suit clung to him. Aaah ... his inner-caveman was back.

"Hi..." she said, somehow managing to stutter over the two-letter word as her eyes jumped back up to his face.

"Hi."

Jimmy coughed. "Er ... hi?"

"Oh, er ... Merri, this is Jimmy. Jimmy, meet Merri. Jimmy is to me, what Candy is to you."

His 'what the fuck' expression was priceless. "I'm your candy?"

Merri laughed and Jimmy remembered his manners, shaking her hand and smiling at her, and now he really needed to fucking let go of her. "So, *you're* Mer—"

"What are you doing here?" asked Jamie, interrupting his friend's lack of finesse.

"The bus stopped across the road and I remembered Candy said they sold sun lotion and swimsuits here..." And then she stopped, clearly realising what she'd just said would take his mind back to that bikini she wore yesterday while he'd lathered cream all over her, and yes, she'd be right. He mentally urged his dick to be still inside his wet-suit ... the foamed neoprene *really* didn't leave much to the imagination.

Her face flushed again. It was bloody adorable.

"The bus? You should've called; I'm borrowing my dad's car – I can drive you around." '*Cause I've got nothing better to do and you're all I think about.*

Yep. Seventeen all over again.

*Sod the Masters degree you earnt in Zoology and Mar-*

*ine Sciences – it means nothing.*

A small smirk played with the corner of her mouth. "You'd have wanted to spend all day driving me around?"

"Depends – where did you go?"

Her smirk turned into a smile and she almost glowed, some element of her coming alive and taking her back to her youth.

Beautiful.

"The climbing centre."

"Oh," exclaimed Jimmy, "the indoor one up near the water park? It's a good place – been there years. They refurbished it about five months ago."

"Yeah, it was good," she nodded at him.

"Did you tell them about your preference for no safety ropes?" he cut in, stupidly annoyed at the two seconds of attention she was paying his friend. *Grow up, you douche.*

She shrugged, turning back to him, her smile still there. "They didn't ask. Anyway ... since you're closed I guess I'll—"

"I'll drive you home."

"In that?" she blurted out, staring pointedly at his wetsuit ... or his crotch.

The slight buzz of the lights overhead was the only thing that sounded as Merri swore under her breath, closed her eyes and bit down on her lip. Oh, he liked her clumsy tongue. A lot.

Her skin, from head to toe, now turned a delightful shade of plum.

His rucksack was in the car and had his change of clothes in it. No, he hadn't been about to drive her home in this ... but *now* he was going to, because catching glimpses of her softness under that prickliness was just too fucking addictive and always had been.

While she battled with herself, he went and grabbed his keys from where he'd thrown them on the counter near the back door on entering the shop. Before she could protest, he had her elbow in his hand and was steering her out the front as he said goodbye to Jimmy.

"Pop back tomorrow for the keys to the boat, okay?"

"Yep. Thanks for the catch-up. See ya!"

"'Bye."

Jamie ignored his friend's bemused look as it fell on Merri, then him, and then back to Merri again.

"You really don't have to drive me home ... I mean to Candy's."

"I know where you meant, and I'm happy to drive you, although you'll have to give me directions."

"It's not far – ten minutes by car maybe."

"It's no hassle at all then, is it." They stopped in front of the Hyundai.

"Wow. That's big."

"Yeah, she's a monster. We call her The Beast."

"Fitting."

He opened the door for her. "Hop on in."

"Will I get out alive?" she asked as she fell into her seat.

"Now where's the fun in knowing that?"

"This is a pattern with you, isn't it? You offer me a ride; I have no idea how it's going to end..."

He stared at her. He didn't want it to end. Not this time. He climbed into the driver's seat and slammed his door shut. "Come out to dinner with me tonight."

Maybe actually *asking* her would have sounded more appealing than the near order he'd just flung at her. It wasn't really like him, but with Merri, there was always this sense of urgency present; like, if he didn't catch her when she was within his grasp, she'd disappear and he'd lose her forever.

He could feel her green eyes burning a hole through the side of his face. He turned the engine on without looking her way, letting his 'request' for dinner hang in the air between them.

Her reply was the last thing he expected to hear. "It's a spell."

He did a double-take while pulling out into the road. In his mind it was a pretty good impression of something out of Looney Tunes. "Um ... what?"

She looked deadly serious – earnest even. "I think it's a spell. You and me; what we're feeling, and the wind and that photo and how everything happened and ... what we're *feeling...*"

"Er..."

"Remember I told you about my mum? That she's a white witch?"

"Yeah..."

"And remember I said those words to you that morning after you dropped me off home?"

"Yeah..."

"That was a spell. I just didn't know it at the time."

"A spell."

"Actually, they were wedding vows, but according to my mum any words can be magically used if you mean them enough and I meant them. The thing I don't get is that you never said them back, and she said that you'd have had to say them back for it to link us."

His head was reeling, a part of him wanting to laugh at what she was saying and another part of him already repeating those *Once Times Thrice* words in his head. He *had* said them, hadn't he? Just two days ago.

*Right before she reappeared back into your life.*

But that was ridiculous.

"I did say them – two days ago."

She looked at him, stunned. "On Saturday?"

"Yes, but—"

"When on Saturday?"

"Merri, it's not a spell."

"When?"

"Which way here?"

"Oh." They'd hit a crossroads. "Left."

He indicated and waited for a clear run. "It must have been about half-past twelve."

"In the afternoon?"

"Yeah – just before half-twelve, I think."

"I don't believe it."

"What?"

"That's when I said the wrong name at the altar. It was *exactly* then."

"Merri, it's not a spell. Which way now?"

"Er ... left again. It *is* a spell. It explains everything. You don't think how we *happened* to meet up again the way we did, at the time we did, was just coincidence, do you?"

"No, I think it was serendipity; like fate – not a spell."

There was a pause, and he turned to catch her expression. She was looking at him in question.

"What?"

"You believe in fate?"

"Not usually, but I'm going with it." He smiled. "Poet here, remember? And then there's you." His tone grew quiet. "You make me believe in a lot of things."

He heard the catch in her breath at the meaning behind his words. Too bad. He wasn't going to go easy on her.

Again, she shook her head. "It's a spell. Take the second right up along here."

"It really isn't, Merri." He turned right.

"It's number twenty-two, up here on the left. You and I *are* the result of a spell – I'm supposed to be married right now, and you're still supposed to be with your girlfriend of ten years. Everything changed because thirteen years ago, I said those words and two days ago, you said them back."

He pulled up outside Candy's cottage, and Merri released her seat belt.

He killed the engine and took his own belt off, swivelling in his seat until he had Merri's full attention. "The spell is not the reason why I fancy the pants off you and want to see you again, and again, every day and night, until I know every inch of you I never got the chance to know before."

For a minute, he thought she might have another panic attack because she seemed to stop breathing. He hadn't quite meant to be *that* forward, but direct had always been the best way to get through to this woman, not avoidance – he remembered that now. She tried so damn hard with her defences, you had to go in all guns blazing.

"How can you be so sure?"

"Because you said those words the morning *after* I met you. I wanted to know you the moment I saw you climbing that cliff like the lunatic you are. If you want to believe that a spell brought us back together yesterday, then fine – go ahead. But it wasn't a spell that brought me to you at the top of that cliff thirteen years ago, it wasn't a spell that insisted I spend that evening with you, and it sure as hell wasn't a spell that had me making love to you. *That* was all me. And you. We never got an ending – we didn't even get the chance to start. For some reason, we're getting our chance now. I thought about you for weeks – for *months* – after that night. The only reason you faded from my mind over the years was because I had to move forward; because I couldn't turn back time, and had to live my life with what I had in front of me. Call it a spell if you must; I'll call it Lady Luck turning the wheel of the universe for us. I don't care what it is – I *want* this chance. If you *don't* want it..." Fuck. If she didn't, then what? Pip was right: he wore his heart on his sleeve, loved too easily, and trusted too much, as proven by this crazy-arsed monologue that had come out of god-damn nowhere. "If you don't want it, then tell me now, because nothing short of that is going to make me leave you this time – not when I don't have to."

He was about to get crushed.

Again.

He could see it in her face.

Her eyes welled up as she stared at him in disbelief, so much so, that she didn't even blink when one of those tears escaped the corner of an eye and trailed down her cheek.

He reached forward and wiped it away. Why not? After all, he'd just laid it all out there for her in that uncomfortably impulsive way only she managed to needle out of him at the most unexpected moments, in the most inappropriate places.

Another tear followed the first.

He exhaled, long and slow. He hadn't meant to make her feel bad. *Great. Lay it on her so thick she feels guilty telling you to fuck off.* "I'm sorry," he said.

"Why don't you ever run?" The question came out nothing more than a whisper. Nevertheless, it bolted through his heart like a lance.

Too late to go back now. "Where would I run to, when this is the only place I want to be?"

She didn't move an inch; just stayed where she sat, letting her gaze wander over his face, still looking somewhat astounded. "Because I ruin everything I touch."

Had she seriously just said that? The lance went in deeper, although this time, for the pain behind those words, reminding him he had no idea what had happened to her over the last decade.

He reached for her hand, and brought it up to his face until her palm cupped his cheek. "How can you say that, when you gave me the best night of my life? You can't ruin me, Merri – see?" He traced her fingertips down his jawline, relishing in their feather-light touch. "Only I can do that."

She snatched her hand back.

He'd lost her.

Or so he thought for an earth-shattering second, until that same hand landed on his shoulder, a leg swung over his lap and soft, warm lips crushed his.

~*~

*"The spell is not the reason why I fancy the pants off you and want to see you again, and again, every day and night, until I know every inch of you I never got the chance to know before."*

That was the point he'd had her. Him and his bloody poems. Him and his persistence.

Anyone else would have scurried away from the insane lady talking about spells. He swallowed up everything she said, like a writer starved of words, and made them matter; made them make sense.

Her hands clutched at his hair. He moaned under the weight of her, their lips perfectly meshed as she moved against him.

He cupped a breast through her dress, and she discovered an ache she hadn't known was there – not a physical one, but the strange, bittersweet ache of joy that tumbled around with loss and pain and yet more joy. "I've found you," fell out of her mouth and into his, and they both groaned as his hands meandered down her back to grasp her backside, pressing her into his erection, the material of his wetsuit far too thick for her liking.

His bare chest made up for it. She forced her lips away from his, ignoring his sound of protest, and placed them on the side of his neck instead, working her way down to its base, to his pectoral muscles which twitched under her tongue, to his goosebumped nipple that had his cock leaping under her thigh...

"Merri..."

Her name reached her ears through layers of ocean water ...

*Drowning...*

"Wait..."

*No. Thirteen years...*

Thirteen years playing out in one second.

The blare of a car horn made her jump, propelling her above the illusionary surface for air. Hoots and whistles grew loud and then faded as the car and its teenage passengers sped past.

She pulled a face.

Jamie grinned. "We're on a residential road."

"Oops."

He cupped the back of her neck and brought her in for another lingering kiss. When it stopped, it took everything she had not to—

Nope. She had nothing.

She smashed herself into him again, needing to taste him, to feel him...

"Merri..."

*Sssshh ... no talking...*

"Dinner ... have dinner with me tonight."

Did he mean dinner, or did he mean *dinner*?

*Oh, crap – Candy...*

With her own moan of protest, she pulled herself back from him. "Let's do breakfast instead."

His eyebrows shot up.

"Oh ... no, I didn't mean... It's just that I was going to make Candy dinner tonight and have some quality catch-up time with her."

"I'm mildly jealous."

She smiled. "You don't need to be."

Her smile fell away when his fingers gently closed around her engagement ring.

His deep eyes bore into hers, searching for the answer to the question he hadn't asked. But she heard it loud and clear.

Guilt rose in her like a tidal wave, bringing tears to her eyes. "You don't need to be," she repeated.

"I can't leave you again, Merri. I won't."

She wanted to erase the hurt in his eyes. She battled with a swell of anger when she remembered what his girlfriend had done to him – this open soul carrying all the trust in life she never had; the one who'd laid her on the sand and shared that trust with her, so that for a glorious hour or two, she had trusted too.

She wanted that again. "You won't have to."

He didn't seem convinced, his eyes still spearing hers, the question in them almost a plea.

She laced her fingers through his and brought their hands up and out in front of them, her ring, standing between them both. "Take it off," she whispered.

Her heart hammered in her chest and she braced herself for the tell-tale signs of anxiety she was so used to.

There was no anxiety. Just a deep certainty, although she was damned if she knew where it came from, or if it was even real – she hoped to god it was real. Maybe she'd been climbing too many trees and walls. Today's little adventure had been exhilarating, leaving her light-headed and feeling … like anything was possible. Maybe that's why she was acting all crazy. Maybe it had all started with the dizzying heights, or maybe it had started with the wind on Saturday, or maybe it had started thirteen years ago with a vow she had unwittingly made her own.

Whatever the answer, over the past forty-eight hours, pieces of her life had begun to fall away, allowing her to see a clearer picture underneath. *Like ice breaking off a sill…*

Jamie muttered something inaudible under his breath, his fingers tightening around the ring. "If this comes off…" He hesitated.

*…Or, like pieces of shattered glass on the floor of a wedding hall…*

"There's no going back. If this comes off, you're mine."

*…Broken.*

Jamie – broken.

*Oh, god!*

"Wait," she croaked. He was the one perfect thing that had ever happened to her, and was she really acting any better right now than his troll of an ex? "I meant what I said before: I ruin everything I touch. I'd never forgive myself if…" She pulled her hand out of his, tears lodged in her throat. She'd already ruined their one night together; everything it stood for – years back … he just didn't know it. "I'm sorry."

"Merri." His tone was low and determined, wrapping around her, and she didn't want to become ensnared by it.

Confusion clouded her. She scrambled to find the door

handle, the air suddenly thick. She finally found the lever and pulled.

His hand encircled her wrist, arresting her escape. "I'll pick you up tomorrow morning at eight."

*What?*

She stared at him, bewildered.

"I meant what I said, too. I'm not leaving you again."

*Stubborn man.*

He held her stare another beat, then let her go.

She gathered herself, turned around and walked up Candy's driveway, refusing to look as he started the engine and pulled away.

Her heart hurt at the sound of it fading – a torturous déja vu – and when she eventually allowed herself to glance back at the empty road, she couldn't help but wonder if she'd just failed some cosmic test.

*Now* the pangs of anxiety climbed up her body.

She trembled as she focused on her breathing and tried to calm herself down. She had done the right thing – she didn't want to hurt Jamie, and she didn't want to cheat on Michael.

*You didn't run away for some noble reason – you ran because you're scared. That isn't right either.*

She heavily shut the front door once inside, and leaned against it, fighting the memory of how Jamie had felt under her palms, under her lips... So different from what had happened that time at her friend's house.

*Yeah ... some 'friend'.*

Shit, she didn't want to think about that. For fuck's sake! What was real and what wasn't? She was messing everything up again and she didn't know how to put it right.

She rummaged through her handbag for her phone and,

for what seemed like the millionth time, groaned in frustration at the zero indication that Michael was even still alive. Every time she tried to make things right, they just went wrong, and that god-awful feeling remained, that she'd just gotten a big 'F' in the great exam of Life.

Would she get another chance?

How many chances was she allowed?

*Once times thrice...* answered a voice in her head. And then, you're out.

# XII
## *Shells*

Candy opened her front door.

It had been a bloody long night and her heart sat heavy in her chest, aching. The past three years had been hard. She didn't know if it all coming to the inevitable end, would make things easier or harder.

She yawned, exhaustion adding to the weight on her breast.

The smell of lasagne clung to the air, even though it was well past ten o'clock. She headed towards the lounge where the lights were on and spied Merri sitting on the sofa, scribbling away in a book as the television blared some Periodic TV Drama into the room.

"Hi."

She jumped up, startled, not having heard her enter.

Relief washed over her features. "Where the hell have you been? I was worried sick."

"Uh ... I texted you."

"No, you didn't."

"I did." She reached for her phone to check her message outbox and... "Fuck." The text hadn't been sent. "Merri, I'm sorry. I thought I'd pressed send, and then..." *Oh, god – six missed calls!* "And then I put my phone on silent." Crap. She felt like shit.

"I made you dinner. It's in the oven, though it'll probably be cold now. I thought we were going to chat and stuff." A note of anger sounded in her voice now her worry had faded.

"I am sooo sorry. I really thought I'd sent this." She threw her bag and phone onto one of the seats while she sat on another. "We'll do tomorrow night, I promise."

"I'm not sure I'll be around."

"Oh ... you have plans?"

"Depends... So where were you tonight?"

"I had dinner round my boss's house."

Her eyebrows rose as she uttered a surprised "Oh."

Candy didn't expand on that – didn't want to go into it; not now. "What are you writing?"

"This?" She closed the book. "It's a journal. My therapist thinks writing things down every day will help my perspective on things and the anxiety levels."

"Good idea. Does it help?"

"Honestly? I'm not sure. I don't write much, just a paragraph each night, but it keeps her happy and it does me no harm."

"Sounds good to me," she smiled. It felt weak. She wondered if she looked as drained as she felt. "Did you do anything fun today?"

Merri studied her face for a bit and then told her about going to the climbing centre, her mediocre lunch out, and then bumping into Jamie at The Boat Shop. "And I *still* forgot to buy my bloody sun lotion," she mumbled. "I'll have to go back tomorrow."

"I can drop you off on the way to work if you like, though you might have to hang around for them to open."

"Actually ... Jamie's picking me up at eight, for breakfast."

"Oooh – a date?"

Merri dropped her pen and nervously fiddled with a strand of her hair. "I don't know. I don't know what I'm doing. He gave me a lift home and ... er ... I kissed him. Lots."

That ache in her heart grew a little less as hope for her friend's happiness filled her. "Wow."

"He blinded me with cleverly structured sentences."

"That scoundrel."

Merri laughed, and then sighed. "Seriously, Candy, I need to speak to Michael. I tried to phone him again tonight – nothing. And his colleagues told me they don't know where he is. They might be saying that because he asked them to, I don't know, but it's as if he's fallen off the face of the planet."

"It's not like you've *not* been trying to get hold of him."

"Usually, he emails me, even if we're having a fight."

"Maybe he's got issues he wants to iron out before talking to you."

She shrugged, looking defeated. "He's not the only one. I'm a mess. I think Jamie's sticking around. I told him about the spell – how I thought that was the reason for everything that's happened – and he insisted it wasn't. Said I spoke those words *after* we spent the night, so our getting together had nothing to do with anything magical, *even though* he said those words – my mum's wedding vows – at pretty much the exact moment I said his name at the altar."

"No way."

"Yep."

"Well, maybe—"

"I wrote a spell to break the spell." She pulled out a piece of paper from between the pages of her journal.

"You did what?"

"Look."

Candy took the page she held out to her. "Once times thrice—"

"Don't say it out loud," she squealed.

Candy rolled her eyes and read Merri's scrawled words silently to herself: *Once times thrice, unbind thine heart from mine, so we may finally part.* Jesus Christ...

"I went with simple, but effective. Okay, so it's almost exactly a copy of the other, but I'm shitty at thinking up rhymes."

"Are you serious with this?"

"Yes. Is it insane?"

"Yes."

"Why?"

"Because Jamie is who you *want.*"

"I won't know that for sure until there's no spell."

"Do you really think a spell can control your heart? What you feel? It can't – it's the other way around: your heart controls the spell. This is the magic, but *you* are the magician. Have you considered the way everything's played out is because that's how you *wanted* it to? Deep inside?"

She threw her a glare. "You sound just like my mum."

"Duh! Because your mum's right. *This,*" she waved the paper in the air, "is you running away from what you truly desire because it scares you."

"If Jamie thinks the spell has nothing to do with anything, then he'll have no problem saying this counter-spell, and if I don't *really* mean the counter-spell with my heart, then nothing will happen when I say it anyway." She crossed her arms stubbornly.

Candy frowned, the stirrings of an exhaustion headache thrumming inside her skull. "You're playing with fire. When people are angry or fearful, they say things they *think* they mean in the heat of the moment, and they say it *with in-*

*tent*, only later to regret it. Remember what your mum taught us when we were little? Words can hurt, or they can heal, and that's *especially* true if you're doing magic – *knowingly* doing magic. If you're going to work magic, you've got to be responsible. It's not black and white."

Merri rose from her seat and snatched the spell from her hand. "It's a back-up."

"And why would you need a back-up, unless you were shit-scared. You've climbed cliffs with no fucking back-up."

"Much to *your* disapproval."

"This is so *not* the same thing. Risking your life, constantly, for superficial moments of exhilaration that never last is foolish, but risking your heart, if only just once, for a lifetime of happiness... Not everyone gets that chance. When the universe throws a flashing neon sign at you all but *telling* you which way you're supposed to go, you *don't* turn away from it."

"Listen to yourself!" She slammed the spell back in her book and grabbed her belongings from the coffee table. "This isn't a fucking love story with a guaranteed happy ever after – this is real life where people get hurt!"

Her anger piqued. "Oh, you're gonna lecture me about real life? You have no fucking idea what real life is in your safe, riverside luxury apartment, in the arms of your safe, millionaire fiancé, while you wait for your safe, corporate monthly salary that allows you to straighten your hair so you can be a more acceptable version of the shell you've become."

She wished she could take back her words in an instant. No, the way Merri lived wasn't who she really was, even if she couldn't see it, but she'd pulled herself out of the gutter to get there. To accuse her of not knowing real life wasn't fair. She pinched the bridge of her nose. The headache was growing. "I'm sorry," she mumbled.

Merri's eyes shone with hurt and it skewered her.

"I didn't mean—"

"Whatever the fuck your problem is with me and Michael, and me and Jamie, and the way I live my life, get it out of my face," she seethed.

Tears clogged her throat.

Merri hurried past her.

"Wait, Merri ... it's because you're *not* living your life."

She turned back in the doorway, her face tight with anger and pain. "Maybe I'm not – so what? The way you feel about it ... isn't that *your* issue?"

She disappeared up the stairs, each footstep final, and slammed her bedroom door shut.

Fuck. They could bicker, but had never really argued in all the years they'd been friends.

She wiped at her eyes. The tears fell anyway.

Well ... that was a fitting end to a crappy day.

And Merri was right. It *was* her issue. A great big, fat, whopping issue that wasn't going to go away.

She needed to tell her.

~*~

Her sleep had been restless.

Merri rolled over and switched off her seven o'clock alarm that was due to go off in ten minutes.

*"You have no fucking idea what real life is..."*

That horrible feeling that followed any argument wedged in her gut. Somewhere in her consciousness, she registered that it was the first time in a long time that she'd *had* an argument, face-to-face, and not collapsed into shambles on the floor.

"And I'm not a shell," she mumbled to the empty room, fighting back a sudden surge of tears. No. If she were a shell, she'd feel nothing at all. The problem was she felt too much.

She kicked off her covers and stood, feeling shitty.

She'd heard Candy leave the house twenty minutes ago and there was still no word from Michael. Would Jamie keep his word and swing by at eight?

Her phone beeped.

> **Yes. I'm still coming to get you. Be ready. J x**

How the fuck did he do that?

And not a peep from Michael.

*Surprise, surprise.*

Merri grabbed her towel, phone still in hand, and headed for the bathroom with a frown. She hadn't thought the counter-spell was a bad idea – it just seemed logical to her: the power of elimination so she could see more clearly. *What the hell is Candy's problem?* she thought for the umpteenth time as she turned on the shower, and then moaned in contentment as she succumbed to the feel of the jet spray kneading her shoulder muscles.

Some time this week, she was going to have to fit in a massage. A trip into Truro wouldn't go amiss.

~*~

The front door opened and Pip and the kids bundled in, all except Pip looking far too chirpy for before eight in the morning.

Jamie placed his half drunk mug of coffee down and grabbed the keys for The Beast. "Hey, it's the rabble."

Choruses of "Hi, Uncle Jamie" greeted him. He looked questioningly at Pip. "What you all doing here so early? You know mum and dad are still in bed, right?"

"I think Becca's coming down with a cold, 'cause she didn't sleep most of the night and I'm exhausted. I couldn't face making four breakfasts – *four*. It was quicker to get everyone in the car and drive here."

There was a race into the living room to see who could reach the TV first. Pippa took a couple of steps closer and crossed her arms as she smoothed out the carpet with her toe. "I also wanted to catch you before you left."

"Aaah."

"You sure you wanna do this? I mean, you're really going ahead with it?"

"With Merri, you mean?"

"Well, are you?"

"Any reason I shouldn't?"

"Besides the fiancé?"

"Yes, besides the fiancé."

"I'm only looking out for you."

"Spit it out, Pip."

She blew out sharply through her teeth. "Fine. I think she's a little unhinged."

Jamie chuckled.

"What?"

"Well, yeah – remember how I met her?"

"You're okay with that?"

"I love her for who she is – all of her – but that was a big bit. Maybe 'unhinged' does it for me. Maybe I don't see her as unhinged, but as free-spirited."

"Whoa," she grabbed his arm to stop him from leaving. "You did *not* just say you love her."

"Well, you know, I might have thirteen years ago... if I'd

been given half a chance to. Isn't it okay to say love and not mean *luuurrrve*?"

And now his arm was slapped. "I'm not bloody joking! You've just come out of a relationship with—"

"With someone who completely flees my mind when I'm with Merri. When I'm with Merri, the last ten years of my life with Claire feels a bit like a dream."

"So ... what is it? Is it the challenge? Do you think you can tame her, or something?"

"God, no. I don't want to tame her, I want to watch her. I just want to watch her be herself – it turns me on like nothing else. It's like seeing a painting or a story unfold before you in the sky. She reminds me of those falcons that—"

"Are you being serious?"

"Yes, I'm being serious." He pinned her with his gaze. "Look, I'm not going into this with the head of some horny teen; I'm going into this knowing I'd never forgive myself if I let a second chance with her slip through my fingers. I don't bloody know how things are going to turn out, but the way I figure it, never knowing is worse than getting fucked over again. In an ideal world, waiting 'til things are more settled would be awesome – great – but maybe the crazy way this has all come about *is* ideal for us. How we met was crazy, why not this?"

A sheen of wetness formed over Pip's eyes. She let go of his arm and stared at him, shaking her head.

Crap. He *hated* seeing her sad. "Hey, come on..."

She pulled back from his touch. "How do you do it?"

He tried not to sigh out loud. He wished he could make it all better for her with a hug, or a meal out, or a joke. "Do what?"

"Keep on believing. Keep on having faith when there's nothing left to hold on to?"

"Isn't that the only time you can have faith? When there's nothing else?" He shrugged. "I don't know, Pip ... I don't think of faith as something you need to have *in* the world, or in some deity or religion or whatever; I think having faith is about trusting in yourself, and trusting that you'll know what to do when life gets complicated. I'm not scared of complications. But I *am* scared of walking away from something I want with every fibre of my being, without even trying to have it. I'm scared of what that'll do to me. Last time, I could let Merri go because I had no choice; this time, I'd regret it forever."

SpongeBob SquarePants squeaked, banged and rattled from the other room.

Sammy laughed.

Pippa stared at him, wide-eyed, her tears blinked away and never shed. "You always did have your soft head screwed on."

He gave her a smile, and brought her in for a hug whether she wanted one or not. "I'm going to take that as your blessing. Now, I've really got to dash."

He made it as far as the foot mat.

"Wait."

He bit his lip, ignored his watch, then turned back to her.

"I don't know about faith – I don't really get a lot of stuff right now – but..." She gazed at the ground as she struggled with her words. "I get that time matters. I get that one careless moment not looking where you should, on a rainy, winter's night, can change five lives in one second. So, when it happens the other way round ... when you get given just one, fleeting moment, to look the right way and make everything better ... take it." She sniffed, her nose growing red, and rapidly swiped at her face, glancing nervously at the living room. "Take it. That's my blessing."

"Pip..."

"No. No hugs. Go already." She made a swatting action at him.

His heart broke for her. "Thanks. Take it easy today, okay?"

"Easy. Yeah. Will do."

"Liar."

She smiled, and he chose that moment to shut the door.

~*~

The shower soon cleared her mind of circling thoughts, and before she knew it, she was downstairs feeling lighter and happier, and counting down the final ten minutes before Jamie's arrival ... and trying to talk herself out of going to breakfast, not that he seemed that easy to persuade away.

Candy had collected flowers from the garden and placed them in a vase on the dining table with a note, but the biggest surprise, which brought tears to her eyes, was the sight of Blue propped up against the vase.

She grabbed her old rag doll, feeling slightly stupid that she was so happy to see her again. She'd ended up pretty much giving Candy the doll, since she had needed Blue more than her in their early school years. She hadn't known Candy had kept her.

Merri picked up the note she'd left.

**Didn't think I'd thrown her away, did you?**

**I'm so sorry about last night. I was tired and stupid things came out of my mouth, although that's no excuse. Ironically, it sort of proved my point about saying things**

*you don't really mean when hurt or angry, LOL. But, in all seriousness, I feel horrible, and I need to explain things to you about what I've been through the last few years. Maybe then my reactions will make a bit more sense. Or maybe not. Anyway, please be in tonight. I promise I'll be here.*

*Big hugs,*
*Candy xxx*

Merri sighed, feeling bad, and reached for her phone.

> Hey, you. Thanks for the flowers and note. And Blue! :) I'm sorry too. I'm sure I must seem crazy to you. I'll be here tonight. M xxx

A clatter at the door made her jump, but it was only the postman.

She went to collect the mail from the floor to put on the table and frowned at the two NHS-stamped envelopes in her hand, along with one from a bank, the usual junk mail, and something addressed to herself that looked like a birthday card from her mum.

But she couldn't pull her eyes away from those god-awful three letters on the corner of those two foreboding-looking envelopes.

NHS.

National Health Service.

She'd had enough of those letters – hated them on sight, although she couldn't deny the skill and expertise that had saved her mum's life and perhaps even hers. Still... Why was Candy receiving mail from the hospital?

*Don't be nosy, Merri. It's probably a reminder for a regular health check or something.*

Both of them?

She froze when she spotted the department the letters had come from, there on the back of both envelopes: Cancer Unit.

No.

No *way*.

But Candy's note replayed in her mind – *I need to explain things to you about what I've been through the last few years* – and the pin pricks made themselves known, up both arms and across her chest.

*Fuck. No. Candy does* not *have cancer. She doesn't...*

Another voice inside her, young and too innocent for such horrid life lessons, screamed, *She's going to die!*

Before the panic could get to her, she all but slammed the mail down on the table and tore into her mum's birthday card.

*It's nothing. You'll talk to her tonight, and you'll see that it's nothing – just you going wild in your mind like you always do.*

Her mother's card slipped out of the envelope along with other things inside the card Merri wasn't prepared for. A folded piece of paper and a small cascade of photographs hit the floor.

*Oh. My. God...*

Her and her dad hugging by the fire next to the Christmas tree; her and her dad making snow angels in the garden; her on her dad's shoulders, both of them with the widest grins... And it sort of went on like that – eight photographs in total, all taking her back places that were both warm and painful. She remembered every single one; remembered the actual events, what she'd felt at the time they were taken, the texture of his woolly coat, the smell of it... Christ, that hurt – her chest – *fuck* that hurt.

With trembling hands, barely holding it together, she opened her mum's card and read the annoyingly small handwriting covering the span of the inside and also the back.

*Dear Merri,*

*My darling, breathe. Don't have a meltdown, okay? Breathe!*

*Chin-up, sweet-pea. I wanted you to have these, because you're not supposed to forget those you love, even though, sometimes, it's easier to. When we have wondrous, magical, fantastical, amazing days that make us feel invincible, we should <u>always</u> remember them and hold them close to our hearts – those days with your father were like that for you.*

*And if Jamie makes you feel like that, then what is the problem? The only mountain here is of your own making.*

*I've also enclosed a letter from your father, written to you, but he didn't want you to have it 'til you were grown up, then with the move to London and my tumour, I admit that I completely forgot, and the letter remained at the bottom of a box. This whole thing with the wedding and Jamie reminded me, and*

I finally found the letter yesterday after work, after our conversation, just in time for the last post, I might add. Maybe some things work out after all!

Read it, feel it, and then let it go, honey.

Happy birthday, Merri. Did you know we nicknamed you Merri when you were a toddler because you never stopped smiling? You were so unbelievably happy over every little thing that made no sense, in the way that only two-year-olds can be.

I know you remember these photos being taken. I know you remember everything about your father. I know because you two were like peas in a pod. You loved each other so much. You must never be afraid to love again because you can, Merri. You are capable of it and it never gave you panic attacks when you were five. Love big, honey. _Big!_

And don't shut out the past, or those ghosts will stay stuck in there forever. You need to let them out and set them free.

Sorry I can't be down for your birthday – the last two days have been so busy I'm wiped out. The clients are quite intense right now – there must be some astrological alignment or something coming into play. I'm planning to make it down for the weekend instead and I'll bring Tequila!

*Happy 29 Years! Oh, hey, wait – it's your Saturn Return! Fuck me, that explains a lot!!! Haha! Oh, I get it now! Oh, sweetie, you are so, so special.*

*Be happy, Merri. Be very, very happy.*

*Big love, hugs and kisses,*

*Mum. xxx ooo xxx*

Numb.

*What the actual fuck…?*

What just happened? She came downstairs from her calming shower, and then the postman tore her life apart.

Saturn Return? Why did her mum always do that? Mention something random, have a little personal laugh about it and then *never* explain it?

And then there were the photos.

Numb.

She supposed numb was better than panic. Different, anyway…

She reached once more for her phone, still dazed, and this time rang her mum's number. It rang out and went to answerphone. She dialled the shop instead, realising too late that they wouldn't be open yet. Someone answered regardless.

"Hello."

"Oh, hi. It's Meredith – I was wondering if Penny was in yet?"

"Oh, hey. Wow. You're her daughter, aren't you? Your mum is just … wow. The last few weeks she has really nailed her readings, I mean *really* nailed them, like, accurately predicting names and places and – god – shit you wouldn't believe."

*Right. Shit I wouldn't believe.* She exhaled towards the sky. "Great. So, is she there?"

"Oh, no, she's not in yet. Man, those readings ... they've been doing her in. She's been going home early the last couple of days. It must be like some kind of thing where the more 'aware' you are and the more 'tuned in' you are, the more it can drain you. Know what I mean?"

*No.* "Uh-huh."

"Are you clairvoyant or anything?"

"Or anything."

"Oh..."

"Could you tell her I phoned to say thank you for the card, and for her to give me a call back when she can?"

"Sure."

"Thanks. 'Bye."

"Oh, wait – when you say 'or anything', do you mean—"

She hung up.

*Not psychic, not magical, can't even see into the next five minutes.*

The doorbell rang and she leapt out of her skin.

*See?*

Was it Jamie?

Probably.

Trying to shake the slight dizziness out of her head, she gathered the photographs, unopened letter and card, and placed them back into the envelope. Her emotions felt frayed – she couldn't deal with these right now.

"I'll be there in a minute!" she yelled to the door and then ran upstairs and slipped the envelope into the front pocket of her suitcase.

Hesitating for one second, she then went for her diary and took out the 'undoing' spell she'd written last night. She felt shitty all over again that some stupid words had caused a small rift between herself and Candace.

Not even bothering to check herself in the mirror, she ran back down, placed the spell with Candy's note under the flowers, found a pen and—

The doorbell went again.

"Hang on!"

*You're right,* she wrote on the paper, just under the spell. *This was dumb. If we know what we want our lives to be, then what does this matter? Speak later. xxx*

A lump gathered in her throat.

*Fuck, Candy, don't have cancer; don't be dying.*

She picked up Blue, stuffed her in her beach bag, hauled it over her shoulder and went to face the rest of the day.

# XIII
## *Fight*

"Is this some new form of art?" Jamie asked, amused.

Merri looked up, startled, still adorable... "Excuse me?"

She hadn't worn any make-up this morning, and she hadn't straightened her hair. He wondered if it was on purpose or because she'd been in a rush. She looked fresh and more 'herself' than the first day he'd clapped eyes on her. "The patterns you're making with your pancake and maple syrup. I can't figure out if they're circles, or butterflies, or if making the pancakes extra mushy makes them taste better."

"Oh..." She glanced down, and then up again.

Her mind had clearly been preoccupied ever since he'd picked her up and he didn't think it was just because of him. But this was Merri and he hadn't expected anything less, and as usual, the need to get to the root of her puzzle, whatever it was, ate at him. What he hadn't expected, was for her to suddenly open up...

"That morning you dropped me off after our night together, I walked home to find my mum awake with two visitors – old friends of my dad's that my mum also knew ... turned out he'd died of a heart attack earlier that night."

...It was dazzling.

Her opening up was as dazzling as her resisting any process of opening up. He felt like she'd just given him a small piece of the world. He also felt her pain. "I'm sorry."

"I was sorry, too, about two things: that he'd died, but also, that the most perfect night of my life got a little bit ruined."

Another small piece.

He wanted to catapult across the café table and take her into his arms, because, like the wind or a flower, this wouldn't last. She would open and bloom, then close and hide. She was like a sylph – some kind of air nymph – there was only the 'now' with her, always had been, and he relished every second of it.

He settled for reaching for her hand across the table, which she didn't pull away from him. "*Not* ruined."

"But it was a little. And then later on – years later – it got ruined again, and it was my own fault."

He waited for her to expand on that, but she didn't.

Instead, she stuck the worn out piece of pancake into her mouth and chewed. "I don't want to ruin what we have, no matter how small it is. That's my biggest fear – that I'll ruin it, or ruin you."

"My biggest is never knowing what it's like to be with you. To me, that feels more damaging than anything you could do to me. And what we have, it's never felt small to me, Merri. It's always felt monumental, and infinite."

She shared a little smile with him. She was in a strange, whimsical mood this morning. It was lovely. He was going with it.

"Look at us," she quipped, "actually talking like grown-ups."

"It's like a revelation, huh?"

She laughed. "It is for me. I've spent much of the past ten years avoiding panic attacks, so meaningful conversations – any situation where I might hurt someone's feelings, or get hurt – are something I've skirted around. This is ... nice. It's freeing. Sort of. Scary – a little – but freeing. The past couple of days ... the anxiety's still there, mostly, but it's like I've got a better grip on it."

"Well, that's good, because I've got a surprise for you."

Her eyes narrowed at that. "Surprise?" She withdrew her hand. "Oooo ... I don't know..."

He laughed. "Trust me, Merri. Do you trust me?"

For a second, he thought she was going to say no, and that would have wounded him greatly, but her guard fell away a little and her green eyes softened. "You know I do. I probably trust you more than anyone."

The sincerity of that took his breath away a little. Hell, if he didn't love her, he was only a hair's breadth away from it.

He pulled what he was looking for out of his pocket and placed it on the table in front of her.

She looked at it, confused. "A key?"

"The key to a boat. I spoke to Jimmy, and he let me have the boat a day early. I didn't want to change your birthday plans tomorrow, but I selfishly wanted some time all to ourselves for your birthday. That time is now. I also ran it by both Pip and Candy to make sure they were okay with it; that I wasn't bursting some bubble by doing this. We have the boat all of today, as well as for the picnic tomorrow. So, say you'll spend today with me. Please."

She looked at him, searching out something in his face. "Aren't you worried I'll say no?"

"I'm more worried for my sanity if I were never to ask."

"What would you do if I did say no?"

"Try and see," he dared.

Her smile turned mischievous. "Well, I'm not sure I've packed everything I need to—"

"We'll stop by yours again, or go buy what you need."

After a moment of deliberation, she abruptly stood, but the twinkle was still there, dancing across her irises. "Thank you so much for breakfast, Mr Corbin, but one and a half hours of your time is quite adequate enough for—"

"Ms Goodwill," he moved to the end of the table to block her exit, "I assure you that the last ninety minutes, although delightful, has taught me everything about what happens to pancake when it's mistreated and not enough about you."

"Are you harassing me, Mr Corbin? There are consequences for that, you know."

"There are consequences for everything, but ... it *would* be a great shame if my sincerity was misinterpreted for harassment." He stood aside. "You're free to go."

She paused, seeming all at once uncertain. "Um ... what?"

"You're free to go."

He almost put a halt to the game, she looked marginally crestfallen. It quickly turned to that familiar spark of anger at the realisation that she'd just lost. With reddening cheeks at his smirk growing wider, she turned on her heel and made to stride out the door.

She didn't get very far.

He grabbed the waist of her sundress, pulled her backwards against him and spun her around. "I win."

"You pig."

"You deviant. Gotta say I'm disappointed. I thought you'd put up more of a fight for us."

At that, her eyes widened. He could tell she had no clue what to make of that statement, not that it mattered – his point was clear: *he'd* fight for them, and he wasn't letting her walk away so easily.

A cough sounded to their right. "Erm ... here's the bill," smiled the waitress doubtfully, obviously unsure as to their intentions on standing.

Jamie grinned. "Thank you."

She left, and he rummaged through his pockets for change.

"I have, you know," said Merri, quietly.

A twenty pound note went down. "Pardon?"

"Some nights I'd wake up drowning, naked – horrid nightmares – desperate to reach the surface even though I knew everything would be gone once I managed to break through, and I was almost right ... almost. You were still there; this bright, beautiful memory against a ton of darkness. And I fought for us, even though a memory was all I had."

Wrong.

He was the one who'd just lost.

He was floored.

"I'd never let you drown," he managed to get out, stunned at the depth of what she'd just confessed.

"I know." Tentatively, she took a step forward, leaned in, and kissed him on the cheek. "You never did." Another small smile graced her features. "I'd love to spend today with you, Jamie. Please get me home for eight, 'cause I need to talk to Candy." Before he could utter a word, she turned and walked out the door towards his car.

Eight o'clock.

*That's ten and a half hours to uncover all her secrets.*

And by fuck, he would.

~*~

Her palms were cold with sweat, but then, they always were

when coming here.

Pippa kept her head down and made her way to the reception to sign in. The lady behind the desk was one who knew her. Most of them knew her here – only a couple of members of staff were strangers to her.

"Mrs Fellows," smiled the receptionist, "it's great to see you."

"Thanks." She smiled politely, then leaned down to fill out the sign-in book with her details. "How is he today?" Her heart beat faster. It was a question that never had the right answer. She wanted to hear "all healed" or "a miracle's taken place". What she got was "good", "better", "the same as usual" and at the very worst, "not good today, Mrs Fellows".

"Same as usual, Mrs Fellows."

She nodded.

"Kids not with you this morning?"

"I've left them with their grandparents."

"Right you are." She took the pen from her when she'd finished. "He's in the same room – you know your way. It should be fine to go straight in. The nurse should be by shortly to see you."

"Great. Thanks."

The receptionist gave her the warmest of smiles. It did little to take away the chill that had just settled in her system.

Pippa made her way to room 208, taking the stairs instead of the elevator today. There were so many day-to-day things she never thought about – couldn't think about. She just took a deep breath on waking, rolled over and got through all those hours one by one. This was the only place where she didn't seem able to do that. Maybe it was the eerie silences on passing some of the rooms, their doorways open, coupled with almost inhuman moans and strange conversations that floated outside others. It was a large care home, this one, filled with patients that were mentally disabled, most of them physically so, too.

*David doesn't belong here.*

But she couldn't think that way, because that thought was the key to the floodgate. That thought was everything that brought the past rushing back and gave David *life* – gave him his personality back, his strength, his capabilities ... everything that was stolen from him.

"Mrs Fellows!"

She jumped.

"Oh, sorry, I didn't mean to startle you," beamed Nurse Kelter, a kind, middle-aged woman who sacrificed her own family's time to be here looking after hers.

Guilt was a bitch.

"I just wanted to let you know that David's doing well this morning. He held a pen for almost a whole minute – even seemed to know what to do with it – and we studied family photographs again after breakfast," she nodded encouragingly. "There may have been recognition sooner than usual, and also lasting for longer. Of course, these things are unpredictable, but it was certainly a highlight."

"Thank you so much."

The nurse placed a hand on her arm. Pippa tried not to flinch. What she wanted to do was run in the other direction. "And how are you doing, Mrs Fellows?"

"Oh, well, you know ... the kids keep me busy."

"Indeed. They're off school now, aren't they?"

"Yes."

"Not here today?"

"No."

"Well, it's never a bad thing to squeeze in some time to

yourself."

*Time to myself. Right.*

"David's been bathed and changed already today, so you can go right on through."

"Thank you."

A patient caught the nurse's eye and she smiled her goodbye before wandering off to deal with whatever was next.

Pippa's gut churned, not with hunger, but with a great well of sorrow that seemed here to stay for good. It always got to her a little, that she couldn't be there when he was bathed or changed. He was her world. She'd seen him naked a thousand times, undressed him, made love to him ... he'd seen three children come out of her fucking vagina.

She had to stop outside his door and rapidly blink back the hot tears of part-anger, part-loss.

*It's fine. Just breathe, and don't think. Don't think.*

Palms still clammy, she grabbed the handle to room 208 and pushed open the door.

~*~

"Keep watching."

"What am I looking for?"

"Just keep watching," Jamie hollered over the steady roar of the boat's engine.

It was only just midday. Morning snacks had been sparkling white wine and syrup-coated figs, and she was being spoilt rotten, Jamie not letting her lift a finger for anything. She could get used to this!

They'd also spent the best part of the morning catching up. He had talked to her about how he'd met Claire, his adoration for Australia, and his job which he loved, but also how his life could be predictable – too planned. According to Jamie, she'd been the only real exception to that pattern throughout all his years.

Merri had taken a deep breath and told Jamie about her slippery slope downhill: the drugs, the unreliable, often dangerous friendships she entertained, her mother's illness and the way she'd found her, and her eventual climb back up.

He hadn't judged at all – just took in everything she said the way he always had: with interest so intense, it was almost uncomfortable. However, there was that one thing she hadn't been able to bring herself to tell him. Not yet.

He came up beside her and slipped a hand around her waist. "I've locked the steering for a bit since we've got a clear course ahead. Shouldn't be much longer now."

She stole a peek at him out of the corner of her eye, and for the first time since arriving at the coast, allowed herself to take in his appearance without guilt. She couldn't discount the fact that he was gorgeous. Whichever angle she studied him from, he was made up of a smooth, gentle masculinity that screamed an unusual combination of 'confident' and 'laid back', and not least when he was out amid the waves. This was clearly his domain.

She glanced back at the ocean, still not sure what she was supposed to be on the look-out for, and leaned back into him slightly.

His arm tightened around her.

Sense was fast slipping away, or maybe it was more than that. Maybe her brain had been thumped so hard, with so much information being thrown at it, it had no choice but to let its guard down. Whatever it was, the fight was getting hard – she didn't *want* to fight Jamie; she wanted to fight next to him, for him, for a future she'd caught a glimpse of, for just one night, when she was sixteen.

Yes, her brain must be short-circuiting. Was she giving up security – stability – for some whimsical notion? Or was the intangible future within her grasp enough? What would she be turning her back on if she didn't follow it? If she didn't try? She had no kids – no ties except a job, which could probably be transferred for a smaller salary – and a fiancé she wasn't sure was still her fiancé. All she had to do was make a decision. It should be easy. What stopped her was fear.

Had her father really left them because he was too afraid to be bound by love? On the surface it seemed a ridiculous action, but she was starting to realise she'd been living a life keeping anything that equated to love at a distance. What if she *was* just like her father? What if she walked into something with Jamie and then wrecked it all because she couldn't deal? Because there was no doubt in her mind she'd fall hard for him if she let herself – she was almost already there.

The photos of her and her father were on her mind. Loss was a cavern from which some never climbed out.

The letters from the hospital for Candy were on her mind. Some people never got the chance to really live and it wrenched her to pieces to think that might be Candy.

Her mother's scribbled words in her birthday card were on her mind. *She* had always lived her life to the fullest – had done it all her way through others' jibes and comments. Fuck ... through Merri's own derision, occasionally.

And Jamie was on her mind. She sneaked another look at him.

"You're supposed to be watching the sea," a hint of amusement riding his tone.

She blushed and mumbled "smart arse" under her

breath, when an odd shape caught her eye directly under the boat.

*What is...?*

There it was again, and another one, slightly larger than the first, and then she gasped as more came into view, her gasp quickly turning into excited squeals. "Dolphins!"

Jamie's smile reached ear-to-ear.

It didn't take long before Merri was bouncing around like a ping-pong ball, leaning over left and right guard rails to get a better view.

"Careful."

"How did you know? I've come out a couple of times in the past trying to spot them and I never could!"

"You have to know when they're most likely to come to the surface, and they like bigger waves – you gotta get the boat going at the right speed. When I used to surf more often down under, sometimes they'd surf right along next to me if I caught the right wave. They *love* to play."

"Play?"

"Yep. That's what they're doing: saying hello and wanting to play."

She couldn't contain herself. Unbridled joy practically burst from her when a couple of the smaller dolphins – baby dolphins? – started jumping over the crests of the waves either side of the bow; waves made by the boat as it hurtled through the water.

Seeing dolphins so close was amazing, and their enthusiastic bounding and leaping were contagious. They sang every time they jumped over a wave and it filled her with ... god, she didn't know what, but it overflowed. It was the same kind of feeling that would fill her with terror, that she held at arm's length, but that was simply impossible at this second, and also seemed wrong – *completely* wrong to be shutting everything out when these sea mammals were basking in the abundance of that same everything.

"How long will they stay for?"

Jamie shrugged. "Fifteen minutes? Half an hour if we're lucky."

And that was Merri gone for the next thirty minutes. She kicked off her sandals and perched as near to the edge of the boat as she dared, surprised that her usual death-wish self had taken a hike. There was no urge to throw herself off the edge, or into the pod of dolphins. She just wanted to watch, because the moment was perfect as it was. Contentment radiated through her, and ... bliss.

Pure bliss.

Only that night with Jamie had conjured the same sense of faultless entireness. She turned towards him, to find him back at the steering, shades on, the wind batting his hair and his loose T-shirt against him. Some profound sense of peace settled deep in her bones, because she suddenly knew: all the bad stuff that had happened in her life – stuff she'd *have* to tell Jamie about – whether it was self-perpetuated or not ... she wouldn't give up that one night with him to make it all go away. She'd give up almost everything else, but not that.

# XIV
## *Gone*

"Hey," said Pip, uncertainly, with half a smile as she walked back into David's room. "I wasn't sure when you eat, and I'm starved, so I went and bought you a ham and cheese sandwich, and a yoghurt from the canteen."

She wasn't sure why she still waited for his reply. She should know by now there wouldn't be one, although sometimes, there was a reaction. Not today.

"Um ... I didn't want you to be hungry if I was eating in front of you..."

He stared at nothing. At a random spot on the carpet.

"Do you want me to help you eat it? I could, um ... here..." She dropped all the food on the top of the only table in the room and proceeded to open the packaging for the sandwich. Shit. Maybe he didn't do sandwiches. Could he chew solid foods properly? Did it depend on the type of food? She'd never had the opportunity to feed him since the accident, and now she did – here she was, about to do this.

Her mind immediately threw up the last time she *had* fed him. It had involved strawberries and whipped cream and a shit-load of laughter and cleaning up afterwards.

She turned away her stinging eyes from him, placed the sandwich down and went for the yoghurt instead.

After finding a spoon and controlling every agonising

emotion that threatened to bubble up inside her, she turned back with another smile and knelt in front of him where he sat. "David?" She nudged his knee with her elbow. "David."

*For fuck's sake, LOOK at me!!!*

"Would you like some yogurt? It's Fruit of the Forest."

The corner of his mouth glistened slightly with a spot of saliva. Had that been there before? Was that a sign he wanted the yogurt? Was she just supposed to go ahead and try to feed him anyway?

God damn it, she should have spoken to someone about how to do this, but she hadn't known she was going to do it until she'd walked back in the room with lunch.

"David..."

*Remember me? Remember your kids? We love you. I love you.*

*I hate you,* whispered some demon voice that wasn't hers, layered somewhere underneath her own declaration. The voice was a trickster. She shut it out and smothered the guilt that arose from even thinking it.

She brought the yoghurt-laden spoon up to his mouth.

The saliva pooled some more and began, very slowly, to slide down the corner of his mouth.

She went for broke, and placed the spoon against his bottom lip and then slipped it between his teeth.

His arm came up from out of nowhere and knocked her sideways.

She yelled as she landed hard on the floor, on her right hip, half in shock and half in pain.

A deep moan sounded from him, more alien than human.

She'd been told he'd done this once before, but she hadn't been there – had only heard about it second-hand as part of a clinical update. He didn't lash out on purpose; apparently, it was more akin to an extension of his emotions, only he wasn't able to express them properly, and since some of his muscular control was now involuntary...

The door to his room swung open and two nurses – one female and one male – rushed in to restrain him.

*Restraining...*

They were restraining him, and it was her fault, and now she couldn't tell whether he was flailing because of what she'd done or because of the restraining. Her heart split open. "I'm sorry... I'm so sorry. I thought he might be hungry. I tried to—"

They ignored her, shouting over her, throwing names of medication around and other words she couldn't understand.

*How did they know? How did they make it into the room so quickly?*

A needle sank into his arm.

She was going to be sick.

She'd done this. She'd brought him pain.

*God*, she was going to be sick.

She got to her feet, her hip smarting – but it was only a bruise – grabbed her handbag and sped out the room, doing everything she could not to run.

She needed to stay and talk with the nurses, she knew that – there might be a procedure they followed when things like this happened; she might have to give some kind of statement and sign something – but her world had just ended, and it kept fucking ending over and over again, over days, over weeks, over the past seven months on god-damned *fucking* repeat...

She took the stairs, two at a time, down both flights, and with her head down, stormed her way into the lobby and out the double doors before anyone could stop her.

*Get in the car, get in the car, get in the car...*

There was only one fumble with the key, just like in the movies when you had to get somewhere quick, and really, that was her life right now, wasn't it? A bloody bad film.

She wasn't sure how she made it out of the car park. She couldn't even feel herself driving the car.

Was this how it was when the truck had hit him? Had he grown numb to it all as he saw it approach? Had everything gone silent except for the ringing in his ears, even though the reality was filled with screams?

Pippa slammed on the brakes, swerved slightly to avoid a pot-hole, and came to a standstill on the left by a verge that didn't even cover the rugged edge of the country road.

A horn blared at her as a BMW sped by, and then there was silence.

Silence.

Until her frantic, wild sobbing broke through it – broke through anger and grief and eight years of marriage, and a home built on laughter, love and trust...

All gone.

~*~

So far, so good. If you could consider your ball sack about to explode 'good' – he really needed to have jacked off in the shower yesterday night after that crazy episode in the car – but somehow, this impromptu boating trip had gone by smoothly. For some reason, Merri had stopped swimming against the tide, her fight no longer against *him*, nor, to some extent, herself.

Learning about some of her history earlier had been, not just refreshing, but a revelation. All the stuff she'd been through ... hell, it made him proud. Proud of *her*. Proud because he knew exactly what she'd suffered to pull herself out of the chaos she had nested in, and it came from the same kind of grit used for climbing mountains with no harnesses. She was like one of the Peregrine Falcons that lived on the craggy cliffs. Those birds were awesome.

And he'd just taken the last step off his own perch, because if he hadn't loved her then, he'd just fallen in love with her now. He was in for the deep haul, even if the jump was insane. Luckily for him, her insane streak was one of the things he adored about her.

He anchored as close as he could to the shore of a small, sandy cove, glad that it was as peaceful and undisturbed as he remembered it. No one ever came here because there was no path down to the beach – you could only reach it by boat.

Merri was sitting, leaning back against the side of the boat; huge, maroon sunglasses on, enjoying the sun, having now lathered herself in factor thirty.

Jamie smiled at the sight. He was so fucking gone, but then he always had been with her. "Ready for lunch?"

She lazily turned her head towards him.

All he could see of her was her small smile for the shades, but he suddenly felt like a deer caught in headlights.

"Does that mean I have to get up?"

"We could eat on the boat, but I thought we might head into the cove. We'll have to wade through some water though – I can't take her any closer in because of the rocks."

She pulled herself up, slowly, still smiling.

*What's with her?*

"Guess the dress needs to come off then."

*God, yes.*

"It's only about waist-deep. I don't think—" And then he didn't think at all. All words flew right out of his head as yellow cotton went over blonde hair revealing...

*Oh, Christ...*

He'd been expecting a bikini – that same one she'd worn on Sunday. He'd prepared himself for that. What he got instead was lacy, pale blue underwear. She hadn't changed into her swimwear yet.

And he couldn't look away.

Not that she wanted him to, he could damn well see that. He'd have to thank the dolphins later.

*Well, you said you weren't going to run; you vowed you were going to do what it took to win her. Can't really complain when you get exactly what you want, can you?*

No. He wasn't complaining, but his dick was throbbing, his nuts felt bruised and he'd just broken out in a mild, cold sweat. He could hear his heartbeat in his ears.

Merri glanced at his now-too-tight shorts, dipping her head down and slightly to one side, and then back up, indicating she was studying the rest of him and fuck if he didn't feel the burn of her travelling gaze through those shades. Both heat, and a dare, were in her smile and in the rise of her eyebrows – the only parts of her face he could really see. And this time, he saw no fear.

Fearless Merri was beautiful.

Fearless Merri was damn scary.

And she had his full attention.

White teeth peeked through her smile as it widened. She made her way to the small steps on the side of the boat and took hold of the hand rails. "Need a dip in the cold ocean?" she taunted, mischievously, before disappearing down the side.

*Get the food hamper.*

It took him a full three seconds to acknowledge his brain's instructions.

Food hamper.

He couldn't even remember what food he'd prepared; couldn't say he felt like eating right this second, unless it was off the delicately curved body now imprinted into his mind.

It was nonsensical, really, how her underwear covered up more of her than that bikini had, yet, he felt he could see more of her in it.

His cock *actually* twitched, and he mentally chastised it for being so porn-star, then gave it a silent apology for all he was putting it through.

A small squeal came from somewhere in the ocean.

*Fuck! Her panic attacks!*

He dropped the hamper and made for the side; looked over and forced himself to calm down when he caught her giggling at the fish – quite big ones – that seemed to want to nibble on her skin as they swam past.

No panic attack then... In fact, she looked as relaxed as he'd ever seen her. "You all right with the cold water?"

"Hmm? Oh, yes, look ... it only comes up to my belly-button. Nowhere near my chest," she grinned.

He did look, and became fixated with her perfectly shaped belly-button – just right for the tip of his tongue to dip into – because if he looked up to see her face, he would have to wander past her breasts, and he'd already spied for the briefest of seconds just how erect those nipples were under that lace, from the cold water.

Swearing under his breath, he pushed himself away from the edge of the boat, picked up the hamper he'd dropped and made his own way down the steps.

The sea felt like thick ice encasing his genitals in some unforgiving curse, and it bloody hurt. He sucked in a breath. The next time Merri got him hot and bothered, he wasn't going to last. He wasn't going to make it through lunch. He wasn't going to make it five more minutes, because the water was getting more shallow and the full curve of her backside, now in see-through blue panties, was pretty much all he could take. "You're a tease, Merri Goodwill," he said, his voice rough.

She stopped abruptly and turned to face him.

For a minute he thought he'd angered her, but she slid her sunglasses to the top of her head and stared at him in complete seriousness, the tiniest hint – almost unnoticeable – of vulnerability under all her other layers. The words that came out of her mouth started a fire in his chest – it was the good kind of burn.

"I'm not teasing you, Jamie. I want you."

~*~

Maybe that was too much; too forward. She was notoriously crap with words and with expressing herself, which is why she did stupid, wild things instead ... like strip in front of Jamie (or near as damn it). She had always believed that actions spoke louder than words, but actions had gotten her into huge trouble before – and now, apparently – so words it would have to be.

She wasn't a tease, although she could easily see the miscommunication there, what with her in her underwear and all... It was just that she didn't know how to say what she wanted to.

And then, all the sudden, she did. It just came out. "I'm not teasing you, Jamie. I want you."

Yep. She'd just gone and put that out there while they were between sea and shore, half-freezing and half-burning.

And Jamie had said nothing.

Still said nothing.

He just stared at her in a way that suggested he was struggling with himself.

Crap.

She'd thought this was also what he wanted after yesterday in the car. Had she read him wrong? He'd been chasing her, hadn't he? Determined to win her affections; declared he wasn't running...

Embarrassment flooded to her face, although, strangely, no feelings of anxiety surfaced at all. She couldn't figure that out, suffice to say that so much had happened in the past few days it must have knocked the panic out of her. Really, there was only so much someone could take. And this morning: her mother's card ... Candy's letters from the hospital...

There was only so much someone could take and that someone *wasn't* her – she could take a lot more. She'd spent her entire life hiding from that fact while others battled with what was thrown at them; hiding because living big and losing big was worse than a mediocre life filled with maybes, in which you could never lose.

Except it wasn't, was it? Or it was fine for a while. But then the child inside you that remembers living big – the child you built a cage around so she couldn't bargain all your dreams for the fickleness of happiness – grows too big for the cage. What do you do then?

She was having some kind of awakening; an epiphany. It was slowly unfurling and she didn't know how to put any of that into words, so in a rare moment of non-anxious honesty, she had said what she actually meant: the whole truth and nothing but the truth.

"I want you," she repeated, even though her face was now so hot she thought her eyes might start watering.

Jamie came out of his stupor and grabbed her left wrist with his free hand, tugged her harder than she would have expected, then led them both towards the cove, still giving nothing away.

Goosebumps covered her legs as they came out of the water, and with the sudden air on her skin, also came sense. What the *fuck* was she doing in her underwear!

*Jesus!*

They hadn't gone to the shops at her insistence that they shouldn't waste any unnecessary time; she was using Jamie's sun cream and her bikini hadn't had the best reception the last time, so this had seemed like a viable alternative. She'd seen Jamie standing there, so chilled out the way he always was ... and it had just seemed like the thing to do, even though it seemed ludicrous now. It wasn't as if her underwear didn't cover *more* than her bikini – it did! Although now, it was all see-through. She hadn't thought that far ahead.

Stupid.

That's what Jamie did to her: made her feel so relaxed, as if everything would be okay, that she *always* let her guard down and somehow stopped thinking.

*But it's nice, isn't it? To* not *think ahead to the trillion-and-one things that might never happen and all their imagined consequences. Isn't it nice not to shut everything out?*

They reached the shore, and he took them a bit further onto the empty beach, where he dropped the hamper. She couldn't tell whether he was angry or not.

She waited for the panic that always arose at the threat of confrontation... It wasn't there.

When he turned to her, still holding her wrist, the look in his eye was a mix of a hundred things, only a handful of which she could name: pain, desperation, anger, lust, determination, and the one that scared her the most: Love.

She didn't know if any of that was good or bad.

He pulled her to him with a small jerk and she bit down on her tongue to stop a gasp when her body met his, but he regained a couple of inches between them when he held her wrist up, her hand out in front. "This," he ground out.

*Oh.*

The ring.

"I'm not in this for fun, Merri, although it is kinda fun – I'm in this for keeps. I'm not on the rebound. You took my breath away thirteen years ago and I'm pretty sure I fell in love with you that night because I'm falling all over again right now. So don't mess me around. Please. If you want a shot at forever with me, this ring comes off. Now."

*Forever?*

Forever hadn't seemed so dramatic when she was getting married, but this seemed more permanent. It was more 'forever' than her and Michael had ever been, and the beauty of it was, she *wanted* it to be forever. She *wanted* it to be permanent. If she could go back in time with the power to change things, she'd never have left Jamie at all, but...

"How do you know?" she stuttered out, unable to stop her words from tripping over one another at his nearness alone. "How do you know I'm it for you?"

"Because I *know.* I know it like I knew I wanted to live and breathe the ocean – I've always known it. You're my ocean, Merri."

Somewhere to the far right, a bird squawked, tumbling a small stone down a rock face as it took flight.

The last of her defences went with it. "Take it off," she said, softly.

He hesitated; didn't look like he quite believed her.

"Take it off," she said again, meeting his eyes, not looking away.

She saw the way his breath hitched in his throat ... and the way he *stared* at her. Only with two people had she ever felt like someone's whole world: with her dad, and with Jamie.

"Take it off," she said again, louder, her voice breaking as an unexpected, delinquent tear escaped the corner of her eye.

And then it was off, ripped like plaster from a wound. Some great weight lifted – just like that time she'd uttered those words, leaning against his scooter – and there was no time to think about the meaning of that because time finally stood still.

Jamie was on her, in her, teeth nibbling her bottom lip, tongue dancing with hers... He pressed her into him and she moaned into his mouth. Hands in hair – hers, his, "Jamie..."

Her legs buckled before she realised his hands were behind her knees, tugging... She took the hint and jumped up, wrapping her legs around his waist and *byyyy fuuuuck* ... his waist wasn't the only thing she was wrapped around. They both groaned out loud as his cock prodded her between her thighs.

He went down on his knees, her back hit the sand and ... he stilled.

"Jamie?" She nudged him with her foot. *Don't stop now – I don't think I can take it...*

He looked at her, his expression pained.

*If he's changed his mind...* That thought was pure torture. It would shred her to pieces.

"Sand and condoms – not a good combination. And I think I went and bloody left them on the boat."

*Oh. Thank. God!* "I'm on the Pill. And I had to get

tested after I stopped using – I have a clean bill of health."
She inwardly cringed at her mention of the drugs. What a
time to bring up that lovely reminder of her life.

Insecurity snaked its way into her. Jamie wasn't moving,
just staring at her in that way he always did, with those eyes
that somehow saw all of her. Had she just repelled him?

Never taking his eyes off hers, he hooked his fingers into
the waistband of her soaking panties and brought them
down.

*Not* repelled.

Holy. Shit.

His gaze wandered down until it reached its destination.

Her breathing grew heavy. It was all she could do not to
close her legs and hide the view from him.

His finger traced her shaved bikini line south, and she
couldn't hold back her moan when he found her core and
just stroked her there; sliding, slick, not entering...

Her hips rocked against his touch of their own accord,
and all at once there was movement.

Two fingers slipped all the way in, knocking the living
daylights out of her. She arched her back to bring him in
deeper.

His other hand spanned her belly, pressing her down as
his fingers pressed up.

*Jesus Christ...*

"You're gorgeous. So unbelievably gorgeous." His voice
was strung tight, as was his entire self; eyes stormy, muscles
taut, shivering with want... It undid her.

Wet heat rushed to meet him where he worked his magic. A sound of need erupted from her, then his hand was
gone, leaving her empty and wanting and just short of
screaming.

Something tickled her inner-thighs, before those disappearing hands gripped her under her rear without warning. She looked down to find him lowering his face between her legs.

Her autopilot kicked in and she jerked back, clamping her legs shut.

He glanced at her, surprised, still fervoured, "Please... I want to. I'd *like* to. Let me do this for you – you let me before."

God, it seemed too much, too personal ... too *intimate*, and also... "No one else has," her voice no more than a whisper. "Since that night... You're the only one to..."

No more words came out. He looked positively stunned at what she'd just admitted. "Are you telling me, I'm the only person to have ever gone down on you?"

She couldn't tell if she was furiously blushing, or if the sun was burning her. "Michael wasn't into it. Giving or receiving. And other guys ... well, there weren't really other guys. Not boyfriends – just flings that never went anywhere."

His eyebrows drew in and hell ... she knew that face. *That* was his determined face.

His fingers pressed into her thighs as she clamped her legs harder. "Please, Merri..." He drew her forward, then lowered his head, this time aiming for her belly-button. His tongue swept around it, and then inside it.

"Ooh." She squirmed. It wasn't right that such a simple, small thing could feel that good – it was *just* a belly-button.

Teeth scraped along her abdomen, until he landed on her birthmark, tracing it with his tongue, mimicking the last time he'd done that.

She couldn't help but smile.

"Please, Merri ... I'll make it feel fucking good, I swear."

His thumb found her slit; slipped inside her as he continued nibbling her, along the top of her pubic bone now...

"Jamie..." This was a battle she was going to lose. "You don't have to... You already did this; it *was* good – I remember what it was like."

His thumb came back out, slid her wetness up, then circled her clit, and she groaned as it throbbed, aching, under his attention.

"You're wrong. It wasn't good, Merri, because I had no idea what I was doing. I know what I'm doing now." He gently blew on her – *right there* – and the ache grew to astronomical proportions.

"God..."

"Please..."

Her legs fell open under the power of his plea and *everything* disappeared the second she felt his tongue on her most intimate place. Her whole world reduced to the size of a pin-head.

He made a low, guttural sound of longing; lost all languor and delved in deep, sealing his mouth around her.

Gone was any mercy he might have shown her.

The next sound ripped from her was a high-pitched wail. She clutched at his hair, not sure whether to press him into her or push him away. He was right ... this was *nothing* like last time. And this wasn't just good, it was the sweetest suffering – raw and hot and drenched in urgency.

He was splitting her open; every flick of his tongue, a lance spearing her to her core.

"Oh, God!"

Blissful agony ... *too much!*

She tried to scramble back.

He held her fast, not letting her go, picked up his pace, every movement of his mouth her entire existence...

She shattered.

Her body convulsed as she cried out in rapture, and still he didn't let her go, but teased her swollen bud, keeping her hard, keeping her ready; keeping her atop her climax and on the brink of another...

"Jamie!"

His touch left her for one second ... two seconds ... and then he was there above her, swimming trunks gone, the head of his cock kneading her sex, and kneading, and then he pushed himself in all the way. "Fuck ... Merri..."

She whimpered out loud, needing more, and he gave her more. No waiting, no holding back; just his driving claim, every pounding thrust undoing her all over again.

Her bra was pushed upwards. A hand found her breast, her nipple; squeezed... "I can't go slow ... sorry, honey ... I need this now."

His words were like fire.

She felt herself clench around him; draw him in...

He growled out every pant, speeding up, rocking into her, taking everything he needed.

Merri saw sparks. Green dots, black dots, multicoloured flashes shaped like the sun's rays behind her closed eyelids, before she came for the second time.

Jamie groaned in her ear, fisted her hair, thrust once more – deep – then stopped, still moaning as he pulsed his life into her.

His warmth consumed her. She locked her ankles around him, taking everything he had to give. An "I love you" slipped out of her before she could stop it, but it made no difference now. Today was thirteen years ago; thirteen years ago was today, and all the time in between was somehow made up for – a chasm, closed.

She dug her ankles into him, pressing him closer, relishing in the feel of him still hard inside her.

His lips fell onto hers as her tender declaration clung to the air around them, and was then sealed with his own.

"I love you, too."

# XV
## Of Spells and Sorrow

Dear Diary,

There *is* one thing I've always believed in: balance. That fine line that determines whether something continues, or ceases to be. Balance can be seen in all things – nature, relationships and the stock market. Yes, the stock market. When shares go up, other shares go down: you put something in, someone takes something out, and vice versa. It is the way of things. It's the way the universe works. Somewhere inside, I knew. I knew my decision that day would lead to a shift in balance.

Or maybe it's the other way around. Maybe the shift in balance brought about my decision.

Remember what I said before? The extraordinary is hidden in the ordinary. Magic is subtle: woven into everyday life. We only see the full picture after it has played out...

~*~

She was back at the top of the cliff. The sky was turning stormy. She was alone against the landscape, which looked barren and grey – usually, it looked so beautiful. The sea threw itself choppily with the wind.

Merri drew her coat tighter around her against the cold and spun in surprise, and a bit of trepidation, when she heard a sound behind her.

She froze.

Tears spilled over, streaking her face... Every emotion she'd ever felt, fighting for dominance within her.

Her dad held out his arms to her; open ... loving ... giving...

She stumbled into them, crying as she fell against him.

He rocked her in his embrace, both of them standing against the horizon, the storm in the distance; and amid the storm, a ray of sun, off to the south: the silver lining trying to break through.

"My little girl," he murmured into her hair.

She shook her head, unable to speak; only wanting to stay there forever, tucked into the safety of his chest. He was wearing her favourite coat. It was woolly and snug and smelled like him.

His heart beat next to her ear – the heart that had stopped.

"Why did you leave?"

He stroked her hair. "Did you read my letter?"

"No. Not yet. I wasn't ready."

"Are you ready now?"

"I don't know. I think so."

"I left because I was also not ready, and I wish you knew

how sorry I am for all the hurt it caused you. I should have known better, but we never really grow up, Merri. We're always learning; thinking the newest lesson has sped us to maturity, and then we feel foolish when the next lesson strips away all we knew before... You're never ready for love, and, yet, you always are. That was what I never learnt. I never felt ready for you – for how much I loved you – and it was only with hindsight that I could see I was ready, by the mere fact that you existed. Love finds you, not the other way around, and you can't run from it. I ran. But you ... you need to stop running."

"I'm scared."

"What of?" That was not her dad's voice.

Startled, she freed herself from his arms and swivelled to see her mother standing behind her, smiling.

"Mum ... what are you doing here?"

"I wanted to see you for your birthday."

"My birthday's tomorrow."

Her smile widened and her eyes sparkled with pride. "Sometimes, we need to take Father Time by the proverbial horns and tell him what for." She leaned to give her a hug and a kiss on the cheek. "Happy birthday, Merri."

"Yes," said her dad, his arm around her shoulder. "Happy birthday."

The three of them came in for a joint embrace, and it had been so long – so very, very, long – since she'd felt the wonder of that. Love swelled within her, a fresh surge of tears surfacing.

Her dad kissed the top of her head. "We love you, Merri. So much."

Contentment settled deep within her, and beautiful warmth. A movement over Dad's shoulder caught her eye and she frowned.

*Jamie.*

*He was running towards her.*

"I love you, too," she choked out. "I'm happy now – this makes me happy."

"Good," her mother said, squeezing her tightly. "Because you're not a ghost. Don't go chasing them. Love big, sweetie, and be happy. Be very, very happy."

*The wind blew.*

*It blew so hard, she thought it might blow them right over.*

*Something didn't feel quite right. Foreboding loomed like an unforgiving shadow, rising from beneath...*

*Why did Jamie look panicked?*

*There was an almighty crack, something gave way beneath her feet...* Oh, God! The cliff!

*Merri screamed, her stomach leaping to her throat as they began to plummet.*

*Instinct kicked in and she reached out with her hand – any hand – her right hand... It found something that jutted out and she grabbed it, hanging on for dear life.*

"No!"

*Where did they go? Her mum? Her dad?*

"Merri!"

*She looked up.*

"Don't look down! Merri, reach up!" Jamie lay flat on the top of what was left of the cliff and extended his arm. "Reach up and take my hand."

"But..." Mum ... Dad...

"Merri, reach up!" A desperate edge to his voice – or was it her voice? "Reach up!"

*The wind knocked against her. She swayed like a leaf being torn from its tree, and on the wind, a whisper; barely there ... her mother's perfume...* "Don't go chasing ghosts..."

*"Merri, please..."*

*Green eyes met brown. He held her there, with his stare. She got the distinct sense that if she let go, his stare alone would keep her from falling. Some risks were worth taking...*

*Gritting her teeth, she put weight on her hand that clutched the rock, used all the strength she could muster, and threw her other arm up towards him.*

*Fingers closed around wrists.*

*She breathed out in relief, and she was rising ... rising...*

She awoke on a gasp, something shaking her.

"Merri?"

It was Jamie shaking her awake.

They were still in the cove, under the shade of some clumped together trees, having fallen asleep in each other's arms after a poor attempt at eating lunch, and round two of making love.

"You were crying out in your sleep. I couldn't make out what you were saying." He kissed her forehead. "Are you all right?"

"Yeah..." She turned slightly onto her side to face him, the dream still making her feel uneasy as dreams often could long after waking. "I was falling. You caught me."

"Sooo ... were you yelling because you were falling or because I caught you?" he grinned.

It was contagious. She shoved him in the chest. "Ha ha..." And then rolled right on top of that broad, tanned chest, treating herself to more Jamie – more *naked* Jamie.

Her treat ended with her lips on his, her astride him. She levered herself up to get a better view of his face. "I was yelling because my mum and dad were there, and they also fell off the cliff when it gave way, but I couldn't save them."

His dark gaze softened. He stroked her cheek. "I wish I could make it all better for you – all the stuff in the past."

She dipped her finger into the middle of his chin, enjoying how his stubble felt under it. "I think you just did."

His half-smile crept up the left of his face accentuating that gorgeous dimple, grown deeper with age.

He took her hand in his and laced their fingers together. "Don't forget we've got the future. I'm going to make you happy, Meredith Goodwill. Whether you want to be, or not."

She laughed. "I have no doubt. I don't know what I did to deserve you."

"You held on."

Her laughter faded as his words touched her deeply.

"Thanks for holding on."

She kissed his fingers wrapped around hers, feeling a little daft she was welling up again. "Thanks for coming home and finding me."

The rest of the day passed by in a leisurely fashion. Lunch got eaten a little bit at a time, over the next two hours, until it was time to make their way back. They attempted to catch sight of the dolphins again, but they weren't around this time.

A pang of longing tugged at Merri's heart when Jamie brought the boat into the harbour. She didn't want to leave him. She wanted to spend the night with him, and going with the theme of non-anxious honesty, she told him as much. It earned her a deep, twenty-second kiss that had passers-by tutting, or looking away.

"Let them stare," said Jamie. "We have the last of our teenage years to live out."

She smiled into his mouth as his kiss ended. "I wish that could start tonight, but I don't think Candy's doing too well right now, and I want to be there for her if she needs me." She didn't go into detail, feeling it too private a thing to share when anything she shared would be speculation anyway, but he surprised her with his own observations.

"I wondered if she was okay on Sunday. She looked really tired – I figured the kids might have worn her out."

"That is *not* outside the realms of possibility."

Jamie laughed. "Boisterous, aren't they?"

"Yes, but fun."

"Definitely fun. I'd like you to come round for dinner soon. A family dinner. Come meet my parents."

She should be shaking, wheezing and on the verge of collapse roundabout now. She felt more healthy and alive than she had in years. "I'd like that too."

He moored the boat, they collected their belongings, and headed for The Beast. She was getting used to thinking of that car as such. "Do you still have your scooter?"

"The Piaggio? She was a gem, wasn't she? But, no. Sadly, she parted from this world a week before I left for Australia. I do believe her tyres were made into rubber stationery though."

Merri guffawed out her laughter in a completely unlady-like way.

The next thing she knew, she was herded to the side of The Beast and pinned there by Jamie's inviting body as his mouth devoured hers.

"Sex," he mumbled into the kiss, which was now travelling across her face, heading towards her ear, her throat... "Here. In this car."

She sucked in a breath as he found a sensitive spot on her neck.

"Teenage years … relive…"

He *had* to be joking. "Now?"

He groaned. "Don't tempt me, woman."

A mini bonfire started somewhere inside her, but no – no, no, no – she had to get home to Candy. But, *god*…

Jamie fumbled for the car keys in his pocket, still pressed up against her, then when he finally found them, he unlocked the passenger door just behind her, not un-meshing himself from her body until absolutely necessary.

"There," he said, opening the door. "Inside, now, before I get arrested."

She smirked, "Yes, sir," and scrambled in, dragging her beach bag with her.

A sudden silence fell, and she turned to find Jamie staring at her again. Surprise, surprise. "What is it this time?"

A slow, delicious, wicked smile spread across his face. "You'll be calling me Sir again."

*Holy—*

The door slammed shut, leaving her squirming in her seat and unwittingly grinning from ear to ear. Because life had just gotten exciting, unpredictable, full and *right*.

And she was enjoying every last, non-anxious second of it.

~*~

Candy shut her front door behind her.

She was purposely home early having felt bad standing Merri up last night. The bunch of flowers she'd left out for her this morning caught her eye, still looking colourful, and underneath them her note to her. Right next to the note, was another piece of paper – the spell Merri had written last night with other words scribbled beneath it: *You're*

*right. This was dumb. If we know what we want our lives to be, then what does this matter?*
*Speak later. xxx*

Candy sighed, not quite managing a smile, but grateful for the sentiment behind Merri's message.

Stupid fight.

She next noticed the mail on the table on the other side of the vase; spotted who they were from. She pulled a face. She wasn't in the mood to deal with those right now. She was floundering through life as much as Merri. What the fuck did she know about what she wanted? If only magic could fix everything.

The doorbell rang.

She dropped her bag on the table, making the round wooden furniture look truly cluttered, and went to answer it.

Pippa stood on the other side of the door.

"Hi," greeted Candy, surprised.

"Hi," she smiled.

The woman looked slightly wrecked, but it was under a cover of 'pulled myself back together'. The only reason Candy could tell was because she saw herself in it. She decided not to mention it.

"I was hoping to catch you. I wanted to drop off the keys to the boat – Jamie has the other set. I didn't know if maybe you wanted to get there early to put up decorations and prepare things or whatever."

"Thanks. Come on in."

Pip stepped inside and Candy closed the door.

"You want a drink?"

"Oh, no. I'm cool. I need to head back to my parents – I left the kids with them all day."

"Whoa, better hurry."

She laughed, then crossed her eyes, reminding Candy just why she liked her so much. "Yeah, it may knock my dad out of early retirement and back to work."

Candace grinned.

"Anyway," she held out the key in front of her, "here you go."

"Great." Candy took it. "Oh! I almost forgot, I have something of yours – at least, I think it's yours."

Pippa followed her into the dining room where she delved into the handbag she'd dropped on the table. "I know I put it in here somewhere..."

"What's this?" Pippa asked. Her eyes were fixed on the spell Merri had written.

"Oh," Candy wrinkled her nose. "Remember I told you on Sunday about Merri's mum and the spell Merri said that she thinks ruined the wedding and all that?"

"Yeah."

"Well, this is her counter-spell against that. Not her brightest idea, if you ask me. She wrote it last night; thought about saying it, and thankfully seems to have changed her mind."

"So ... you really do think Jamie and her together is a good thing?"

"Sure. Why not? In all honesty, I kinda think they're meant to be, and I don't think you see that often, you know? People who are just *meant* for each other. She wrote that thing 'cause she was scared. If she'd written it with a clear head and no trace of fear, I'd have been more willing to hear her out, but she was riding on past hurt. That's never a good basis for magic."

Pippa glanced at her, thoughtfully. "You're really into the whole 'magic' thing, aren't you?"

"I guess. When I was a kid, Merri's mum was like this

strong, independent woman to me. She was always so sure of herself and just let you be yourself without stifling you." She let out a snort. "Exactly the opposite of my mother. Anyway, it wasn't like she drummed her lifestyle into us or anything, but I just always kinda got it – I got the way she thought about things – and when I was older I asked her more about it. Merri was never so into it."

Pippa's eyes were back on the spell. "I had a friend in senior school who said she was a witch; that said she got it passed to her from her grandma. I always thought it was a shame she went around wearing black and being all emo – no one ever took her seriously. But there was a time at a beach party, after a huge oil-spill, she did this ceremony to hex the people that had done it—"

"Yikes! Merri's mum wouldn't have done that – she'd have done something like a spell to protect the wildlife, or to protect the beach from future spills."

"Yeah, well, exactly one week later someone was found washed-up dead on the shore. He'd gone swimming at night and not seen a man-of-war jellyfish, and got stung to death. Freaky thing was, he as one of the crew on the ship that had spilled the oil."

Candy whistled.

Pippa nodded. "Tell me about it."

"Oh, I've got it!" She pulled out the black onyx earring she'd been looking for. "I found this wrapped up in my beach towel when I unfolded it to put in the wash. Merri said it wasn't hers."

Pippa reached for it. "Excellent! Yep, that's mine. Thought I'd lost it playing with Becca in the garden. Speaking of which, I really should head back."

"Of course. Merri should be home in a bit anyway. Any news on how her day with Jamie went?"

"Not heard a peep."

"Hmmm ... I'm going to assume that's good news."

Pip smiled as she headed for the door. "Let's hope so, or I'll have to put up with love-sick Jamie all over again. Once of that was enough. Twice because of Claire has me wanting to rip her eyeballs out."

Candy opened the front door to see her out. "Third time lucky, then."

"Third time lucky," agreed Pippa, waving her goodbye without looking back as she walked down the driveway towards her car.

Candy shut the front door once more, wondering if she could fit in a shower before Merri's arrival. That bone-tired feeling was seeping its way into her again, not that it had ever really left the past few weeks.

She went to clear the table for dinner first, frowning to herself, because something felt strange – out of place. She couldn't pin-point it.

When she finally figured out what it was, she didn't know whether to be worried or bemused. She was intrigued more than anything else, as to why on earth Pippa would have taken it.

Merri's spell was gone.

# XVI
## *Trickster*

There was something wickedly sinful – in a deliciously naughty way – about walking around in public having just had sex.

Merri bit her bottom lip as she slid the key home, unlocking Candy's front door.

She was still a little plump between her legs; still a little slick – still horny as fuck. And she couldn't stop grinning. She wondered if anyone could tell. She felt kinda wild; a little primal ... she hadn't felt this way in forever and it was like a breath of fresh air. She could breathe. She could *breathe*. Her lungs felt bigger – stronger.

"Hey, you!" called out Candy as she entered the hallway. "I thought I heard the door. How did it go?"

Straight to it, then.

Her friend's eyes sparkled in both curiosity and hope.

"I can't believe you and his sister were in on this." But she was still smiling – couldn't bloody help it.

"It was totally his idea!" she protested. "All we did was say yes. And judging by the expression on your face your little boating trip was ... good? Fun? An out-of-this-world fuck-fest?"

"Candy! Honestly!"

"Well, which was it?"

She walked into the living room and fell onto the couch. She was too blissed out to tease her for long. "All three."

Candy squealed. "For real?"

She nodded.

"Oh, my god."

"We're going to give things a go."

"Oh, my god! As in, properly? As in, a couple?"

Merri held up her left hand.

Candy looked confused at first, and then like Merri had just told her she'd won the Nobel Prize when she spotted her naked ring finger. "Shiiiiiit!"

"Yes. Properly. All I need to do now, is tell Michael. Something I should have done first."

"Fuck that – you tried to do it the right way. No, this *was* the right way. Sometimes it's a case of now or never."

And on that subject...

Merri's heart beat a bit faster, but she was controlled. She could do this. "Candy," she tucked her legs under her and propped herself up on her elbow, resting it on the arm of the sofa. "Are you okay? And what I mean is... All right, what I mean is, that you've been looking really tired – exhausted in fact – and I feel like a horrible friend for not noticing when you came up to London for the wedding. You said in the note you left about needing to tell me what you've been through the past few years..." She left that sentence hanging, watching Candy's face closely.

It fell slightly, and a mask went on, although it was a thin, half-hearted mask that didn't really do its job the way it was supposed to. "I did say that, didn't I?"

"Yes, you did. So ... what's going on?"

She visibly gulped, looking more than worried.

It put Merri right on edge, her whole self sinking, as hope plummeted. "You can tell me anything, you know that, right?"

"I ... I think so. I just ... this one's really hard, and I don't know where to start." A sheen lay over her blue eyes, setting off the blue of her cropped hair. Fuck. Was that why it was so short? Because of...

"I picked up your mail this morning," she threw out there. Candy had been pushing her for some kind of conclusion with Jamie. Tit for tat – she wasn't squirming her way out of this. "The letters from the hospital ... from..." Crap it, her voice grew thick. "From the cancer unit."

And Candace wasn't looking at her anymore, but down at the floor, chewing away on the corner of her lip. A tear splashed on the laminate wood next to her foot, and Merri lost all decorum.

"Bloody hell, Candy – do you have cancer? What kind? Is it bad? Is it terminal?" *Argh! Stupid tears!* She swiped at them, angrily. She had vowed to be strong for her. Merri-turned-puddle was not what her best friend needed.

Candy looked up at her, surprised, cheeks still wet. "What? You think... Oh, shit..."

"Are you dying?"

"Merri!" She leapt at her where she sat on the sofa and threw her arms around her. "You daft cow! I'm not dying."

*Not dying.*

*NOT dying.*

"Oh, Christ," she blurted out, squeezing Candy tight and attempting to dry more tears.

"I don't have cancer."

*Oh, thank GOD.* And she did. In that second, she mentally sent her gratitude to any and all deities that might or might not exist, relief cascading over her.

"But..."

Merri's skin prickled at that one word.

Candy pulled back, disentangling herself from their hug. "Someone I'm in love with does. Those letters are info I asked for about what I can expect towards the end. Someone I love is dying – soon. Maybe just weeks left."

"Someone you ... Jesus."

A long, heavy moment passed between them.

"Candy ... I'm so, so sorry."

Merri wondered how the hell it could be that she didn't know she had a boyfriend. Had she asked? She was sure she must have asked at some point over the past four days. Had Candy just skilfully avoided answering? Wasn't there some quip about not having sex since forever and some not funny joke about ovaries shrivelling up? "I didn't know you were in a relationship."

"It's complicated." There was that mask again. Why? Complicated how? Unless...

"Oh, do you mean ... I sort of assumed that ... is it a 'she'? I mean, I am *totally* okay with that, if that's the reason why you never said anything. I automatically thought 'boy-friend', but—"

"Merri..." She was shaking her head and obviously struggling with what to say. "It's ... shit, I don't know how to... It's even more complicated than that. And I don't want you to hate me, or be weird with me." Her voice quivered and it broke Merri's heart.

"You can tell me *anything*. How can you not know that? God, some of the stuff I've been through ... I haven't told anyone, not even my therapist because I wasn't ready and I didn't know how to explain the way things happened in a way she wouldn't judge me, even though I know she's not supposed to judge 'cause she's supposed to be neutral and everything, but that doesn't mean people don't—"

"What things?"

"Oh, no you don't. You first."

They hit a stalemate. Both of them caught between wanting to pour out all their aches and pains, and not wanting to annihilate every wall of protection they'd built around all that shit.

Merri's phone rang.

She sat-up, shocked, and became still as a statue.

"Merri?"

"That's Michael's ring tone. It's Michael." Only now did it hit her she hadn't once checked her phone today.

God knew how many seconds passed with them both staring at each other as her phone got louder and louder.

"Answer it," said Candy.

"But—"

"Answer it. You've been waiting days for him to contact you. Talk to him."

She dove for her bag and brought her phone out. She shot Candy a look, "This conversation is *not* over," and pressed the answer button, her heart literally pulsing in her throat. Okay, well, not literally, but it bloody well felt that way. "Hello?"

"Meredith?"

It was more than strange hearing his voice. It sounded so familiar, but also a little alien, so much had happened the past few days. A small ball of anger made itself known at the base of her stomach. "I've been calling you for *days*."

"I know, I'm—"

"Would it have killed you to text an 'I'm fine', or *anything* to let me know you hadn't jumped off a bridge?"

"Merri, listen—"

"Listen? Are you kidding? I have things to tell you, *important* things, and I didn't want to do it like this – feeling frustrated and angry with you – and you didn't even let me say I'm sorry, god damn it, because I *was*. I was *so* sorry that I said what I did, and that I hurt you, but you just—"

"Merri, where are you? You need to come home."

"I'm with friends after you buggered off and left me not knowing *anything*."

"I know, and I will explain, but I need you to come home now. I've been away abroad."

*Abroad? Where?*

Her anger heightened as a horrible thought seeped in. "Did you go on our honeymoon without me?"

"No. Business meeting. I got home this afternoon. Went to see you; you weren't there and your bag and toiletries were gone. I couldn't get through to you on your phone – kept saying the call couldn't be connected—"

*Aah – must've been no signal in that little cove—*

"I tried to phone your mother, but couldn't get through—"

"Just as well," she grimaced. "Not sure what language Mum would have used with you—"

"So I went round to her house."

*Ugh. This isn't going to end well.*

Candy squeezed her hand in sympathy, clearly seeing the exasperated look on her face.

"I think Mum has evening clients at the shop on Tuesdays – she won't be home yet."

Silence.

A really weird one that felt all wrong.

*"... those readings ... they've been doing her in. She's been going home early the last couple of days."*

Her skin prickled.

Dread carried a certain ice with it, and you could never escape its cold. She heard Michael take in a breath, even though the breath itself was quiet – eerily quiet.

"*The last few weeks she has really nailed her readings, accurately predicting names and places and – god – shit you wouldn't believe.*"

Candy rose to her knees, concern etched all over her face. "What's wrong?" she mouthed, silently, and then she winced when Merri's grip tightened painfully around her hand.

She looked down.

Knuckles, pale – ghostly white.

"*Mum ... what are you doing here?*"

"*I wanted to see you for your birthday.*"

"*My birthday's tomorrow.*"

"*Sometimes, we need to take Father Time by the proverbial horns and tell him what for.*"

No. Oh, god ... no.

And awareness, as it dawned on you, carried mighty swords that could split you in half with one strike.

"Merri," said Michael.

"No." *Don't say it!*

"I found your mother dead. I'm sorry, sweetheart. Suspected brain tumour, but there'll be a coroner's report. You need to come home – you're her next of kin. They won't let me do anything else. You need to confirm her identity. There'll be papers to sign. I'm so, very sorry."

~\*~

Jamie pulled into the drive the same time his sister did. She looked a little sullen. He was grinning like an idiot and had given up trying not to.

"Have you been out?" he asked her as they both stepped out of their cars.

"I've been out all day. Went to see David, then drove

around for a bit, and then popped in to see Candace to drop off the spare key to the boat."

"We must have just missed each other. I dropped off Merri about fifteen minutes ago."

"Oh, I left there about an hour ago and did a quick food shop 'cause we're low on some stuff. You had a good day? I'm guessing by your goof-ball expression the answer's a 'yes'?"

"Ooooh, yeah."

Pippa rolled her eyes, but smiled. "So your sappy boat trip idea was worth it, then?"

"It was worth the last thirteen years. It was worth everything."

"God," she muttered as she unlocked the door to their parent's house, "you are *such* a drip when you're in love."

"And you're a moody cow. Why didn't you tell me you were going to see David? I'd have liked to come along."

"And miss the last thirteen years of your life condensed into twelve hours of an alternate reality?" she gibed.

"It was eight hours ... and no, but we could have gone another day together. You don't have to do this on your own anymore."

"Yes, Jamie," she argued, her voice hard, "I do."

"Hello, you two," called out their mother, poking her head around the door to the living room.

"Mum!" yelled Becca from god knew where, and then, there she was, speeding down the stairs like a gopher on Red Bull.

"Whooooa!" exclaimed Pip. "My little princess, do *not* break the stairs."

"Mum!" She threw her arms around her legs, and Pip leaned down for kiss. "Did you get me anything?"

"Er ... no. Did I say I would? I did get Spaghetti Carbonara for dinner, though."

"Ooo, that's my favourite!"

"I know."

"Pippa," said their mother, taking her shopping bags from her. "Aren't you staying here for dinner? You know you can."

"I feel like we've been here, stealing your food, every day."

"Nonsense. It's lovely to have a full house again – isn't it, Geoff?" she called out to Dad.

He grunted an affirmative from the living room couch.

"See? Stay."

"If we could, that would be great – thank you, so much."

She waved her thanks away.

Pippa scanned her immediate surroundings. "Where are the boys?"

"In the garden with the football."

Becca frowned. "If we're staying at Nanna's for dinner, then are we still having Carbonara?"

"We'll have it tomorrow, sweet pea, sorry. But you *love* Nanna's dinners."

"*And*," added her Nanna, bending down to Becca's height, "I make the *best* desserts."

"That she does!" agreed Jamie as he ascended the stairs. Listening to the chit-chat filled him full of fuzzy feelings. Yes, he was a drip, so fucking what – he'd missed this when away. Big time. Australia was fun, and wild, and full of natural delights, but nothing quite matched the warmth of family, no matter where that family was. It was one of the things about being with Claire that had never sat right with him: her nonchalance about wanting a family. He'd found his passion in his career early – he would have been happy to step into fatherhood years ago.

"Uncle Jamie?" shouted Becca after him. "Did you have fun on the boat? Are we still going on the boat tomorrow?"

"Yes, pipsqueak, we are, and yes, I had lots of fun."

"That's good ... you probably won't have to go to the nunnery, then."

"Eh?"

Pippa laughed out loud, looked more than a little sheepish, and gestured for him to ignore her.

What *exactly* had his sister been telling her kids about him?

He unpacked when in his room, almost tripping over a ball of wool that had fallen down from ... somewhere – could have been from bloody anywhere. He placed it in the top of the nearest wool bag and carried on unpacking.

His phone was dead.

He plugged it in, not bothering to switch it on just yet, grabbed a clean towel and made his way to the bathroom, not that he wanted to wash Merri off him. He *definitely* didn't want to wash her off. By god, the *feel* of her...

*Okay, brain ... back up, buddy.*

But it was no use. She filled up his senses.

Humming John Denver, his thoughts were already on seeing her tomorrow.

~*~

The next few minutes went by as if someone else was driving her body. Arrangements were made. Michael had booked a private flight for her from Newquay to Gatwick with a click of a button, or so it seemed. A chauffeur would be taking her to Newquay Airport in an hour.

She had filled Candy in on everything after hanging up, her voice sounding distant as she retold it all, and Candy had broken down in a heap.

Candy had adored her mum.

Now, after showering in ten minutes flat, she was in her room, packing, and trying to get through to Jamie for the third time. She only had his mobile number, not his land-line, and it was going straight to answer phone. Typical. When she'd wanted to reach Michael, she couldn't, and Jamie hadn't left her alone. Now that she wanted to reach Jamie, he wasn't there, and Michael was the one throwing her the line.

She didn't want to text Jamie what had just happened, but she'd chickened out leaving a message the first and second times, not sure that she could say the words she needed to. Third time's a charm...

The answering machine beeped. "Jamie, hi. It's me – Merri. Um..." *Mum's dead, Mum's dead, Mum's dead* ... "Michael phoned, and my mum's passed away. It was sudden and ... shit ... this is all shit. I'm sorry. I have to go home and sort out all the legal stuff and the funeral and whatever else there is... I didn't want to text you. I don't want to be leav-ing this message... Anyway, I'll call again when I can, okay? Um, I'm being picked up in about fifteen minutes and I've got a flight to London booked from Newquay. I'm sorry about the boat party tomorrow, but you guys go ahead and have it anyway, and take Candy with you, please? She loved my mum – she's really upset. I love you. I really do. Please wait for me, just a little longer," and her stupid voice cracked. "I want to come back and see you as soon as I can. 'Bye."

Her hand shook as she hung up.

Her heart sank even more.

As she packed the last of her things, she found Blue. She took the rag doll out of her beach bag, placed her in her suitcase, then took her out again and carried her down the hall to Candy's room.

She knocked.

"Come in."

Merri opened the door to find Candy sitting by her window, eyes red and wet.

She attempted a smile. "Here," said Merri, and placed Blue on her pillow. "I'll feel better knowing she's looking after you."

The heaviness that clung to the air was palpable.

"What about you? Who's going to look after you?"

Merri looked out the bedroom window, following Candy's gaze. Cliffs, rooftops, and a small shimmer of sea between them, filled the horizon; all of it blanketed in a dark, rose-grey haze now the sun had mostly set. And just to the right – almost too far to see from the window – stood the silhouette of that small cliff where her life had changed forever. But she'd come back.

Somehow, she'd made it back.

*"...don't fuck up your life because you're scared, honey. Don't go chasing ghosts..."*

She'd known.

Her mother had known she was dying, or at the very least, that something was up. And it was no surprise to Merri, although it did stir her anger somewhat, that she hadn't gone to the doctors. After the emergency surgery last time, and the radiotherapy, plus all the meds she'd had to take and the ghastly side effects she'd suffered, she had sworn if the tumour came back, she'd go down a different route. They'd never fully discussed what that 'different route' would be.

Merri breathed in the summer air and let it fill her lungs; let it heal the well of grief with its natural alchemy.

It had been her mother's choice, and she had to let it go – she'd always done things her own way, anyway. She'd even refused chemotherapy treatment alongside the radiotherapy last time, much to the oncologist's disgruntlement. She could practically hear her mother's reasoning ... *"I'm just glad I have the choice, or what is living for?"*

Choice or no choice, life happened. Sometimes in terrifying ways, but also in ways filled with indescribable beauty not found anywhere else – the dolphins she'd seen this morning sprang to mind, as did her afternoon with Jamie ... the whole day, in fact, had been enchanting – magical – and she was grateful to have experienced it, especially going through all this now. To shut out the terror was to shut out the beauty. The only thing to do was let all of it in.

*"I love you, Merri – you know that, right? I don't mean just as a mother – I mean, I love who you are. Every single bit of you."*

She placed an arm around Candy's shoulder and dropped a kiss on her head, her own tears brimming. "I'm going to be fine."

And, for the first time in too long to properly remember, she truly, wholeheartedly believed it.

~*~

He couldn't run fast enough ... couldn't drive fast enough...

Jamie thumped the wheel of The Beast with his fist.

If he'd *just* turned on his phone earlier... *"I'm being picked up in about fifteen minutes and I've got a flight to London booked from Newquay."*

"Fuck!" he yelled.

He'd all but flung himself down the stairs, shot past everyone as they were sitting for dinner with a "sorry, got to go!" thrown at their startled faces and had broken more than one highway code to get to Merri. Thank god he lived in a sleepy village that the police almost never bothered with.

Her message replayed in his mind. *"It was sudden and ... shit ... this is all shit. I'm sorry."*

He had to be there for her – *had* to be. She'd told him about her mum that morning, and the way she'd talked about her... She was everything to her; was all she had left – had been. Damn it.

*And what about Michael?* butted in the voice in his head, adding a sting to his stress. The same sting that had 'Claire' stamped all over it.

"Fuck," he said again, then turned, without slowing down, right into Candy's drive behind her car, and slammed the brakes on.

He opened the door, leapt out of the Hyundai, and was pressing the doorbell before his feet had even hit the top step of the porch. "Merri!" he yelled.

Silence wasn't golden – it was a hard, cruel bitch.

"Merri!"

Sound.

Movement.

"Sssshh!" Candy's tired, pinched face came into view as the door swung open. "My neighbours *like* me, and I'd like to keep it that way."

He pushed past her and into the hallway, which earned him a scowl.

"Come the fuck in why don't you."

"I got her message about her mum. Where is she?"

"She's gone."

*Oh, god.* He squeezed his eyes shut, his heart squeezing with them.

"Twenty minutes ago or so."

He was screaming inside – a raging caterwaul which re-verberated off his eardrums and bounced around his skull.

Maybe he could still catch her. "Newquay Airport?"

Candy crossed her arms, watching him warily. "You're too late. It's a private flight she's got booked – even if you made it there before the plane took off, you wouldn't get to see her. She'll be in first class, or in some private lounge, or whatever the hell happens when you're stupidly rich – I don't know."

"Stupidly rich?" He seriously needed to calm down. He was so far out of his comfort zone he was a dot to himself.

"You know who her fiancé is?"

He shook his head, feeling slightly dizzy.

Fiancé.

*She has another man.*

Well, duh. That wasn't exactly new information. Only, now, with the magic of the day behind them and reality beating him hard in the chest, he suddenly wasn't sure if this thing over the last four days that meant everything to him had been more of a holiday to Merri.

"Michael Fortune. As in the Fortune family? The ones that own the airline and a small bit of the media and whatever else they have. As in, 'step aside Richard Branson, there's a new Virgin in town'."

He didn't laugh at her shit joke. He felt bruised. Yes, he'd heard of the Fortune empire – he'd flown back home on their fucking airline. God... She'd never said. What would Merri be giving up to be with him?

*She's gone back to him.*

No she hasn't.

*Yes, she has.*

No. She hasn't. She had told him she loved him in her

message; that she'd be back as soon as she could.

*He'll hug her; she'll hug him back; she'll cry on his shoulder and he'll comfort her. She'll be in another man's arms tonight ... tomorrow morning.*

Candy stared at him like he was crazy and he didn't blame her. He must look a state. There was anger and loss, and hurt for Merri and *her* loss, and a stake through his chest that Claire had put there – that he'd had the blissful illusion of believing was somehow gone. Which was stupid. You didn't wash away ten years in four days.

But with Merri, thirteen years had been nothing, hadn't it? Seeing her again on Sunday ... it was like no time had passed at all.

Doubt flooded into him, and he wasn't a doubtful person by nature.

What did he do now? Wait for her like she'd asked?

Waiting seemed wrong – they'd waited too long. She was suffering and he wanted to be there, with her, holding her, helping her; suffering with her.

*Someone else will be doing that.*

That was too much – it hurt *too much*. Picturing Claire with someone else had been painful, but *this*... Imagining Merri curled up with someone else was unbearable. It didn't just hurt him – it also hurt his seventeen-year-old self who had known her first; who had always belonged to her.

Candy returned into the hallway and Jamie blinked in surprise. Immersed in his inner-turmoil, he hadn't even registered that she'd left.

She held out a piece of notepad paper to him.

"What's this?" he asked, taking it from her.

"Merri's address in London. You won't make it there before her, but you should at least be there for her as soon as you can."

He stared at it like an idiot.

"What's the matter?" she asked him, a trace of irritation laced around her question.

"Will she want me there? I mean – *he'll* be there." His tone *definitely* gave away how he felt about that.

The woman's face darkened. "Merri's mother just *died*. Merri took off her ring for you today – she made a commitment – and she *loves* you, that's as plain as the nose on my face. Yes, Michael will be there with Merri. Yes, you'll have to witness their interactions if you go there, and no, I don't know how she's going to handle that, but this is the part where you step out of the shit your ex left you in and man up, because *you* made a commitment to her too. What Merri *wants* right now is you, and what she *needs* is for you to be able to deal, and no, she didn't tell me this, but I know it. I know it because the only name you say at the altar when you're about to get married, is the name of the person you want to spend the rest of your life with."

That was a lot of lecturing. And a lot of info. His mind was still whirring with it. "Altar? What?"

Her eyebrows rose. "She didn't tell you?"

"She told me she said someone else's name at the altar."

Candy threw her arms up in the air. "God help me! *Your* name, Jamie."

He stood stock still, just staring at her; stunned.

"'I, Meredith, take thee, Jamie.' It was *your* name she said at the altar; it was *you* we spent a whole chunk of time discussing on her hen night – it's always been *you*. If you feel about her half as much as she feels about you, and you in fact *haven't* been on the rebound and leading her on this entire time, grow a fucking pair and take just a *little* more pain. Because the reward at the end of it? It'll be worth it. Some people don't *get* rewards at the end of their pain."

That stake in his heart went in deeper, but this time, it was Candy's words that did it. He looked her right in the eye. "I've *never* led her on."

"Then what are you still doing here? Go and be the man she needs, before someone else is."

His hand folded around Merri's address. "Thanks."

"Okay," she sighed, then made a sweeping action with her hands, "now get the bloody hell out of my house."

"Wait."

"What now?"

"The key to the boat." He took it off his keyring and dropped it into her hand. "I know you've got Pippa's one, but I won't be there tomorrow now."

"Thanks. I don't know if I'm gonna—"

"Please consider going. Pippa's ... she went to see David today. I don't think she's doing too good."

Candy went silent, another soft sigh slipping out of her. "I'll try. I'll make sure she gets the key, but I can't promise anything else."

He smiled, feeling a little calmer. About everything. "Thank you."

She nodded.

He left, and heard her shut the door behind him. He climbed into The Beast, reversed her out of the drive, then pulled over onto the side of the road.

After a telephone call to his dad to say he was borrowing the car overnight – which his dad wasn't best pleased about (he decided not to mention it might be for a few days) – he was on the road following the Sat Nav on his phone to London, making a mental list of all the things he'd have to buy on the way: toothbrush, toothpaste, socks, underwear, change of clothes, phone charger.

The bottom of the screen estimated the time of arrival

to be three in the morning: five hours. He would have to add an hour for shopping and petrol.

He'd leave a message on Pip's phone and explain everything when he got a proper chance to stop, but for now, he wanted to make some headway, because Candace was right with her rather intimidating pep-talk. And waiting simply felt wrong this time, when he could be there for her. Time could take a hike – it wasn't going to make the rules anymore.

# XVII
## *Acceptance*

It was one in the morning before her flight landed in Gatwick. Her phone was still in flight mode, and she couldn't quite deal with taking flight mode off and hearing or reading whatever messages Jamie might have left – it hurt too much.

And Michael was here.

She'd expected a chauffeur to be waiting for her at the gates – perhaps Lionel, or Antonio, both of whom she knew a little – but it was the man himself.

She noted how tired Michael looked – his golden-brown hair, unusually disarrayed; his stubble setting off the slight shadow under both eyes – and surmised that it couldn't be just from the news of her mum. He had said he'd flown in himself, earlier that day, hadn't he? She guessed he hadn't slept in over twenty-four hours.

"Merri," he greeted, with a small smile, and there was genuine warmth there.

Relief rushed through her and she was grateful for the warmth. It was honestly nice to see him, because there *was* an element of security between them and always had been.

"Hi," she replied, and then settled into his offered embrace, letting a little of the heartache wash out of her. The safety net of Michael was nice. It was not the crux of her life anymore, and he wasn't who she wanted to be holding her, but she would take it for the moment because her grief demanded it.

She was still mostly numb, memories of her mother sitting somewhere on the surface of her aura (and now she was even starting to sound like her) as the fact of her death kept hitting her afresh.

A firm kiss landed on her head. "I'm sorry, Merri."

"It's okay. Thanks for being here."

"What else could I do? Come on." He took her suitcase and handed it to the man standing next to him. Ah – so *that* was the chauffeur. She hadn't seen this one before. She smiled her hello to him and he nodded at her, "Ms. Goodwill."

Michael took her hand. She didn't resist. "If you need to sleep in the back of the car, you can. It's a limo."

"I don't think I'll be sleeping for a while."

"I understand."

They made their way through the crowds.

"I spoke to the hospital and made an appointment for tomorrow morning for you to go in and identify your mother's body – 10:30 a.m."

Her stomach churned at the thought.

"I'll be there with you."

That was a comfort, and she gave his hand a squeeze in thanks, but it wasn't him she wanted there.

"You'll have to sign some papers afterwards – it won't take long. I'll take care of anything you need me to."

They finally stopped in front of the limousine and the chauffeur, whose name she still didn't know, held open the door for her. She got in and sat down, and Michael got in the other side.

The click of the boot told her it was being opened. A

clunk told her when it had shut.

Mr Chauffeur arranged himself into the driver's side and the limo started to move.

Merri suddenly felt exhausted.

A hand fell gently on her knee and she looked up at Michael, next to her. His hazel eyes met hers and he smiled, but not before she caught him glancing at her ring finger – minus an engagement ring.

She placed her hand on top of his and laced her fingers through his. "I've got some things to tell you. We've got a lot to talk about."

His thumb stroked the side of hers. "I have things I need to say too. There's time." He leaned forward and gave her a kiss, on the forehead this time. "Everything's going to be all right."

A lump gathered in her throat and she blinked back tears. She leaned into his arm and rested her head there. Those words sounded good. It was what she needed to hear. Somehow, he knew, and he said them again. "Everything's going to be all right."

The peaceful silence of acceptance fell around them as the lights of London sped by either side of them. She ached for Jamie inside, but, right now, she was appreciative of the way Michael simply let her be. His distance allowed her room to breathe; his cool touch, not too intimate, allowed her to feel grounded. She knew she did the same for him. In one sense it was beautiful, and she felt sad for the impending loss of it, because she did need to let it go, but she could now see it wasn't enough. After being with Jamie, only he was enough. Only love – the big kind that engulfed her – was enough. It was true oxygen. It was what you got if you climbed high enough. The altitude made it harder to breathe, but also, easier. It was a paradox. *Love* was a paradox.

*"The thing is, Merri, with you ... everything that's supposed to be wrong, is right."*

She didn't know when she began to nod off – didn't think she could – but somewhere in her subconscious, she registered Michael's arm come up around her so she wouldn't fall forwards. She shifted in her seat and turned a little towards him so her head found the crease of his armpit through his shirt – that was *so* much more comfy... And when she finally drifted away, it was with dolphins in a sparkling, blue ocean, as they sped her home to Jamie; her mother's whisper on the breeze ... *"Be happy, Merri. Be very, very happy."*

~*~

Candy let herself in, not expecting anyone to be up at this hour.

Tim was up.

He looked as haggard as she felt, but also, as kind as always. He gave so much of himself away, she sometimes worried she'd turn up one day and there'd be nothing left of him.

"Hi," she said.

He stood and held his arms open for her.

She walked right into them, tears falling, unable to help the quiet sob that fell out of her.

"I couldn't sleep after talking with you on the phone," he said. "I wanted to be with you; selfishly hoped you'd turn up, but didn't want to pressure you to come over. I know how tiring it can be right now with Lauren at the stage she's at."

"I didn't want to be alone."

"You're not." His hand cupped the back of her neck and he tilted her head up. "You're not." He kissed her, and she melted into it.

He drew back a fraction. "I'm sorry you're going through this."

She wasn't sure if he meant Penny's death, Lauren's illness, or if he was apologising for his own distance from her. It hurt – his distance – so when his lips found hers again, she held onto every last touch of them; every last stroke of his tongue on the tip of hers.

God, this would be nice – to get lost in sensation and forget everything else for a while.

*Forget...*

She sighed into his mouth, and to her delight, he responded with a deeper kiss, his hand pressing harder against the small of her back.

"Tim," she whispered, an urgency to his name she hadn't intended to be there; then, her hands were cupping his face and he was drawing her to him.

*Oh ... it's been sooo long...*

He walked them backwards until the backs of his calves met the armchair. He went down, taking her with him, and she didn't waste a second in straddling him as best as she could in the confines of the cosy seat.

She moaned and ground herself into him, and then tried to push away the disappointment that rose when she couldn't feel his hardness. No hint of an erection at all.

Again.

"I'm sorry," he whispered.

She shook her head against his apology, still kissing him, their kiss all intensity. Her hand found his belt and pulled at it until the buckle came loose, and then she was doing the same to his button.

"Candy, stop."

She pressed her hand against his crotch.

Still nothing.

She could fix this.

She brought his zip down, rubbing his soft cock through his briefs.

"Candy..." He took hold of her hand and she almost screamed. "Please stop. I'm sorry." He kissed her shoulder along the strap of her sun dress; pulled it down and then nibbled across the top of her breast. "Just let me pleasure you. The rest doesn't matter."

The dynamics of their relationship had changed since Lauren had become ill, not that a multi-relationship was ever easy in the first place, but theirs hadn't been hard – not really.

Lauren was the one who had interviewed her and given her the job at the country life magazine she and Tim owned. She had liked Lauren straight away – her zany humour; her open, straightforward manner, without being harsh. Lauren didn't have a harsh bone in her body, but she could be firm, and Candy had felt at the interview she would be excellent to work for.

She hadn't met Tim until her first day there. The moment she'd laid eyes on him, almost five years ago now, there had been a mutual attraction between herself and Tim, and it had been the fiery kind that got you burnt.

But it had been Lauren she'd fallen in love with first.

She hadn't seen any of it coming. In fact, three months into the job, she had handed in her notice, because the heat between Tim and herself was palpable even though nothing had happened between them.

Lauren had been devastated, and when she'd queried her decision to leave, Candy had crumpled and confessed her feelings for her husband.

That was when, to her astonishment, Lauren had told her Tim felt the same way and that she didn't mind.

Dumbstruck, Candy had listened to her explain they were a polyamorous couple.

As well as her husband, whom she loved dearly, Lauren also had another boyfriend, Simon. However, he lived up in Bath, so they couldn't always see each other as much as they'd like.

An hour later, after one of the most intense conversations of her life, Candy had been given two weeks off work to decide how she wanted to proceed. She had been assured that her role was safe and that their relationship at the office would only ever remain professional, and that under no circumstances was she allowed to feel guilty for her feelings for Tim. It was as it was, and he would never impose his own feelings upon her or make her feel uncomfortable. She was also free to leave if she wished and they would be happy to keep her on until she found a job elsewhere.

The choice was left with her.

Candy had spent those two weeks re-evaluating everything she knew about herself. Her mind had been blown and her eyes opened to something she had never considered possible. 'Polyamorous' was not a term she had even known existed. Sure, it wasn't the norm, but her and 'the norm' hadn't always seen eye-to-eye anyway. And she'd never been a discriminatory person.

She had made the decision to stay.

Another three months had flown by and the atmosphere eased between all three of them. They worked well as a team and in Candy's heart she knew they'd become more than a team. Now that the barriers were down and openness was not only common sense, but appreciated, feelings blossomed within her for the both of them. Feelings she hadn't fully expected; that she'd had no idea what to do with; that were becoming harder and harder to ignore.

Of course, she knew they must have known, but they had said nothing and hadn't pushed.

Everything had changed one afternoon as they were closing up to leave work, and Candy had found Lauren crying in the staff room as Tim was running some design work to the printers, hoping to catch them on time.

Simon had left her.

She'd seen it coming, but it still hurt, and she hadn't told Tim yet, as he would also be hurt by the fact that she was. He'd also been fond of Simon, although had never pursued a physical relationship with him.

With Tim out of the office, Candy had automatically, instinctively, taken on the role of carer; hugging and comforting Lauren, affirming that Simon was mad for leaving – saying all the usual things one said to someone who'd been dumped – and even now, she couldn't say who kissed who first.

It was mutual, and needed.

Tim had returned in the middle of their make-out session, the both of them half-naked and lost in each other. He'd witnessed their passion in silent appreciation, and then his hand had found Candy's back while his lips had found the side of her neck, and it was no problem – no problem at all. Because the three of them fit.

For Candy, it was like walking into a three dimensional jigsaw puzzle, and finding the missing pieces were her exact measurements. When she stepped into it, she stepped home, and everything made sense – *everything*. All her awkwardness within past relationships made sense; how she never quite connected; how she never quite felt fulfilled even though all the stops were pulled out to make those relation-ships work.

She'd simply needed a different set-up; a different kind of dynamic based on her own perceptions of loving and giv-ing, and trust and honesty. A perception she'd always crushed because she'd thought it wasn't acceptable.

It was a fucking revelation.

The year that followed was, hands down, the best year of her life. She'd found herself, and she'd found it within a polyamorous threesome. Who'd have ever bloody thought it.

She'd moved in with Tim and Lauren five months after they'd 'officially' entered into a relationship, renting out her cottage, and that had worked too.

Seven months after that, Lauren had been diagnosed with breast cancer, and she'd been diagnosed late. It had been so unexpected. She had only been thirty-two.

Her age also meant that the cancer had spread like wild-fire.

Once again, everything had changed. Devastation didn't just happen to forests, nature, and villages caught up in the earth's fight for survival. It happened to the soul.

They had all been crushed, and no one more than Tim. Lauren was the spoke of their wheel – she was the one who kept them all together and 'together' was fast fading with her.

They'd tried to continue on as normal at first, but as her treatment started, it became harder with her long bouts of sickness and exhaustion. Perhaps the worst thing was seeing the flame of hope die from her eyes over the stretch of three years.

The more ill she became, the more Tim had pulled away from Candy, even though Lauren scolded him for it. And when he *was* there emotionally, he wasn't there physically.

His impotence was the least of their worries, but it was an extra dent in their breaking structure.

Moments like these, right now, on the armchair, were rare nowadays. His fingers inside her were not what she wanted – she wanted him whole, in heart and body, as she'd had him countless times before – but the intimacy he was giving her was akin to gold, so she took it.

He rewarded her with a small groan when she clenched around his digits, rocking against him as his tongue and teeth teased her bare nipples, her sun dress now bunched around her waist.

A surreptitious nudge with her knee told her he was still flaccid.

She, however, was reaching her peak.

"Ooooh," she moaned.

"Please," he softly uttered, against her breast, and she came on the breath of that word as it gently licked her skin.

It wasn't quite the wild chemistry they used to whip up, but it was something, and it brought tears to her eyes.

She held him to her as her orgasm eased. "Thank you," she whispered.

He found her lips for another kiss, which she gladly returned. "That was beautiful; you were beautiful. Be patient with me, Candy."

"Always," she replied. What else could she do? She loved them both. "How has she been today?"

"Tired – more than usual – and her breathing's been a bit laboured at times, but she has managed to eat more, and she's still doing things for herself, like washing and using the toilet."

"That's good."

"She's refused a higher dose of painkillers – again."

"Stubborn woman."

"Indeed. And she's been asking after you. She always asks after you."

"Merri's gone home now to take care of things there, so I can be here again, like I was before."

"Are you sure? It's not easy."

"You know I'd never have left if I didn't have guests."

"I know. Did you manage to tell her about us? I know you wanted to."

She shook her head. "The conversation was leading that way, and then she received the news about her mum... To be honest, I can't say for sure I wouldn't have chickened out. You know what my parents' reaction was. If I lost Merri..."

"She sounds more open-minded."

"She is, but she's going through her own shit right now."

"Well, there's no rush to tell her, is there?"

"No. It's just that," she cupped his face and rested her forehead against his, "when you're in love, you kinda want to shout it from the rooftops. We've been together for four years – the three of us. Not being able to tell anyone ... it's hard. It hurts."

"I know."

"And one day there'll be a funeral." Her voice broke. "I want to go to the funeral. Tim, I want to be there for Lauren and for you, no matter what anyone thinks."

"I know," he soothed. "You will be. God knows, I wouldn't survive it without you there. I won't let anyone keep you away, I promise."

She swallowed back her tears and got herself in check. "I think I'd like to go to bed now. I'm running on empty."

"Okay. Did you bring everything you need? If you need to use my toothbrush—"

"It's all right. I washed up for bed before I came over 'cause it was so late, and I didn't want to risk disturbing

Lauren."

"All right. Let's go."

She climbed off him, letting her dress fall to the floor as she pulled her sandals off.

He picked the dress up after her, folded it, and placed it on the back of the armchair – a lovely, instinctive gesture that implied how well they worked together. It was a tiny symbol of solidity in their crumbling framework.

She gave him a small smile, even though her heart ached with loss. She wondered if they'd survive after Lauren was no more, or if they'd lose each other too.

As quietly as possible, they entered the bedroom.

Lauren's breathing was heavy, and not quite regular. The scent of her cancer medication – just a tinge of it – hung in the air. Her body was full of it. It seeped out her pores and she breathed it out her lungs.

Candy pushed away the stark reality – too stark for the soft black of night – and quietly got into bed, slipping herself under the covers.

She cuddled up to Lauren, wanting to be close; not wanting to wake her, but sometimes her sleep was light – especially if she refused to take her sleeping pills. She stirred.

"It's okay," whispered Candy, "it's only me." She dropped a kiss on her shoulder, and then settled her head on the edge of her pillow and wrapped an arm around her waist.

"Candy?" she croaked.

"Yes, I'm here."

Lauren let out a long, relieved sigh, and it was worth it – that sigh of love and gratitude was worth everything it took to be here.

"I'm not going anywhere. Now sleep."

Lauren clasped her own hand around Candy's, at her waist.

The mattress depressed and Tim slid up against Candy, hugging her to him in the same fashion.

When life kept chucking you bad stuff, you took every moment of good that came your way. This was one of those moments.

Nestled in the warmth of the two people she loved, knowing it wouldn't last long, Candy closed her eyes, focused on how strong Penny had always been – found her strength in that – said a prayer for her as she shed a tear for her passing, and then she let sleep take her.

# XVIII

## Promises

Her chauffeur's name was Blair.

She knew, because Michael had called him Blair as he'd asked him to wait for further instructions downstairs in the car.

"Thank you, Blair," Merri had said with a smile as he'd placed her suitcase down by her front door.

"Happy to help, Ms Goodwill," he nodded, and then he went and followed his orders.

"I'll take this from here," said Michael, picking up her suitcase, and she sort of missed climbing her own mountains in that second.

*I don't mind carrying my own stuff, you know.* But instead she replied with a "thanks" as she unlocked her door. He was only trying to help; to make things easier for her. She didn't need to get tetchy just because she was tired. "Come on in."

She flicked on the lights as she entered, shut the door behind them, and kicked off her shoes, not bothering with where they landed.

Michael stared at her with curiosity, then shook his head and asked, "Where would you like the suitcase?"

"Oh, anywhere is fine. Just drop it where you are."

He did, still staring at her. "You're different," he stated, softly.

*I am?* Her heart skipped a beat – guilt was the culprit.

An awkward silence ensued. "Would you like a drink?" she asked, as if he didn't know his own way around the flat he'd stayed in so often, for days and weeks at a time.

"Oh, no. I'm fine, thanks."

"Okay. Um ... about tomorrow..."

"Yes. There'll be a car outside for you at nine forty-five to take you to the hospital. I was going to meet you there at ten-thirty, but I might be five minutes late depending on my schedule. I've got a—"

"Actually, I was wondering if you'd mind me doing this on my own."

He looked at her, taken aback.

"Not that I don't appreciate everything you've done," she added quickly, "and the car tomorrow morning would be fabulous – I just meant the part where I see my mum. I don't know how I'll be with it and I think it might be easier on my own; to have that space to process ... things..." She trailed off, unsure of what Michael was thinking.

"What about your panic attacks?"

It was her turn to look surprised. She hadn't actually thought about her anxiety for ... almost twenty-four hours?

She had no explanation. She didn't know if there *was* one. Could anxiety disappear as suddenly as it had appeared in the first place? Could a decade of panic attacks just ... not happen one day? "They seem to have faded ... not sure how or why. It might be just a temporary lapse, but I'm going to be fine. I know I am."

"Maybe it's the shock."

"Maybe..." *No, it's being with Jamie. It's about not being scared to live big anymore...* "Um ... I have to give this back to you." She went for the wallet in her handbag, opened it and fished out her engagement ring.

Christ, this seemed a little tactless, but she didn't quite know how else to do it. When was a good time to break up with someone? Was there a good way to do it?

He tentatively took the ring from her, stared at it for a beat, and then shocked the hell out of her with what he said next. "Tell me about Jamie."

"What?" Her eyes were going to pop out of her head. "Jamie?"

"Yes." He made his way to her sofa and gestured for her to follow him. There was no anger in his features at all, just interest.

After a moment of hesitation, she sat down next to him.

"Jamie was the name you called me at the altar, wasn't it? And you were right on the phone – I didn't let you explain. I didn't let you apologise; I just blocked you out and I'm sorry. I was dealing with my own ... revelations ... over what had happened."

Oh, wow... This wasn't a conversation she could avoid forever. She took in a breath, wondering where she should start. There was nothing for it – he deserved the truth. *Well ... here goes...*

"Jamie was a boy I met when I was sixteen – I met him the day after my sixteenth birthday, actually. I fell for him instantly and he fell for me, and ... we were each other's first. I left the next day to come and live in London and I never saw him again, until," she glanced up to catch his expression, which gave nothing away, but he was definitely listening, "we bumped into each other on Sunday. This Sunday, just gone."

His eyebrows rose so damn high he almost looked like a caricature of himself.

*Great. Gotta love that look of disbelief.* "I know it

sounds completely unbelievable, but that's exactly what happened, I promise. Turned out that he'd been living in Australia for ten years or so, and had just flown back home on Friday. We bumped into each other, and..." *he kissed me...* "we got on like no time had passed at all."

There was a pause while Michael contemplated what she'd said. "Do you still have feelings for him?"

She gulped. "Yes."

"Is that the reason this ring is not on your finger?"

She looked down. "Yes. I'm sorry."

"Don't be sorry for the truth. A harsh truth is less damaging than a tender lie, and the worst lies are the ones we tell ourselves."

She raised her head. This was *not* the response she'd been expecting.

"Your mother always stood by her harsh truths. It was something I admired about her."

She welled up.

"I'm sorry I didn't try harder to get along with her."

One tear broke the barrier of her eyelid and slid down her cheek. She didn't bother to wipe it away. Instead, it fell onto her jeans, spreading into a fuzzy-looking, dark spot.

"I did a lot of thinking after Saturday. One of the things that hit me – like an avalanche, really – was that I've never wanted to take you down my road, into a world where you wouldn't be loved in the way you really need to be. My parents pushed me and I went with it, and that's an old, fucking habit I need to break. I don't love you, Merri," his voice grew tight, "and I'm terribly sorry about that, because I feel very deeply for you, and I consider you a true friend, and I mean a *true* friend. I know that if I told you my secrets, you'd guard them as tightly as you guard your own – and I know you do have secrets – yet, I still never told you any of them. I was prepared to marry you; to drag you into my life with all its baggage and have you go in blindly, while I divulged nothing. That wasn't fair of me."

"Wait. I ... I wanted safety. And distance. Distance from my own emotions and past hurts, and you provided me with that. This isn't all on you. I ... don't think I ever really loved you either. And that's really hard for me to say – harder than I thought it would be – but I walked into this relationship with my own motives. So, I'm sorry too."

He glanced up at her, his gaze steady. "What a pair we are." And then he smiled. It was big and at ease, and she'd never once seen it on him before. She saw the boy in him right then, untouched by the cruelties of knowledge, and it was startling.

He cleared his throat. "I'm not going to go into all the hellish details, but I was sexually abused by my aunt when I was ten. It carried on for six years until she was found out. Needless to say, it messed me up no end. It also messed up my family. The aunt in question was my mother's sister, and my mother, out of all my family, probably pushes me the hardest – into work, into achievement, into success... They push me so I will forget, but also, so they will forget. So they can paint over that inconvenient part of my life and tell themselves it's all okay because I turned out all right in the end. Of course, I've never forgotten. No one has."

*Holy fuck! Talk about a bombshell!*

"You deserve to know the reasons why I've always found intimacy hard; why you may have found our sexual relationship difficult at times. You deserve to know it was not about you; that it had nothing to do with you, and I'm sorry I never explained that to you before."

Suddenly, she felt vulnerable. Painfully vulnerable, and she knew exactly why: a part of her *had* thought it was about her, and worse, had thought she'd deserved it. It was a jarring clarity: she had stayed, partly because she thought she *deserved* it. God...

"I..." Where were the words? *Please help me find the words...* "When I was nineteen—"

"Don't." He put a finger to her lips. "Don't tell me *your* deepest, darkest secrets. Don't waste them on me. Tell the one you love."

"But you just told me yours."

"Because I'm never going to love anyone, Merri."

She didn't know what she must have looked like on hearing that statement, but he smiled sadly, leaned in slightly, and stroked her bottom lip before pulling back. "I'm not capable of love, not in that way."

"How can you say that? You don't really believe that."

"Oh, I do. There were a couple of girls in my late teen-age years ... I thought maybe I could love them. They liked me; I got to know them... In both instances, we clicked, and it always went well until it became physical. That's when all I saw was my aunt, even when I was with them, and any love I might have felt stopped right there – turned to repulsion. It's hard to explain, and no one should hear such stories anyway. I dare say you were the closest to love I ever got. And unlike me, you *are* capable of love, Merri. Show your scars to the one who can heal them, when you find him, if you haven't already."

*Poor boy,* she thought. *Poor ten-year-old boy. That was Liam's age, wasn't it?* Dear god, that thought made her want to hurl – it was vile. What had happened to Michael was vile and she was sure she hadn't heard the half of it. "I wish I could heal your scars."

She remembered their love-making that time, when she'd touched the marks on the backs of his thighs – how he'd reacted. It all sort of made sense now. A really dark sense. Part of her wanted to ask about those marks, but another part of her knew he was right: she *wasn't* the one to heal them, because Michael was now her past, and Jamie was her future.

"I wish I could heal yours too," he said, sincerely. He took one of her hands, opened it, placed her engagement ring in her palm and then closed it around the diamond-tipped gold. "Happy birthday, Merri. Keep it. There'll never be another fiancée for me. It's yours. Do what you want with it: bury it, lock it up, wear it, sell it for money – I don't mind."

It was funny how that ring meant more, now, in this second, than it had when he'd slipped it on her finger. "I'll remember you. That's what I'll do with it."

"Then, I'm honoured."

"It might be asking too much, but ... do you think we could still be friends? Maybe further down the line, in a year or two?"

His eyes crinkled at the corners. "You don't have a choice, I'm afraid. I'm going to be checking in on you regularly until the funeral, and then afterwards."

She laughed. "Thank you, and I mean for everything. And I'm sorry I messed up in front of your family and said the wrong name at the altar."

"Don't be." He sighed, leaning right back into the sofa and putting his feet up on the coffee table in front of it. "They need to get used to the mess. They need to see the mess for once. You didn't say the wrong name at the altar, Merri – you said the right one."

~*~

*I left because I wasn't ready, and I wish you knew how sorry I am for all the hurt it caused you. I should have known better, but we never really grow up, Merri. We're always learning; thinking the newest lesson has sped us to maturity, and then we feel foolish when the next lesson strips away all we knew before... You're never ready for love, and, yet, you always are. That was what I never learnt. I never felt ready for you – for how much I loved you – and it was only with hindsight that I could see I was ready, by the mere fact that you existed. Love finds you, not the other way around, and you can't run from it. I ran. Make sure you never do.*

It was almost exactly the same.

There was a little bit more than what he'd said to her in the dream – stuff about not sending her birthday and Christmas cards; how he had always been on the move with his next project – but the bulk of it was word-for-word.

Merri put her father's letter down on the floor next to her, along with the photos. She was sure she should be surprised, perhaps shocked, that she'd had a premonition of sorts through her dream. But she wasn't – she was her mother's daughter after all.

With a half-sad smile, she brought her glass of Baileys to her lips and took a sip, which was naughty, because it was nearly four in the morning, and she'd already brushed her teeth, and was sitting here by the sofa in her sleepwear ... but she hadn't been able to sleep. Perhaps the little nap in the limo had done her over for the night.

Michael had left almost two hours ago after offering to stay on the couch, which she had declined.

She grabbed her pen and journal from on top of the coffee table, the book still open, and carried on where she had left off a little earlier.

*Do I dare say that my mother was right? Magic does exist. But it's not in the ether, and it's not some intangible thing we can't see or sense. It's the extraordinary hidden in the ordinary, playing out before us often, but only in small amounts, so that we're tricked into missing it when it happens.*

*But sometimes, if we're lucky – or perhaps luck doesn't have much to do with it – it grabs us and shakes us so we can't miss it, even if we want to.*

*Then, things get hard, because once you know magic exists, you have to decide whether to be the bystander, or the magician ... and we were all born to be magicians.*

She paused, thinking about what she'd just written: *we were all born to be magicians.* Words her mother would be proud of, she thought, but the words themselves didn't have to mean anything abstruse, they could apply to anyone's life – Michael's, Candy's, Pippa's, hers... She didn't want to watch her life play out before her, she wanted to direct it.

*And what would you direct into it right this second?*

Oh, that one was easy.

"Jamie," she whispered.

Her intercom buzzed.

She looked around her startled, not sure why she thought answers would appear out of thin air.

*No ... not a chance.*

The buzzer sounded again.

Goosebumps raced over her skin. His name left her lips once more, and then she just knew.

Just. Knew.

She jumped up, ran to the intercom and pressed the buzzer without saying a word. Speaking to him would be great, but she wanted to see him now; sooner than now – yesterday.

She unlocked her front door, yanked it open, and then raced down the stairs.

She swore she smelled him before she saw him; that crisp freshness of ocean and beaches, combined with his own scent – the one she'd always known and had never forgotten.

"Merri?" she heard him call out, unsure.

She was making a small racket going down the stairs, but she was still out of sight ... one more flight ...

"Merri, please don't be mad, but I had to come."

She couldn't reply. It would take up valuable milliseconds.

"Merri?"

*One more corner...*

The sleeve of a jacket ... the edge of a rucksack ... the side of a face ... *him*.

His eyes met hers, relief fell over his countenance, and he didn't get a chance to say or do much else.

She catapulted into his arms as he dropped his bag and swung her legs around his waist. Her hands sank into his hair; his grasped her backside, and her lips locked onto his. "You came back," she murmured into them. "You came back."

"Of course I bloody did. I always will."

"No. You'll never have to again." Because she was never leaving him again. "That's a promise."

# XIX
## *Fixed*

It was six a.m. The kids weren't up yet.

At some ridiculous time in the early hours of the morning, she had received both a message from Jamie explaining why he and Merri weren't coming along on the boat trip today, and a text from Candy saying she'd be at the harbour at nine and that she had both keys.

Okay. Fine.

She hoped that meant Candy was also coming along for the ride. She didn't feel like she wanted it to be just her and the kids today. She was fraying, she knew that, and didn't quite know how to fix it. That was a first for her – she was normally the fixer; it's what she did.

So, she was all out of options, and that's what she told herself as she lit the small tealight against the rising sun, already too bright.

*You are not seriously going to do this,* snarked the voice in her head.

*Out of options!!!* she screamed back.

Like it was going to work anyway. Like she had a clue what she was doing. Was this ceremonial enough? Was she supposed to wear special clothes, or something?

Whatever.

She put down the extinguished match and then brought forward the piece of paper she'd borrowed—

*Stolen*—

She scowled... *Borrowed* from Candy's house.

*Once times thrice, unbind thine heart*
*from mine, so we may finally part.*

God, she was trembling. This felt like murder or something. If this actually worked, and David and her ended, would it be like she'd killed him?

Vomit surged up her throat. She swallowed it back down with a grimace.

*You don't want to do this.*

No, she didn't.

Her eyes filled with tears. She really *didn't* want to do this, but if the kids ever witnessed what she'd seen yesterday – if he ever did that to them...

A sob threatened to break through.

*Hold it together, for god's sake.*

And she was tired. No, she wasn't just tired. Even exhaustion wasn't strong enough for the bone-deep fatigue she carried.

Doing this 'spell' was stupid. It wasn't that she didn't believe spells could work if done by the right person – like a witch, or Wiccan, or something (was there a difference?) – but she just wasn't that *into* spells, and she was pretty sure she *wasn't* the right person.

*Just walk away from him, Pip. You don't need a spell to do that. Just let him go.*

Except she couldn't do that either. She was nowhere near being able to do that.

She took a deep breath, her tears now free-flowing, and began. "Once times thrice..." her voice sounded really weird, like hearing herself recorded ... "unbind thine heart..." she almost choked ... "from mine, so we may finally..."

*Fuck...*

"...so we may finally..."

"Mummy?"

Shit!

"Becca?" She spun around, hiding the spell behind her back. "What are you doing here?"

"I woke up," shrugged her daughter.

Of course. A four-year-old's answer.

Becca frowned. "Mummy, are you crying?" and then, "What's that smell?"

"Smell?"

Burning.

*Burning!*

"Oh, god!" she shouted, then turned to find the paper alight from where she must have unknowingly – *stupidly* – held it over the flame of the tealight.

*Water!*

Nope. No water in here.

She spied the large pot plant outside the window. That was going to have to do.

Rushing over to it, with Becca at her heels going on about calling the fire brigade, she slid up the window, reached out and rammed the paper into the cool, damp soil of the plant, flames down, smothering them as best as she could.

She hissed when her index finger got slightly burnt as she pressed it all under the soil, and then pulled a face when she noticed that one of the leaves had gotten a little singed.

David had liked this plant.

"Mummy, is it 999?"

"Yes – I mean, no! No – you don't have to call emergency services okay? We don't need a fire engine, it's all right, I've fixed it."

Becca cheered. "Well done, Mummy! You fix everything."

That cruel voice in her head burst out laughing.

With a sigh, she pulled the paper out of the soil, some of it crumbling away into ashes. Pretty much the whole note Merri had written at the bottom was gone, as was a small corner of the spell itself.

Wonderful.

So much for giving this back.

A loud wail sounded from Sammy's room, making Pippa jump. Her heart sank. *Not another nightmare.*

A small, but strong gust of wind whipped the spell from her hand. "Hey!" she yelled to no one.

Candy was going to be mad.

She went to make a grab for it, but Sammy let out another scream, and that's where her feet led her – to her son – Becca right on her heels, as always.

She was just going to have to grovel to Candy and Merri. The whole thing had been a stupid idea anyway.

"Sammy," she said, running into his room. She forced herself to calm down so she wouldn't frighten him further. "Sammy..." She took his shaking body into her arms and whispered soothing words. "Mummy's here ... everything's fine, darling. Everything's fine."

Becca perched on the bed next to Sammy and laid her little hand on his back as Pippa rocked him back and forth.

"Everything's fine."

If she said it enough times, maybe she'd start believing it herself.

~*~

The alarm on Merri's phone sounded.

Seven o'clock.

Not that they'd slept.

She reached across Jamie to turn it off.

He stroked her naked torso, and the soft skin on the underside of her breasts.

She smiled as she felt his erection stir against her hip. "You have a lot of energy."

"You have a lot of boob."

She laughed. "These things? They're tiny."

"They're not tiny – they're perfect."

"Glad you think so."

They had talked about the plan this morning. She still wanted to see her mum on her own. She knew it would be hard, but having Jamie to come home to would make it a hundred times easier. She glanced at his face and caught his eye. "I'm glad you're here."

He smiled, softly, and ran his hand up her back to cup her neck. "That makes two of us. I know this might sound wrong after everything that's happened, but," he ran his thumb down her jawline, gazing at her openly, with every feeling he'd never hid from her, "Happy birthday, Merri."

Still smiling, she lay her head on his chest, enjoying the sound of his heartbeat. "Thanks. I want it to be a good day – it will be 'cause you're here. Are you going to be okay while I'm at the hospital?"

"Have you got a PC I can use?"

"I've got a laptop."

"That'll work. I thought I might do a search for jobs in my field, in the UK, just to see what's out there."

"But you miss Australia."

"I'd miss you more."

"I'd consider going there with you."

"Let's wait and see – no rush. We've got a couple of months to decide, but wherever we go, we go together."

"Agreed." She kissed him in the centre of his chest.

He lazily drew circles on her lower back, his eyes closed, his face dreamy and full of the future. "I want a life with you; I want a family with you … I want everything with you."

That earned him another kiss, his words, alone, pumping the blood through her heart – or they might as well have.

But a shadow fell at the word 'family', although the shadow was not as daunting as it would have been just a week ago. Was now the right time to say what she needed to?

The sun streaked through her bedroom window. Maybe it could burn away the darkness if she let it all spill out.

She decided on yes. She wanted a clean slate, especially with him, and she wanted to come back to him, after seeing her mum, knowing they could begin properly.

"Jamie?" She slid her body further up his until she was level with his eyes.

"Mmmm?" he asked, those eyes still closed.

Her entire future hammered in her chest as her past slipped out. "I was pregnant."

His lids flew open. His gaze settled on hers, looking both startled and confused.

"No," she answered, seeing the question forming in his mind. "Not from that time – not yours." Her fingers pressed into his pectoral muscle. *Please let this be okay...* "I was nineteen. It was during the peak of my time using drugs. E was my favourite – Ecstasy. It took me to places I couldn't reach; these amazing highs, but it also took parts of my memory, like when you've drunk too much and you can't remember anything the next day... Anyway..." She paused.

His jaw clenched, but he remained silent, waiting for her to explain. He brought a finger up and stroked down the length of her nose – his way of saying it was all right.

She let out a long breath. "One night, I was at my friend, Alison's house. I say friend, but none of them were really friends, just part of the crowd. She was having a party because her parents were away. I knew half the people there, and half of them, I'd never seen before. I was looking for a fix. I'd been on smokes all day and they made me nice and spacey, but I never got that euphoria from them and I wanted it. I knew Alison kept a stash of E somewhere in her bedroom, so I sneaked up there and searched for them; finally found them under her mattress. Usually, I'd take half a tablet, but I was feeling ... I dunno. I dunno what I was feeling. I took a whole one. It was stupid, taking from someone else's stash when you don't know where they've come from, but around that time, I was sinking fast, spiralling, and that joy that I could get from a pill – I couldn't find that anywhere else.

"I sat on the floor in the bedroom and waited for it to kick in. I didn't want to go downstairs to all the noise – just wanted to be on my own for a bit.

"After about ten minutes, these three guys walk into the room."

Jamie tensed.

She couldn't help but tense with him, but she closed her eyes and forced herself to stay calm, so she could finish the story. Half of her didn't want to; another part of her needed to purge it all.

"They were looking for some place private to cut coke. I thought they were going to ask me to leave, but they sat down there with me and started cutting in front of me, and chatting – meaningless stuff that I don't remember, but I remember they were chilled out, and all right to hang around, and then ... they offered me a line. I refused 'cause I hated mixing drugs – I never got the full effect from each one when I mixed – but they kept pushing, and wheedling, and then they dared me... I was so god-damned stupid.

"I did it. I snorted a line – just one, and they laughed; I laughed with them, and then..."

She had to swallow hard.

Jamie's warm hand rubbed her back; anchored her.

"And then, it was morning, and I was waking up in Alison's bed with all three of them next to me. We were all naked, and I didn't remember a thing. I don't know how we got there. I don't remember touching them, or kissing them ... but I could feel..."

She was shaking.

Both arms came up around her.

"I could feel what had happened – inside me. I didn't know ... I didn't know if I had wanted it, or if they ... if they'd forced me...

"I thought I was going to throw up, but I didn't. They were still sleeping – totally out of it – so I sneaked out of the bed, found my clothes and left, and I shut it all out, because that's what I always did. I just shut it out. I never told Alison, and I never saw them again.

"That was the first time I'd had sex since you."

She heard him suck in a breath.

"I ruined it – that perfect night we had."

"Merri," he whispered, but she wasn't listening – couldn't stop now, she was almost there...

"I'd start to wake up after that, at night, as if I'd had a nightmare, but I could never fully remember what it was. And it brought me back to what had happened, which would make me feel sick. The only thing that calmed me down was remembering you and our night together. That was so special; it was so ... *special*." Something tickled her chin and she realised she was crying. The teardrop fell from her chin and onto Jamie's chest. "I didn't know I was pregnant until I'd had a miscarriage two months later. There was all this blood – I was so scared – but that's not the worst bit. That's not the worst bit."

He kissed the next falling tear.

"I didn't stop," she choked out. "I killed a baby, and I didn't stop taking drugs. I used to pretend I was a mother when I was five years old; I had this rag doll I carried around and I took it everywhere, and fed it and put it to sleep, and when I was little it was all I wanted – to be a Mum – and I killed a baby, and I didn't stop." She was in floods now, words pouring out. "I only stopped when I found my mum, almost dead. It was like something snapped and fell away, and for one tiny second I saw the light. I saw how I was fucking everything up, and I saw what I could grab to pull myself out – last chance, 'cause I'd used up all my others – and I took it, and it was So. Fucking. Hard."

And she was gone.

That was it. That was everything.

She spent the next however long crying, Jamie cradling her in silence.

At some point, he turned them on their sides, and brought her into him, and there they lay until she was all dried up.

With the calm, came unforgiving awareness. She wasn't sure she could look at him. "Do you hate me?"

She'd spoken too quietly, but she couldn't say it any louder, and she couldn't repeat it 'cause she wasn't even sure she could handle his answer – she'd hated herself. If he felt about her, the same as what she'd felt about herself, for years... It didn't bear thinking about.

She had started to forgive herself exactly seventeen hours ago, when their making love had sealed some invisible divide. She couldn't put it into words, but she knew it to be true. But now that he knew ... if *he* couldn't forgive her...

He turned her towards him and it took everything she had to meet his eyes. The sun shone across them, turning them almost bronze, just like that morning she'd said good-bye to him against his scooter. She saw herself reflected in them.

When he finally spoke, his words were more powerful than anything she'd ever uttered.

"I love you more."

~ * ~

Death had a certain peace about it.

Her mother's skin was smooth – flawless. If she was feeling whimsical, she would say it even looked like she might have a small smile on her face.

But she couldn't feel whimsical with the staff in the room with her.

"Yes, that's her."

And that's all she needed to say.

The sheet went back over, and she was led out of the room and given papers to sign and a ton of information about death certificates, coroner's reports, funerals and what-not, that she'd already decided she wouldn't be reading through today.

After it had all been done, she stopped at the hospital chapel before making her way home. No one else was in there.

She walked to the front where the candles were displayed, found some matches, and lit a new one.

"For you, Mum. Thank you, for loving every single thing about me."

She stared at the warm, orange flame, taking in its gentle sway, and then turned to leave. Halfway up the aisle, she turned back. "Oh, by the way. I *am* going to be happy. I'm going to be very, *very* happy."

Every lit candle flickered, even though there was no breeze in the room.

Merri smiled, everything shimmering as she welled up. She said goodbye, and walked out.

She knew grief wouldn't just disappear with goodbye. It was so fresh, she knew she was still partly numb to it; that she was just going through the motions... She knew the next few months were going to be hard. But her life was waiting to begin.

She was ready to start living it.

# Epilogue

Jimmy dumped the rubbish sacks in the big bins outside. He could do with clearing this up a bit. The back alleyway of the shop always looked a little bit like an apocalypse had hit it.

*I'll just add that to my list of one hundred things I need to do tomorrow. And people think I've got no responsibilities. Ha.*

He picked up cans, leaves and random bits of newspaper, and other paper – all sorts of fucking paper – that had blown in from elsewhere and chucked them in the bins too. All except for one, which caught his eye. It had been burnt.

How weird.

But that wasn't as weird as the weird shit written on it – from what he could make out, anyway, 'cause some of it had been burnt off.

Absent-mindedly, he wandered back into the shop, trying to make head or tail of what exactly he was reading. He hated unsolved puzzles. If he came across a puzzle of any kind, he had to fix it, and this was a puzzle.

He went straight for the pen pot, uncapped a biro and hesitated for a second, wondering if he should ruin the strange perfection of his scorched find. He'd already completed the puzzle in his mind ... that missing word that had been turned to ashes. He didn't know what it was originally, but he was pleased with his alternative. It had an element of hope about it. Just for the hell of it, and because no custom-ers were present right this second, he read his find back to himself out loud.

"Once times thrice, unbind thine heart from mine, so we may finally..."

He brought his pen to the paper and filled in the blank.

## START

If you loved this story, you'll be pleased to know that book two, *Summer's End*, is available to purchase. As the breeze picks up, Pippa and Jimmy find themselves fighting a surprising and growing attraction towards each other. Struggling with sorrow and loss, Pippa may be required to take a leap of faith for a future worth having.

Available as an eBook and in paperback
from all good book retailers.

Please enjoy the opening chapter overleaf.

# SUMMER'S END

## *Prologue*

*H*er hands shook; the candle flickered. "Once times thrice..."

The shadows on the walls moved like ghosts.

But why was it dark? Wasn't it supposed to be morning?

"...unbind thine heart..."

Wind whistled through the open window. Distracted by a loose wisp of hair covering her eyes, she shook her head to be rid of it, then found herself looking around her, at her bedroom – their bedroom – at the bed.

There she lay, asleep.

Oh. This was a dream – she was dreaming. Why?

She looked back down at the piece of paper in her hands. Because you never finished the spell.

The stupid spell. That's right – she'd lost it. This was her second chance to get it right.

"...from mine, so we may finally—" The wind blew out the candle, plunging her into darkness. "No."

It wasn't pitch black – she could make out some shapes. She looked down at the paper. Despite the faint light, she couldn't decipher the last word. What was it? What was it?

"It's okay, you can say it."

She jumped, startled, and turned towards the voice – the one that came from her bed. It was no longer she who lay on it, but a man that sat upon it, his silhouette enti-

*cingly familiar; his voice she knew too well.*

*She took a step to the left to try and see him better. "David?"*

*"You can say it, Pip."*

*"Say what?"*

*"The last word."*

*"No. I can't." Even from here, in this light, she could see the blood covering his head; staining his shirt.*

*"Why not?"*

*"You're not dead."*

*"I'm not living."*

*"You're alive."*

*"But not living."*

*"Stop saying that."*

*"It's true."*

*She shook her head in denial.*

*"Don't you remember?"*

*"Remember what?"*

*"This." He held up a small, red envelope.*

*She shook her head again, this time in confusion. "What is that?"*

*He smiled a sad smile. "You didn't want me to write it, but I had to."*

*"What are you talking about?"*

*"The tree."*

*The tree ... Oh – that tree. Their tree. "You went back to the tree?"*

*"I felt it was important. They were things I wanted to say. I want you to open the envelope. But first, you have to say the last word."*

*She shook her head, vigorously; stubbornly. "I don't want to."*

*The window was flung fully open, and wind rushed*

around the room. She let out a cry as everything went flying, the spell torn right out of her hand. Again. "No!"

She might not be ready to say it, but neither was she ready to give it up. Had she blown her second chance? She wasn't sure she'd get a third. "Stop!"

The paper flew right out the window, just as it had before, but this time, she chased it – swung her leg out of the window, paying no mind to the drop as she landed on her front lawn, expecting to feel pain shooting through her ankles; feeling nothing instead, such was the way of dreams.

The wind took the paper speeding through the air. She ran after it, not really knowing where she was going. All the streets looked strange, and they shouldn't because this was her home – this was where she'd grown up. But nothing looked like home.

She sprinted like a deer escaping the lion's claws; or perhaps she was the hunter running down her only meal. She ran so fast, she almost didn't stop in time, and yelled in alarm when the road ended right in front of her – gave way to a cavernous drop of which she could see no bottom, only unending darkness.

The wind teased the paper above her, directly over the massive hole, far too high for her to reach; then, the wind became a breeze, dropping the spell – her only way out – onto the other side of the ominous canyon. With a soft rustle, it tumbled along the ground, rolling even further away, down two monstrously high walls that formed an alleyway, until she could no longer see it.

Her face threatening to crumple, she swallowed back tears.

"What are you going to do now?"

She turned around, and there David was, still bloody and pale, but standing now, his hands in his pockets as he looked beyond the rip in the road to where the paper had disappeared.

"I don't know." A drop of blood fell from his head to the cement under their feet, in time with her first drop of tears. "David, you're hurt."

He stared at her, strangely. "I'm okay."

"You're not okay. You're bleeding. Let me clean you up."

"You can't. This is as good as I get now. But you can get better." He pointed at her chest.

She looked down, shocked to see blood staining her own top, spreading outwards from the centre of her breast. Every time her heart beat, more blood pooled, and the stain got bigger. "I ... I don't know how to fix it."

"It certainly is a puzzle." He turned back to the broken road. "But sometimes to find the answer, you have to take a leap of faith."

Her eyes widened, not sure if he was insinuating what she thought he was.

"You need to jump."

Fear clawed at her. "I can't jump that. That's huge. I'll never make it."

"That's why it's a leap of faith."

"No. It's suicide. That gap's got to be at least twelve feet wide."

"But they made it across." He now pointed to the other side of the canyon.

She strained to see as far as she could down that dark alleyway that looked like it swallowed all living things. She heard the sounds before she saw the glimmer of light: laughter.

Children laughing.

The glimmer of light grew, until the alleyway looked a little less foreboding, and she could now see the source of

the light was the sun, shining on a patch of grass. Three figures bound gleefully around in it, playing.

Her breath caught. "Becca ... Liam..."

"And Sammy. There they are."

"Why aren't they in bed?"

"Because it's morning, Pip."

She turned back to him, confused.

"You're just standing in the dark."

Something cold landed on her nose. She looked up.
"Snow."

"And you're standing in the cold."

It was cold, and getting colder with every snowflake
that fell. She wrapped her arms around herself. She was
wearing summer clothes. "Come with me. Jump with me."

He smiled, eyes glistening with tears. "I have to stay
here."

She broke, a sudden sob escaping her. "I can't do it
alone."

"You won't be alone. As long as you take that leap."

She looked back at her kids – her world – they were her
world now. And they needed her. She had to try for them.

Shaking uncontrollably – or perhaps the shivering had
set in from the cold snow, now falling thick and fast – she
stepped back, and back again, taking step after step until
she was sure she had a long enough run for the jump. Never
gonna make it...

"You're going to make it," David said. "I love you." His
voice cracked. "You're going to make it because I love you."

"I love you, too."

A gun fired.

The starting pistol! RUN.

Oh, god... Quick! She wasn't prepared for this sudden
urgency that dominated everything. With the blood on her

*shirt blooming with the pounding of her heart, and snow swirling up a blizzard, she took off against it all, the soles of her bare feet burning as they hammered against the cement of the road. She ran faster than she ever had before, because she had to make it. Had to make it for her kids.*

*The edge was there before she knew it, and ready or not, she took the leap, felt her feet leave the safety of everything she'd known, no matter how unfamiliar it all seemed now. Only in mid-air did it occur to her she might actually live. She might actually make it, though it was too soon to tell. The edge was so far away.*

*She threw her weight forward; pushed air with her feet. She could see the landing, but ... God, no! She wasn't near enough!*

*A scream pierced the air.*

*It was Sammy, staring up at her.*

No! They aren't supposed to see this! They aren't supposed to see me fail!

*He opened his mouth, and screamed again.*


Pippa woke up, heart thudding, sweating, eyes wide open, trying to grasp at what was happening.

Screaming...

"Sammy." She leapt out of bed, opened her door, and half-ran to his room, almost stumbling – she felt so disorientated.

He was having another nightmare. It was the same most mornings – they always seemed to wake him at about six-thirty.

She rushed into his room, a disturbing sense of her own bad dream pressing on the edges of her consciousness, but anything she might have remembered was obliterated by her son's need. "Sammy..."

He was tucked into a ball under his covers, eyes still closed, crying.

"Sammy, wake up. Mummy's here." She gathered him into her arms, and held him against her as he came out of his terror.

Finally awake, he flung his arms around her, and buried his head into her neck, shaking and sobbing.

"I've got you. You're okay. Everything's okay."

*You're going to make it.*

She frowned, trying to get at the abstract memory as she pressed Sammy closer to her. Had David been in her dream? She couldn't recall, and it frustrated her more than she'd like. What she remembered most now, was that last day they'd shared. It haunted her persistently. He'd been in the garden, laying down the new patio just a few hours before the accident. It had begun to snow. She'd told him he was mad for laying it now – wait 'til the spring, or summer. He'd replied, if it didn't get done now, it would never get done at all.

He'd been right. That square patio tile still lay there, untouched from where he'd left it after they'd wisely decided there were better things to do in the house on a weekday when the kids were at school, and he had a rare morning off work.

They'd made love instead.

She'd squealed and thrilled at his winter-chilled hands from his labour in the garden. The moment had been bliss. He'd wanted to stay home all day after that – make love again. He'd boyishly teased he'd throw a sickie – something he hadn't done since he was seventeen – but the meeting he'd had that afternoon at his architectural company was far too important; the very last of the year before being handed his big partnership.

*"Sod them. They don't have you for a wife – they don't understand."*

*She laughed. "Don't you dare – you have to go. You've been waiting for this since forever."*

She brought her mind out of the past, and kissed the top of Sammy's head. His crying had eased; turned into sniffles rather than sobs. "You okay, my man?"

He nodded against her, but didn't let her go.

She sighed to herself, and sat there, cradling him. She had nowhere to be in a hurry, anyway – not at six-thirty in the morning. And it seemed like Becca hadn't been woken this time by Sammy's screaming. If Liam had, he'd stayed in his room.

What day was it?

*Thursday.* That's right – yesterday, they'd gone on the boat trip for Merri's birthday, sans Merri. *Might as well return the boat keys to the shop first thing, since you're up.*

Unbidden, an image of an ominous tunnel (or was it a long, narrow path?) came to mind, a field at the end of it, lit with sunshine.

Had she dreamt something like that? She racked her brain to no avail. It shouldn't make a difference, but she had that 'uneasy' feeling that always followed a disturbing dream. Remembering would be helpful so she could put it behind her.

She went back to planning the day out in her mind. She'd take the kids to her parents' house first, then drop the keys off at The Boat Shop, be back before ten, then the rest of the morning and afternoon would be theirs to do what they liked. There weren't many free days left; she'd have to go back to work soon, and the kids would be at school.

The house fell silent now Sammy had quietened down.

Loneliness pulled at her heart. It always seemed silent now.

She glanced at the doorway, imagining a dishevelled, just-woken-up David standing there with a smile and a cup of tea for her, asking how Sammy was; asking if she'd like him to take over.

Emptiness filled the space instead.

And silence reigned.

# *More Titles by Dianna Hardy*

### *Dark Paranormal Fantasy Romances:*
The Witching Pen series
Eye of the Storm series
After the Storm novelettes
Blood Never Lies (duet novels)

and

'Til Death Do Us Part
(an adult retelling of The Little Mermaid)

### *Gritty Contemporary Suspense / Romance:*
Broken Lights

### *Poetry:*
A Silver Kiss (Vampire Poetry)

# About the Author

Dianna Hardy is an international bestselling author of (cross-genre) fantasy fiction, most notable for her dark paranormal fantasy and the raw, intense *Eye of the Storm* series. But her heart-warming *Once Times Thrice* series proves she thrives in the light as much as the dark. Whatever your poison, what she loves most is to bring you stories that are action-packed, fast-paced and not short of heat, with the focus on character development, relationship dynamics, and the plot. She writes full-length novels and short fiction.

She currently lives in South Hampshire, UK with her partner and their daughter, where she writes full-time.

Official site:
**www.diannahardy.com**

Facebook:
**www.facebook.com/authordiannahardy**

Twitter:
**www.twitter.com/thewitchingpen**